Blue

SELECTED SHORT STORIES
Volume Two

by
Wodke Hawkinson

USA

Dedication

In memory of Dennis

*You could not have known how much you would
be missed by those who truly loved you.*

Contents

Preface

Dear Reader,

Welcome to the fiction of Wodke Hawkinson. Thank you for coming!

As you may know, Wodke Hawkinson is the pseudonym of PJ Hawkinson and Karen Wodke. As a writing duo, we find many ways of bringing out our creative writing styles, both together and separately.

In our first short story volume we mentioned one method of writing we enjoy, that of using the same story line or list of characters. In the last volume we were inspired when a son-in-law dropped his cell phone into a pond while fishing. This volume we used characters donated to Karen on HubPages. She then lent PJ a cupful of the same characters and we went to work. Karen produced *Ruby, Pete, and Rex the Cheat*, while PJ followed a completely different line and ended up with *Life of a Beat Cop.*

Since each of us has her own twisty way of looking at things, Wodke Hawkinson enjoys the mixed talents of two minds instead of one.

In Volume One we introduced our intention of putting in one humorous, simply for fun, and quite frivolous story, one that seemed to be abundantly, copiously, and profusely loaded with adverbs. We have continued this wordy theme in Volume Two. See if you can spot the mysterious, grandiose, and yet rather short, story.

Check out our already published works *Catch Her in the* Rye by Wodke Hawkinson, *Half Bitten* by PJ Hawkinson, and *James Willis Makes a Million* by Karen Wodke.

We'd also like to mention two upcoming novels, *Betrayed* and *Tangerine,* in addition to a new short story collection: *Alone,*

Selected Short Stories, Volume Three. All will be coming your way within the year.

A book takes readers to places they've never been before, places they could otherwise never go. Thank you for traveling along with us as we venture into unknown realms.

Wodke Hawkinson

"A book is the only place in which you can examine a fragile thought without breaking it, or explore an explosive idea without fear it will go off in your face. It is one of the few havens remaining where a man's mind can get both provocation and privacy."

~Edward P. Morgan

"Reading is sometimes an ingenious
device for avoiding thought."
~Arthur Helps

Death Hates His Job

G hated his job. It wasn't just a strong dislike, it was actual loathing. He thought about it as he pulled on his blue jeans and gray t-shirt, and bent to fasten his black boots. With a feeling like weariness, which was surely impossible for him, he shrugged into his black hoodie and slung the case that held his blade over one bony shoulder like a quiver of arrows. For a while he had missed the long robe, but he had to admit his current attire was much more comfortable. G tried to keep up with the times. Good old G. Reaper. That was him, long-time acquaintance of Father Time, and colleague of Mother Nature. Often the couple laid down the groundwork for his projects. But still, for all their contributions to the effort, the buck stopped with him. He was Death.

He cringed as he slipped out the front door of his apartment on the first floor of an old Victorian and noticed his neighbor, the elderly Violet Thistlewaite, rocking quietly in the porch swing. Her skull looked delicate as an eggshell where her pale scalp peeked through the thinning white hair. Knobby hands clutched the edges of her shawl as she turned her head toward him and stared with vacant eyes as if she could see him.

"Who's there?" she called out timidly.

It gave him the creeps. He chuckled; he had nothing to fear, especially from a frail woman with poor vision.

Death was universally hated and feared, except by the insane and those in terminal misery. Over the eons, this disdain had begun to eat at him. Somewhere along the way he had developed the regrettable capacity for remorse and a sharp cognizance of his own unpopularity. Always reviled and despised; friendless, basically. His presence was rarely welcome. Most never realized he was there until the last second, right before the harvest. As he glided down the walk and passed through people, leaving them aquiver with a vague apprehension, he came to a decision. He simply wouldn't show for his first appointment. Maybe he would go to the park instead and scare a few pigeons. None would land near him, even when he brought bread crumbs for them. Still, he enjoyed watching them bob around, trying to snatch the food without coming too close. They reminded him of necks stretched across guillotines. His thin lips curled down slightly at the recollection. *I hate this job.*

Or perhaps he would wander downtown and see how many people could perceive him, probably as a chill draft or the crawling sensation of eyes on their backs. He could always tell the sensitive ones; they would shiver or glance nervously over their shoulders. They knew not what they felt, only that it was bad.

Feeling slightly less dejected, he swept around the curved walkway to the street, traveling with long strides though his feet never touched the surface below him. He headed for the shopping district to do a little people-watching.

Several hours later, after drifting aimlessly around the world, curiosity overcame him. What, he wondered, had happened with Mr. Swenson, the elderly man he was supposed to have visited that morning at the nursing home? He couldn't resist the urge to check.

Instantly he was outside the window of Mr. Swenson's room peering in. From the grimace the old man made, the tears that ran unchecked down his wrinkled face, and his tortured movements, G could tell there was great pain. In fact, the poor human was in agony. G chastised himself for neglecting his duties before passing through the wall into the room. Leaning over the wretched figure on the bed, he pulled his blade from its case and swung. Swenson's face immediately settled into an expression of peace as his soul departed.

So, this is what happens when I don't show up on time. Worse suffering, he thought, his heart heavy with remorse. *I truly hate this job. I try to do a good thing, and look how it turns out.*

Moments later, Mrs. Swenson hobbled into the room holding onto the arm of a husky nurse aide, a cup of coffee in her other trembling hand. She looked toward the bed and the cup slipped from her fingers and hit the floor, splashing coffee over her loafers. G watched as her face crumpled and tears rolled down her lined cheeks. She tried to reach the bed, but the aide stupidly held her back.

"He's gone," Mrs. Swenson cried as she pushed weakly against the young man. "Let me go to him."

The nurse aide relented and supported her as she approached the bed. "Oh, Jimmy," she whispered, reaching to caress the still face of her beloved. "My sweet Jimmy."

G turned away and slipped from the room, one hand clutching his black hood, his cadaverous cheeks sucked in against his teeth, his jaw tight with despair. It was almost always like this. And he hated it. He hated being in so many places at the same time, having so many abodes all over the planet that none really felt like home. The massive weight of familial grief, centuries of it, pressed down on him, invisible, thick, and choking. Like heavy smog. There was no joy in this work, no satisfaction. If there ever had been, he couldn't remember when.

He was finished with this job; no more would he do it. He retired.

Had the world been paying attention, they might have noticed that for one whole day nobody anywhere died. Death was sitting on a park bench, making pigeons uneasy, and sinking into a deep depression. Someday it would be discovered and marveled at on the evening news, one whole day without death. Remarkable. Ordinarily, an idea like that would amuse G, but not today. He was too morose. He had never been so conflicted.

Perhaps he should seek counseling. Even that wry thought failed to raise a sardonic sneer.

Unbeknownst to G, people around the world were suffering horribly. Pain endured past life's expiration date is beyond any pain known. And with G sitting on the park bench, agony ran rampant.

G realized he had nothing to look forward to except watching pigeons. He had nothing to do, nowhere to go. An idea formed in his mind. Since he had no other purpose than raining sorrow onto humanity, there was no good reason for him to continue. He himself must die. He would commit suicide. But how does someone who is not alive, take their own life? It was a weighty question. He rose from the bench.

Deep in thought, G deliberated as he traveled. He looked in on some of the people in his date book, the people who should be gone by now. He didn't like what he saw. In most cases, there was torment, either physical or mental; in other cases, a sour tradeoff. Die now this way, or die later in a worse way. He watched as one man lifted the gun to his open mouth and laid a quivering finger on the trigger as tears streamed down his face. Since G was scheduled to slide his own bony finger over the man's and press, but did not, the man simply shook with his internal conflict, unable to proceed.

At another location, G saw a young girl run in front of a car. *What purpose would it serve for that child to die?* he mused bitterly as the vehicle swerved, missing her by only a small margin. G was to have held her back so the car would hit her, but he wasn't doing that job any longer. It no longer suited him.

G felt justified as he began to turn away from the scene. This tiny girl would live now; she'd enjoy her childhood, marry, have children. She would live her life never knowing how close she had come to dying. G abruptly grabbed his head, pressing his temples with bony fingertips as images flooded in, and he perceived her future. He saw this precious youngster, somebody's darling, thin and bruised from disease, lingering in a hospital bed in misery as her family stood helplessly by.

So, in this case anyway, Fate had determined she could go quickly or she could go slowly, but she most definitely was targeted for demise. "So unfair," G murmured to himself. "Who calls these people home?" He still knew very little about his boss. He just followed orders without question. Or he did, until now.

He looked back at the girl and felt no happiness over her close escape, no joy, for he knew what she must later endure. Because of him. Because he failed to do his job.

Who will take me home? He felt a wave of pity for himself. In one fluid movement, he unsheathed his blade, swept it in graceful arc across his throat, slicing it neatly. Immediately, he felt his skin, tissues, and fibers draw back together, closing the wound as if it had never happened. *How ironic*, he thought, *I am Death but I myself cannot die.* He had feared as much.

Gradually, he perceived a presence. He turned quickly, his movement disturbing the atmosphere around him like small ripples on a still surface. Over his shoulder, he caught a glimpse of a shimmering figure just as it vanished. Puzzling over this, and the general state of things in his world, G began to sort the facts as he knew them. He shuffled them in his mind.

Slowly, he began to comprehend his relationship to these humans, the ones who should be here no longer. He grasped the greater purpose in a flash of insight. With a stab of grief, he realized he must return to the job; things were worse with him gone. He couldn't justify staying away only to wallow in his own suffering.

That, and the fact that he could not do away with himself, forced G to return to work.

G determined that if this be his purpose, the very least he could do to assuage his guilt was to endure some punishment of his own as atonement. He sped to his first missed appointment, but this time he did not vanish immediately after the swing of his blade as he usually did. He stayed instead, to watch.

Surprise filled his soul, if a soul he indeed had, when he noticed a form draped over the dying woman as she sat in her living room chair. It was the same figure he had glimpsed following his suicide attempt. This being began to swell as the woman's life drained from her. G noticed that the pain seemed to lift from the woman, as if the being were absorbing her agony, mitigating the shock of separation from her body as her mortal life ended.

And, if this weren't unsettling enough, when the last of life's force had drained from her, the being lifted into the air and floated upwards. Darkness slowly emanated from its body as it rose, releasing pain into the atmosphere where it dissipated like mist. A glow replaced the darkness, growing brighter as the being ascended. G stood transfixed.

Far above, there was a break in the fabric of the world; bright light emitted from the breach. The being lifted its arms towards this opening. Rays of soft radiance poured from its fingers, soared upwards, and joined with the brilliant illumination above. Agonizing streaks of light burst overhead; and quick as the break had appeared, it was gone.

G stared. Slowly the being drifted down until it was face to face with him. Shimmering, sparkling, and luminous, the being looked into G's eyes with compassion before fading away. G felt as if his heart would burst. An angel! For this creature could be nothing else. He had heard of angels, but to find they really existed was beyond thought. Had they always been there? He wondered if his suicide attempt had opened a new awareness in him.

Over the next few days, G saw the angels again and again. Now that he knew what to look for, it was easy to spot them…the beings of light, mute yet compelling.

In his long existence, G had been part and parcel of countless grisly atrocities and scenes of stunning malice and gore. He had never noted the presence of angels before, but now he saw them on every job, always lying over the mortal remains, fulfilling their duties, ministering to the dead and dying, easing souls toward their destinations.

G was just coming to terms with his unique calling when

one assignment rattled him so that he broke from his routine.

He approached the suicide bomber on the dusty road and looked through the man's eyes to the crowded market ahead.

Oh, no. Not all those people! G cringed as a rebellious thought insinuated itself in his mind. He glanced at his time-piece, then over to the angel waiting by the side of the road, well away from the soon-to-be deceased. Before G could resist the impulse, he swung his blade many minutes before he was sched-uled to do so. The blast rent the air as the explosives inside the backpack ignited and a nearby shack crumbled.

G looked around. The angel had not moved, standing as if frozen in time, a single tear trickling down its porcelain cheek.

G sheathed his blade and slid away, shoulders hunched. He should feel good; he saved many lives. *But, at what cost to the survivors?* He didn't want to know. He would be visiting each of them soon enough. Of that he was certain.

G returned to the pigeons. As he tossed bread crumbs to the birds, he reflected on all he had learned. Although he still didn't care for his job, he'd recognized the necessity of his work. He'd come to terms with his place in the world and now knew it was beside the angels. In time, maybe he would be allowed to move into the higher realm and become as they were, vessels of light and mercy. One could hope.

G stood. There was work to do.

Back to the Past

Rusty stood in thought. He was remembering. Eyes. The eyes................ Rusty went slowly back in time.

Slithering along on his stomach past the gully where his worst enemy, the Strangler, lay, Rusty Tanner made as little noise as possible. Following behind him, also on his belly, was Rusty's faithful companion, Boris. Boris was a giant wolf, trained to do Rusty's bidding. Rusty and Boris went still as they heard a shifting of the weeds in the gully where the Strangler hid. Suddenly from the gully burst a long-haired black cat that promptly jumped on Boris, who, with a yelp, leaped straight up in the air and took off across the field with the cat hot on his trail. Rusty fell on his back giggling wildly.

Rusty Tanner was eight years old, a lanky red-haired ball of energy. He had a scattering of freckles across his nose and cheeks and was considered cute by all of his mom's friends. His 'wolf' was actually his dog, Rascal, a short-haired, short-legged, soft chocolate brown dog with deep brown eyes. Rusty's cat, Harry, with his vivid blue eyes, was guilty of breaking up the capture of the Strangler.

"Rusty," called his mom, "it's time for lunch."

"Coming," Rusty shouted as he brushed off the leaves and grass from his clothes and made his way to the house. He lived on the outskirts of a small Kansas town and had the whole world at his back door as a playground. The farm actually consisted of eighty acres, and although Rusty could tell you this fact, he didn't really have a concept of the area. He only knew that he had lots of room to play within the boundaries set by his parents. The Tanner home was a two-story non-working farm house, well tended, with a neat lawn and a tire swing hanging from the old oak tree next to the house. Besides Rascal and Harry, they had a pair of parakeets named Blue and Green. Rusty had named them after the colors of their feathers.

Rusty entered the house through the back door. His mom took one look at him, sighed, and pointed to the restroom. "Wash!" she demanded.

Rusty looked at his hands in confusion, and then mumbled under his breath, "I brushed everything off, jeez." But he obediently went and washed his hands and face. Sitting at the table he started to bolt his sandwich down.

"Take it easy, this isn't a race," his mom said and Rusty slowed his chewing a little bit. Rusty sat watching his mom as he ate. She didn't work outside of the house and was home every day, and Rusty liked having her there. She grew an enormous garden. She canned vegetables, made jelly from their fruit trees, kept the house cleaned, and her husband and son well fed. She took care of his cuts and always had a warm arm to hold him when he didn't feel good or was sad. On top of that, Rusty thought that his mom was very pretty although he would never say so.

When he was done eating, Rusty jumped up, took his plate and milk glass to the sink, and headed for the door. "Hold up there young man," his mom said, "did you forget that we were going into town? We need to buy groceries and stop by the drugstore."

Rusty's face fell. "Aw, do we have to?"

"We'll get an ice cream soda at the drugstore and also stop and see your dad. So go change clothes," his mom encouraged with a smile.

"Whoopee," Rusty hooted and took off for his room. He returned in a few minutes, still pulling a shirt over his head.

10

Rusty liked going to the post office where his dad was the Postmaster. He liked to watch the machines sort the mail and was always fascinated by their speed and accuracy. Plus, and here was the kicker, everyone always treated him as if he were special. In addition, the promise of an ice cream soda had him licking his lips, never mind that he had just eaten.

It was summertime, Rusty was out of school, and going to town only happened about once a month. Rusty's mom drove the two miles to town while Rusty counted chicken hawks; he had seen twelve by the time they pulled onto the blacktop, passed the grade school, and entered town. Rusty leaned out the window, waving to kids from school that he knew and wishing he could go play with them, but knew there wouldn't be time. Although, he just might slip in some time to look at comic books at the drug store, and maybe Tommy or Billy would be in there looking at them too.

They parked at the curb near the post office. Rusty bounced ahead of his mom, peering into the drug store window, but waited at the door of the post office for her to catch up. They entered together and almost immediately a voice boomed out, "Mr. Rusty, how are you doing?" The voice came from the desk clerk, Mr. Patterson, a tall, thin man with a balding head, piercing black eyes, and a startling deep voice. Mr. Patterson always called Rusty 'Mr. Rusty', and Rusty always came back with, 'doing fine, Mr. Patterson, doing fine', just as he did today. They grinned at each other and Mr. Patterson turned to Mrs. Tanner and said, "The boss is in the back." Mom smiled, thanked him, and led Rusty into the interior of the building.

Here was the part of visiting the Post Office that Rusty liked the best. First, his dad, a medium-height slender man with dark red hair and blue eyes, shook his hand as if he was a grown up businessman come to visit. Then he would rumple Rusty's hair and say, "How's it going buddy?" Rusty would always shake hands solemnly and then beam when his dad rumpled his hair. He told his dad about stalking the strangler.

"Did you catch him?" his dad asked.

Rusty sighed, "No, a big black cat surprised my wolf friend and scared the Strangler away."

"Well, better luck next time," said Rusty's dad. Then his dad told him he could go and watch the machines while he talked to Rusty's mom. "Just be sure to stay out of the way. And remember, the machine is dangerous, so don't touch it."

"Yes sir," Rusty exclaimed and took off to the machine area.

The machines were run by the biggest man Rusty had ever seen, a man by the name of Clyde. Clyde was easily six foot-five inches and weighed probably two hundred and ninety pounds. He had light-colored skin, the blondest hair that hung to his waist in a single braid, huge beefy hands that could do the most amazingly detailed work when necessary, and a soft Cajun drawl that always made Rusty grin.

Clyde was watching the progress of the machine and straightening misaligned stacks of outgoing mail when Rusty walked over. They talked quietly about how the machines were running, and then Rusty asked about Clyde's dog. Clyde had a mischievous dog which he had named Ralph. Now he gave Rusty the details of Ralph's antics the day before. "Ah cum in de back do yesteday an dat dog done had ahl ma close out a de closet and strung ahl oer de flo. He do get so mad at me when ah go an leave him lone too long." Then Clyde threw his head back and laughed a quiet laugh. Rusty laughed with him and then Clyde asked him if he would like to load some of the mail into the machine loader.

Rusty's face lit up and he said, "Sure I'd like to do that if you think it'd be okay. My dad said not to touch the machine."

"I reckon it'll be jest fine." Ya don't hav ta touch de mashine to put de mail in de tray." He showed Rusty how to place the envelopes in the loader, and Rusty loaded about fifty of them and watched the machine sort the letters he had loaded. It was great fun, but then his mom said it was time to go. Rusty high-fived Clyde and said that he would see him next time.

"Latda ma frien," Clyde said as Rusty left with his mom.

Between the Post Office and the drugstore, Rusty told his mom how neat it had been to load the sorting machine. "Was that safe?" his mom asked.

"Sure," Rusty said. "Clyde would never let me do something dangerous."

"Well you're right about that," Rusty's mom replied. "Your dad says that Clyde is the safest operator he has ever had. He sure knows that machine."

Rusty and his mom went to the drugstore, and he was delighted to find Tommy at the comic book stand. "Hey Tommy, any new ones?" Rusty asked.

"Get a load of this," Tommy said excitedly, holding out a superhero comic. "This guy can melt things just by looking at them."

"No way!" Rusty ogled the picture in the comic. "That's neat." The boys flipped through the comic and then started goofing around, talking about the different things that they would melt with their eyes if they could.

"What would you melt?" Rusty asked Tommy.

Tommy thought for a minute and then said, "The blackboard at school when I don't know the answer to the teacher's question. How about you?"

Rusty thought for a minute and then said, "Bucky Thompson's fist when he's bullying us around."

They laughed uproariously over Bucky looking at his missing hand. The boys knew they only had a short time before Mr. Spinner, the store manager, would run them off from the comic book rack. He'd say, "If you're not buying, you're not looking."

Rusty's mom finished making her drugstore purchases and called Rusty over to the soda fountain. "See ya later," Rusty said with a sigh. Although he had many friends at school, his house was far enough out of town there was no-one close by to play with and it was fun talking to Tommy.

His mom let him order a chocolate ice cream soda at the soda fountain and it was deeeeelicious. As they left the drugstore his mom reached over and wiped a whipped cream mustache from his upper lip. "Hey," Rusty exclaimed, "I was saving that for later!" He and his mom laughed and finished shopping before heading home.

"Can we stop by the library?" Rusty asked. They did, and he got six books to read: one about pirates, one about cowboys, two Hardy Boys, and two about Tom Sawyer. He started reading one of the Hardy Boys mysteries on the way home and was already thinking about sneaking up on criminals by the time they returned home at three-thirty p.m.

Rusty took his books inside and then headed for the barn, with Rascal at his heels, so that he could set up a spy lab in one of the empty stalls. First, he dragged in an old bench that his dad didn't use and then ran to the house.

"Mom," Rusty called, entering by the backdoor. "Do you have a magnifying glass, envelopes, string, flour, pad of paper, and a pencil that I can have?"

Rusty's mom cocked an eyebrow at him. "What are you up to now?" she asked.

"I'm setting up a spy lab in the barn," Rusty told his mom importantly. "I need all this stuff so that I can catch criminals."

"Ohhh," Rusty's mom said, as she remembered the books he had checked out in the library. "Let me look around." She found all of the things he had asked for and then said, "Let's check in the storage room real fast. I think I have something in there you might be able to use." They went into the storage room and his mom rummaged around for a minute. Finally she handed Rusty an old camera and telephone, neither of which worked anymore. Rusty was ecstatic. He rushed back to the garage and started setting up his 'lab'.

By five-fifteen p.m. when his dad got home, supper was ready and Rusty had to stop for the day. He looked longingly out the door several times, but his mom shook her head and said, "No more tonight. Its bath time, then you can watch TV for one hour, and then its bedtime."

Rusty knew better then to complain, so after supper he took his bath and then allowed as how he would rather read than watch TV, if that was okay.

"That's fine son," his mom and dad said. "We'll be up to tuck you in later."

When his parents came up a little later, Rusty was sound asleep with an open book lying on his chest. Rusty's mom took the book, noting that it was a Hardy Boys book, pulled the covers up, kissed Rusty on the cheek, and told him she loved him. Dad leaned over to give him a quick kiss on the forehead and also expressed his love. They turned off the light, but left the door opened slightly so that the hallway nightlight shone through.

That was the end of one day in the life of Rusty Tanner. Everyday he did similar activities and though he always had fun, he wished that he had someone to play with. So many of his 'adventures' would have been tons better with at least two people, but he got by okay.

Then, one balmy summer day that started no different than any other day, everything suddenly changed. He woke in the morning, made his bed and straightened his room, washed his face and brushed his teeth, and got ready for a day outside. After breakfast, he left by the back door with Rascal at his heels. On the rear stoop he stopped and gave Harry, who began to purr loudly, a good roughing up and then he headed off to play.

A little later, Rusty burst through the back screen door, banging it against the outside of the house. "Mom, Mom!" he screamed, running past her and into the living room.

His mom, who had been in the kitchen preparing to make jelly, quickly followed her son into the living room. "Honey, what's the matter?"

"Mom," Rusty said breathlessly. "Mom, Mr. Jenkins just told me that his kids are coming for the summer. I didn't even know that he had kids. They live in Philadelphia, Pennsylvania, and he said that they would be here Friday. Where's Philadelphia, Pennsylvania? Can I go over to the Jenkins's house on Friday? Can I, can I?"

"Slow down," Mom said, after digesting the information pouring from her son. "Let's wait until Friday and then we'll see. We can probably go over to meet them after they get settled in, if it's not too late." Then, Mrs. Tanner got out a map of the United States and showed Rusty where Philadelphia, Pennsylvania was and where their town was in Kansas.

"Wow," Rusty commented. "That's a long way away; do you think they can get here by Friday?"

Laughing, Mrs. Tanner said, "Oh, I imagine if Mr. Jenkins said they'd be here by Friday, they'll make it."

Mrs. Tanner thought about what she knew of Mr. Jenkins. He was the new sheriff in town. She and Mr. Tanner had met him and found him to be a very likable man. Five months before, Mr. Jenkins had bought the house just across the road and down a bit. From their conversation, she had learned that he had recently been divorced and that he had children who lived with their mother. Evidently his divorce was due to the fact that Mrs. Jenkins was unable to handle the stress level of being married to a policeman. She had decided to end the marriage. They remained on friendly terms, which was good since they had children together.

Mr. Jenkins's house was close enough for Rusty to walk over. Mrs. Tanner hoped his kids were Rusty's age, as she knew that summertime was a lonesome time for him and he needed playmates close by.

"Did Mr. Jenkins say how old his children are or how many?" Mom asked.

"Noooo," Rusty dragged out, "just that I would like them."

"Well, this is Tuesday, so you have to wait three days to find out. I don't want you bugging Mr. Jenkins about this, understand?"

"Yes ma'am," Rusty said reluctantly.

The next two days, Rusty would leap down the stairs each morning asking if it was Friday yet only to find out that it wasn't. Most of the time he would spend playing somewhere in sight of the Jenkins's house just in case they came early, which, of course, they did not.

Finally the big day arrived. "Now don't you be hanging around the Jenkins house all day," Mom told Rusty. Rusty said that he wouldn't, but he spent all day out by the road watching the Jenkins house slyly. He played with his army men on a hill, he stood on his head, and he collected every roly-poly he could find, which his mom would later find in a paper sack by the backdoor, the two hundred-plus insects in it giving her quite a fright.

After waiting for what seemed hours, Rusty saw the Sheriff's car turn onto their road at the far corner. He craned his neck trying to see the kids, but he couldn't. Finally, they turned into their driveway and two kids got out. Rusty strained to catch a glimpse and almost let out a whoop when he saw that they were boys and looked his age. Deciding to act like a spy in a movie, he tried not to be seen by slithering on his belly down the ditch a hundred feet or so and sneaking behind fallen branches and big rocks. Finally, he was close enough to see well and stopped with his mouth hanging open, staring a couple of more minutes. He forgot about being a spy as he jumped up and made a bee-line for home. Banging into the house through the back door, he hollered, "Mom, Mom." This time he saw her at the refrigerator defrosting the freezer. "Mom," he hollered again, "they're here. They look just like each other. You can't tell them apart. Are they mirrors?"

"Okay, calm down," said mom. "What are you talking about now?"

"Mr. Jenkins's kids. They're boys. They must be mirrors 'cause they look just like each other. I mean, JUST LIKE," Rusty said excitedly. "They've got blond hair that's kinda long, but not too long, and they look just like each other."

"Ah," Mom said. "They aren't mirrors; they must be twins."

"What are twins?" Rusty asked.

"Twins are two children that are born at the same time to the same mother. They can be identical or fraternal. Identical twins look alike while fraternal twins usually don't," Mom explained.

"They must be *idental* then," Rusty said, "'cause they sure look alike." Mom had Rusty say 'identical', until he had it right, and said that he shouldn't go around calling them twins because they actually were just brothers. Rusty didn't care what he called them; as long as they had names, he'd call them by those.

"Can I go over there now?" Rusty asked, hopping from one foot to the other. Mom told him to wait forty-five minutes and showed him on the clock when that would be. He stared at the clock the whole time and as soon as it reached the spot she had showed him, he jumped up and shouted, "Now?"

"Yes, now," she said with a small laugh.

Before she had the last word all the way out, Rusty had banged out the back door and was already in the front yard. "Rusty!" Mom hollered. "Wait for me." She caught up with him and they made their way over to the neighbor's house.

As Mrs. Tanner and Rusty approached the Jenkins house, Mrs. Tanner admired the trim single-storied house, comparing it to her own two-storied house. The Jenkins house was painted white with dark blue shutters, while her own house had bright red shutters. Both were well kept. The Jenkins lawn was freshly mown and there was a row of neatly trimmed bushes at either side of the front steps. They knocked on the door, and the Jenkins family stepped outside to greet them. Mrs. Tanner and Mr. Jenkins talked while the children introduced themselves.

Looking at the boys, Mrs. Tanner knew that they must be identical twins because they certainly did look alike. Their names were Colton and Corbin and they were eight years old, just like Rusty. She smiled, knowing these two boys would help keep Rusty occupied for the summer!

Colton and Corbin were so alike it was almost uncanny, from their straight blond hair which came to the top of their collars to their brilliant blue eyes. The only thing Mrs. Tanner could see that was different was Colton had a slightly misaligned front tooth.

"Have you arranged for a sitter yet?" Rusty's mom asked Mr. Jenkins. "Because if you haven't, I wouldn't mind keeping them during your daytime shifts."

"That would be wonderful," said Mr. Jenkins, looking stricken since he had failed to think that detail out. "But, the boys' sister will be here in two weeks. Will that be too much trouble?"

"Not at all," said Mrs. Tanner. They soon worked out the details; then, Mrs. Tanner went home, after giving instructions for Rusty to come home in one hour. Rusty and the other two boys were already hard at play.

Almost from the first words exchanged, the three boys were inseparable. Rusty was thrilled that his mom was watching Colton and Corbin because then they could play all day long; and although he knew they had a sister that would be coming soon, he didn't really listen. Who cared about a girl anyway?

The next two weeks passed quickly. Rusty showed Colton and Corbin the spy lab he had made. "Wow," Colton said, "Maybe our dad will give us some stuff too so we can be partners."

"Sure," Rusty exclaimed. "You can never have too much spy stuff."

The next day Colton and Corbin came over and brought some really neat stuff. "Here's a pair of handcuffs," Corbin said. "They don't work, but we can act like they do."

"NEAT!" Rusty shouted as he checked them out. "What else you got in that box?"

What they had were a can of mace (empty), two more magnifying glasses, a pair of old boots so they could leave tracks and investigate them, scissors, glue, and lots of other things. The three boys got busy and soon had their spy lab set up.

"So," Corbin said, "what do we do now; how will we get someone to call us so that we can look for criminals?"

"We'd better write an ad to put in the paper," said Colton.

Rusty sure wished he had come up with that idea, but since he hadn't, the least he could do was write down what they wanted the ad to say. He grabbed a sheet of paper and a pencil. Licking the lead he said, "Okay, what should we write?"

After a lot of hemming and hawing, they picked a name for their lab, made up an address and phone number, and wrote the following:

New SPY LAB opened
Need bad guys to look for
Send letters to SPY LAB at 16 Spy Lab Road
Or call us at 2936

The boys looked this over and decided that it would do. They stuck the letter in an envelope and Rusty said that he would give it to his dad to put in the paper; and although all the boys knew that Rusty wouldn't really give it to his dad, they pretended that they were open for business and that they might have to wait several days to hear anything from their 'ad.'

A couple of days later, Rusty's mom took them to the swimming hole way back on the Tanner's land. They took a picnic lunch and hiked to the pond. On the way there, they saw a snake that had smooth scales, the belly yellow and irregularly patterned with black, a black head, body and tail profusely speckled with small yellow, cream or white spots. Rusty's mom told them this was a King snake and that it was not poisonous, but that it would still bite them if they got to close. The four of them made a wide berth around the snake and continued down the path. When they got to the pond, they disturbed several box turtles that had been sunbathing on a branch that was sticking out of the water. They disappeared with several 'plops' as soon as the three boys got close.

"Can we get in now?" asked Rusty.

"Do you remember the rules?" Mom asked.

"Yes ma'am," Colton said.

"Tell me," Rusty's mom said.

The boys rushed to give her the answers. "Don't go past the markers," Corbin said. Rusty's dad had put out painted markers along the edge of the pond that he could move as Rusty's swimming skills advanced.

"Don't hold each other under water, dunking is okay but don't hold anyone down," Colton said.

"Right," Rusty's mom said. "But there is one more; what is it?"

All three boys tried to look like they didn't know what she meant, but then Rusty giggled and said, "Oh yeah, don't splash you!" "

You got it," Mom said, settling down by the water to sunbathe with a book. "Now, go have fun."

None of the boys needed further encouragement. They hit the water running, creating huge splashes that didn't quite hit Rusty's mom, but almost did, making them laugh uproariously.

They swam and played for about an hour and then Rusty's mom said it was time to head back home.

"Ahhhh," all three boys moaned, but Rusty's mom gave them a look, after which they came out of the water and put on their shoes for the trek back to the house.

After the boys got out of their swim trunks and into their clothes, they headed for the spy lab. When they entered the barn, Corbin said, pretending, "I think I hear our phone ringing."

The three boys ran for phone and Corbin grabbed it off the hook. "Spy Lab," he said in his most professional voice while grabbing a pad of paper and a pencil. "Un-hunh, yes, okay I got it, we'll get right on it, thanks!" Corbin turned back to the other two boys and said, "We've got a case."

Rusty and Colton gathered near Corbin and looked at what he had written: Mr. Crabtree says that a bad guy has been peeking in the window of the Tanner house. See if you can catch him.

Corbin said he needed to use the bathroom and would be right back. "You guys get the investigating equipment ready, okay?" he suggested as he left the lab. On the way out, he snuck the old pair of boots with him. He went to the side of the house and used the boots to make prints in the ground and then left the boots under a bush so they could be found. He quickly used the restroom and returned to the other boys.

When he got back to the lab, he found Corbin and Rusty ready with magnifying glasses, fingerprint dusting powder (flour), and the camera. They started off towards the house. "We better proceed carefully in case the criminal is still present," Corbin whispered, and the three boys snuck to the corner of the house.

"Did Mr. Crabtree say what window the bad guy was peeking in?" Rusty whispered.

"No," Corbin said. "Let's start here and work our way around." All three boys crouched down and moved around the corner of the house. "Let's watch the ground for prints," Corbin said craftily.

"Good idea," said Colton.

Suddenly, Rusty, who was in the lead, gave a surprised yelp. "I found prints!"

Corbin snickered under his breath but Colton said, "No way! Really?" He crowded forward to see.

The prints stopped under a window that opened into the laundry room. "We'd better dust for prints," Rusty said.

"Right," said Corbin. "Let me have the kit."

Rusty handed Corbin the bag with flour and Corbin sprinkled some on the windowsill, discreetly pressed in one finger, and then blew on the dust. He promptly sneezed when some of the white powder blew up his nose.

"Take a picture Rusty," Corbin said.

Rusty aimed the camera at the fingerprint and pressed the button. "I'd better take two," he said, pressing the button a second time.

They continued around the house searching for more clues. "Get down and look under the bushes in case the criminal left something behind," Corbin suggested to Colton.

"Good idea," Colton said, and dropped to his knees. Almost at once, he jumped back with half a yell, and then laughed at himself. On the ground, near where his hand had been, was a lizard. It had six light yellow stripes down its back and Rusty knew that it was a Six-lined Racerunner. He also knew that they weren't very common to the area, but they saw them now and again because of the sandy quality of the ground. These types of lizards liked the heat and this one was sunning itself on a rock where the warm light shone though the bushes. Colton tried to grab it, but with its impressive speed, it darted away before he could get close.

"Leave it alone. We're here to catch a bad guy," Corbin chided Colton.

Colton threw his brother a disgruntled look, but continued down the bush line on his hands and knees. All of a sudden he stopped. There ahead of him was something in the bushes. Creeping closer he saw that it was an old pair of boots, and although he recognized them, he acted like he had never seen them before. "Look at this;" Colton told the other two boys. "There's a pair of boots here."

Rusty looked over his shoulder and said, "Don't touch them; let me go get an evidence bag." He quickly ran to the lab and got a paper sack and a pair of old tongs his mom had given him. Returning, he asked Corbin to take a picture and then used the tongs to put the boots in the bag.

"I think we've found all there is to find," Corbin said. "Let's go look at the evidence in the lab."

At the lab, the three boys each looked through magnifying glasses at a piece of paper that was supposed to be a developed picture of the fingerprint they had taken. Rusty scratched his chin in contemplation. "You know," he said slowly, "I think I've seen this print before. Let me check the files." He went to the end of the shelf and rifled through a box of old papers. "Ha!" Rusty exclaimed triumphantly. "Here it is. He held up a sheet of paper with a bunch of figures on it that might have been an old grocery list, and showed it to Corbin and Colton.

They both looked at it excitedly and asked, "What's the name on it?"

Rusty pretended to examine the paper closely and then said, "His name is," he paused. "Gregory Peckard!"

"Let's inform Mr. Crabtree immediately," Colton exclaimed.

Corbin picked up the receiver of the phone and dialed a number, waited a second and then said, "Mr. Crabtree, this is Corbin from the Spy Lab. We know who was peeking through the windows. It was Gregory Peckard. Pick him up right away." He listened for a moment, said thanks, and hung up the phone. "He said the check is in the mail," Corbin exclaimed and all three boys high-fived.

"Want to shoot a game of hoops?" Colton asked one day. "Our dad put up a basketball hoop for us."

"Sure," Rusty exclaimed, after which they played basketball everyday for a week before the novelty wore off a little bit, and then they only played a couple times a week. They were all bad, only making a basket once out of every twenty shots, but they had fun. Rusty asked for a basketball and his dad brought one home for him.

Other times the boys rode bikes on the trails Mr. Tanner had made for Rusty. The trails wound through the trees and were full of hills and turns. They played hide and seek and every other game they could think of. And, they talked. "What's the place like where you live?" Rusty asked.

Corbin said that it was totally different than their dad's house. With their mom, they lived in a big town and only had a small yard to play in because they lived in an apartment house.

"What's an apartment house?" Rusty asked.

"It's a big building that has a bunch of houses in it. We live on the third floor. There's an elevator, but Mom usually lets us run up the stairs. She says that it zaps some of the energy out of us," Colton said.

"Wow," Rusty exclaimed. "I've only rode an elevator once and it was real neat."

"I guess," said Colton. "It seems kind of boring to me."

Rusty was amazed that anything that cool could be boring, but he didn't say so.

One day something happened that Rusty would never forget. He was on the way to Colton and Corbin's house when he saw one of them standing out on the drive beside their house. It was a chilly day and whichever one it was had his hood pulled up and was facing away from Rusty. Rusty had his basketball with him and he yelled, "Heads up," and tossed the ball to the other boy. The boy turned around, caught the ball, whirled and shot a perfect shot through the hoop with no net. None of them had ever done that before; they weren't very good. Just as the boy turned back to Rusty, who stood with his mouth hanging open in amazement over the shot, the front door of the Jenkins house burst open and Colton and Corbin flew out calling, "Show off" to the kid that had made the basket. Rusty looked at them with mouth agape and then at the boy who had shot the basket.

The hood on the other boy had fallen back and long blond hair tumbled out from under it. It wasn't a boy; it was a GIRL. And not just any girl; it was a girl that looked just like Colton and Corbin except for the length of her hair. Rusty stared. "Who are you?" he asked.

Colton answered, "This is our sister, Carson. Remember, we told you she was coming?"

"Yeah, I remember, but you didn't tell me she looked like you!"

Well," Corbin said, "we're triplets."

"What are triplets? Rusty asked. "I thought you were twins." Rusty forgot his mom said not to call them that.

"Triplets are like twins but with three kids," said Carson.

Later that day, Rusty strutted through the back screen door of his home and with an air of superiority told his mom that Corbin and Colton weren't twins.

"What do you mean?" asked his mom.

"They're triplets," stated Rusty. "They have a sister too; she just got here today."

"Really," Mom said. "Well, isn't that something. Do you like her?"

"I don't know. I guess. I mean, she's just like Corbin and Colton; you can't hardly tell she's a girl," Rusty muttered, turning a little pink.

That summer, and the next five, flew by for the four children. Each summer Carson, Colton, and Corbin would arrive a week after school let out and go back to their mom's a week before school started back up. They would swim in the swimming hole, climb trees, play board games when it rained, and talk for hours about what they wanted to do when they grew up. As the years went by, Rusty found himself more and more drawn to Carson, until he could almost admit to himself (but no-one else; gross, liking a girl) that he loved her.

Then disaster struck. Mr. Jenkins took a job in Philadelphia so that he could be closer to his children all year long. There would be no more summers of fun. There would be no more Corbin, Colton, and worse yet, no more Carson.

The Jenkins family moved and Rusty fell into a blue funk the next summer, even though he was now old enough to ride his bike into town to go swimming at the local pool or play at the homes of school friends. Rusty, Carson, Corbin, and Colton tried writing for a while, but they were just kids and slowly the letters tapered off. Rusty received only sporadic letters from Carson when something really noteworthy happened, and then she too stopped writing. Eventually, as children do, Rusty moved his friends to the back of his mind and then out of it completely.

Then, a letter arrived, six years after the Jenkins had moved and just like that, his friends were back in his mind. The letter was from Colton telling Rusty that he had gotten into Kansas State University. Rusty was going to the same college, and the two friends would be reunited. Colton's letter told Rusty that Corbin had enlisted in the army and was going to Vietnam and that Carson had taken a job at a local modeling agency. The letter brought back waves of memories, and Rusty looked forward to seeing Colton again.

Rusty and Colton reunited at college. Rusty didn't look much different than when he was a kid, just taller. Colton's hair wasn't quite as blond as it had been and was on the long side. He had the body of the wrestler he was. As it happened, the two boys ended up in close-by dorms. They'd meet occasionally for sodas and deliberate over the possible fate of Corbin. They'd say a prayer or two for his safety.

Both boys were unsurprised that Carson had gone into modeling. Rusty said that he had always thought she was the most beautiful girl he knew, and now he guessed she had proven him right.

"Jeez," Colton groaned, "that's gross."

Rusty turned red and changed the subject.

Unfortunately, as these things seem to go, the two boys had grown apart and had little in common. Although they enjoyed seeing each other, they didn't spend much time together, saying hello when passing in the hallways, sitting together occasionally to shoot the breeze and talk about their families, but little else.

Then Colton tracked Rusty down to tell him that Corbin had been shot in action. He didn't know how badly his brother was hurt, and he was beside himself with worry. Rusty had Colton contact his advisor to explain the situation so that he wouldn't get failing grades during this time of crisis. Rusty and Colton talked every day with Colton giving Rusty updates on Corbin. During this time, Rusty and Colton started to fall into their old friendship and both seemed to forget they had fallen out of it.

Colton rushed up to Rusty one day and with a hitch in his voice dropped the news like a bombshell. "Corbin had to have his left leg removed below the knee. Mom says his letters are upbeat and that he is doing physical therapy. As soon as he is able to get about, he will be honorably discharged. He'll be coming home."

Rusty and Colton continued to talk, both horrified by the results of the gunshot that Corbin had withstood. Colton worried that he wouldn't know how to treat Corbin, but Rusty assured him that Corbin would still be his brother, not some stranger, and that he should treat him like he always had.

Six weeks later, Colton told Rusty that Corbin was coming home. "He'll be there the day after summer break begins." Colton was shaking so badly that Rusty asked whether Colton wanted him to come along. He didn't want Colton to go alone in the shape he was in.

Colton decided that, yes, he did want Rusty to accompany him home. As they neared Philadelphia and the Jenkins home, Rusty felt himself grow more and more nervous. He began to think that he should have stayed at college and not made this trip. How would it feel to face Corbin knowing that he had lost a leg? Then he reminded himself of what he had told Colton, that it was still just Corbin, and that he should treat him as he always did.

Ok then, how am I going to feel seeing Carson again? This last thought gave Rusty pause. "Is Carson coming home too?" Rusty, stuttering and turning slightly red, asked Colton. "I mean, is she going to be there to see Corbin too?"

Colton gave Rusty a strange look. "She actually lives in Philadelphia, but she's staying at Mom's for the next few days. She wants to be there when Corbin gets home," Colton said. "I kind of thought you guys still wrote to each other. I guess I was wrong."

"I haven't talked to Carson in a long time," Rusty said somberly. "I lost track of all of you until you and I got into the same college. I didn't know where any of you were. Sometimes I'd think about you all and wonder where you were, what you were doing, but I didn't even know how to get in touch with you, how to find you. I'd lost your address years ago. I didn't know if any of you had gotten married or anything like that. Hell, I didn't even know if you were still alive. I mean, I didn't know anything, nothing at all." Rusty sounded injured.

Colton looked thoughtful. "I guess I never thought about it. When we all get together and start talking about the past, your name always comes up. You know, now that I think about it, it is usually Carson who brings your name up." Colton gave Rusty a speculative look but said no more.

The two boys continued into the city and to the Jenkins home. Rusty had never met Mrs. Jenkins and wasn't surprised to find that she looked remarkably like her children. She had a very pleasant disposition and Rusty instantly liked her. Standing next to her was a distinguished-looking gentleman who Colton introduced as his step-father, John Manson. He guessed that meant Mrs. Jenkins wasn't Mrs. Jenkins at all, but was instead Mrs. Manson. He was glad he found out before he greeted her. "I'm glad to finally meet you, Mrs. Manson, and it's nice to meet you too, sir," Rusty said to Mr. and Mrs. Manson.

Mrs. Manson hugged him and said she felt she already knew him from hearing the kids talk about him every year when they returned home from their dad's house. She then said that Carson was waiting in the family room and that Colton and Rusty should go on through.

Rusty followed Colton into the family room and almost lost his breath at his first sight of Carson in seven years. She was stunning; blond hair cascaded over her shoulders, blue eyes sparkled, and her lips were red and luscious. His voice left him. He knew from the warmth of his face that he was blushing. Carson looked up when they entered, glanced at Rusty without recognition, then jumped to her feet and threw her arms around Colton. "Colton, what are we going to do?"

Colton slowly removed himself from his crying sister, looked her firmly in the eyes and said, "Get it together, sis; don't let Corbin see you like this. We have to be strong for him so that he can be strong. Remember, it's still Corbin. His leg doesn't make him who he is!"

Sniffling, Carson said, "You're right. I know you're right, but it's so hard. I mean, he's so much a part us that I can't believe that this could happen."

"Well, it did," Colton said. "Now we have to be here for Corbin and forget about ourselves. We need to act as natural as possible, okay?" Noticing his guest standing by the door, Colton said to Carson, "Say hi to Rusty."

Carson looked bewildered and glanced from Colton to Rusty. "Rusty," she said. "Rusty?" She looked at Rusty a moment and understanding came into her eyes. "Rusty," she said flatly. "Oh, I didn't recognize you."

She turned back to Colton and Rusty sat down in a chair feeling as if he had been slapped, as if his heart had been yanked out and stepped on. He couldn't understand why Carson had treated him this way. He had thought that they would probably hug just like she and Colton had. He sat down quietly and waited while Carson and Colton talked.

Finally, Colton told Rusty he'd show him to his room. Rusty couldn't wait to escape from Carson and quickly followed him. Colton looked at Rusty after they got to the guest room and asked quietly, "What did you do to her?"

Rusty, still feeling as if struck by a truck, said, "Nothing. I haven't even talked to her since you moved. We all wrote a few times, but then we just kind of quit. I haven't heard from her for over six years."

"Well she's sure got a mad on for you," Colton said matter-of-factly. "But I'm sure she'll get over it." Colton left Rusty and he lay on the bed and thought back to the days Carson, Corbin, Colton, and he had spent together. He found himself smiling often and soon drifted into sleep.

Rusty was awakened by the sound of Carson calling out, "He's here." He got up from the bed and moved to the window. Looking out, he saw that a cab had pulled up to the front of the house. A young man with scraggly hair and a stringy beard got unsteadily out of the cab, balanced precariously, and reached back into the cab for a pair of crutches and an overnight bag. He tossed some money into the cab and made his way laboriously to the front of the house. Rusty noticed that one leg of the man's pants was pinned up below the knee. "Corbin," Rusty whispered to himself.

As if sensing that someone was looking at him, Corbin glanced up. Rusty waved and Corbin stared a moment. Rusty thought he saw Corbin mouth the word "Rusty", and then he waved a hand in the general direction of Rusty and started towards the door of the house.

Rusty waited upstairs for a while, combing his hair, brushing his teeth and generally freshening up, giving the family some time together before he made his way downstairs. He followed the sounds of voices and found everyone in the family room.

Rusty walked in and Corbin hollered, "Rusty, how the hell have you been?"

Rusty and Corbin shook hands grinning at each other. "I been fine, how about you, I mean apart from the obvious?" Rusty asked with the grin leaving his face.

Corbin grimaced, "I've definitely been better, oh yeah, definitely better!"

For a while Corbin spoke. He told them about getting hit by the bullet. He told them how the wound had gotten infected and his dismay when he heard that he would have to lose the leg. Then, he gave them some good news. He was to be fitted for prosthesis as soon as the leg had healed completely. He should be able to walk again, eventually. Everyone was heartened by this news and the mood lightened.

Corbin then asked to be excused; he said that he really needed to clean up. He'd flown in to the States and immediately boarded a plane for home. "I didn't take time to groom," Corbin said with a laugh. "All I wanted was to get home to you all."

Colton allowed that his brother looked like a bum and Corbin threw a pillow at him. This helped to lighten the mood further. Corbin made his way with difficulty up the stairs, accompanied by Colton, who carried his bag. It would become obvious over the next few weeks that Corbin had told them all he was going to about his time in the war; although, it was possible that he spoke to Colton about it when they were alone together.

Mr. and Mrs. Manson said they had things to do and left Carson and Rusty alone together. Carson stood and started to leave without a word, but Rusty stopped her. "Carson, why are you mad at me?"

Carson paused right inside the door and Rusty thought that she was going to walk on; but, she stopped, squared her shoulders, and turned back to him. "Why do you think Rusty?" she asked haughtily with a glint of anger and hurt in her beautiful blue eyes. "Did you think that you could just walk in here and act like we're old friends, like you never deserted muh..us?" Rusty thought she almost said 'me' but then caught herself and changed it to 'us'.

"Huh?" Rusty was puzzled. "What do you mean, deserted you? I don't understand."

Carson looked at him and after a moment she spouted out. "You never called, or wrote, or anything. It was like you just decided you didn't like me anymore." Rusty noticed that this time she said 'me' and not 'we' or 'us'. He also noted that tears glistened in her eyes. "I thought you liked me. Why did you stop?" she cried.

Rusty was confused. "I did like you; I liked you a lot, and I've never stopped," he said. "I never stopped writing. I mean, I did stop, but then, we all stopped. Not because I didn't like you; just because I was a kid and a boy I guess, so when you stopped, I stopped too. Do you see what I mean? Of *course* I like you! How could I not!"

Carson appeared speculative, the look in her eyes far away. "You're right," she said hesitantly. "I guess I'd forgotten. We did all quit writing, me last of all I guess, but we all quit eventually. What with school and all, I had forgotten that we all quit. How could I forget that?" She looked at Rusty with anguish in her eyes.

"Life pulls funny tricks with our heads," Rusty said. "At least I know it does with mine. How about we start over? I'll go out and come back in." He left the room.

A few minutes passed and Rusty re-entered the family room. Carson had sat down on the couch and jumped up when Rusty entered. "Rusty," she screeched gaily and threw herself into his arms. Rusty grabbed her up and spun her around, then he held her like he would never let go, finally able to savor the greeting he had expected on his initial arrival.

Finally they separated and Carson gave a self-conscious giggle. "Well, I guess we're made up," she said.

"I guess so," smiled Rusty.

They sat on the couch and talked; they spoke of the times they had spent together as kids. Rusty told Carson that he would never forget the first time he had ever seen her, the time she made the amazing basketball shot. He told her that he remembered the first time that he had noticed her eyes; that her eyes weren't exactly the same as Colton and Corbin's eyes after all. It was a rainy day and they had been at Rusty's house playing a board game. Rusty had just landed on one of Carson's properties with a hotel on it, and Carson had whooped, "Pay me two thousand dollars." Rusty looked dolefully at his money and then up at Carson. There was a gleeful look on her face, and that was when Rusty noticed that her eyes didn't look at all like her brothers'. They sparkled and glittered. He had never noticed her brothers' eyes look like this. Her eyes were beautiful, and from that point on he snuck peaks at them every chance he got.

They talked until Colton and Corbin came back downstairs. Corbin had shaved and his hair was pulled back neatly in a hair band that Rusty suspected was Carson's, since it was pink. He looked more like his old self, only thinner. Corbin's mom would take care of that with her good cooking. At the dinner table, the conversation was stilted to begin with. Gradually they fell into old patterns, and the talk became freer and more lively as they found that Corbin was still Corbin and not some stranger in their midst.

Rusty stayed most of the summer, only going home for a couple of weeks. By the end of the summer, it was quite obvious to everyone that Rusty and Carson were a couple. Carson visited often, and she and Rusty had been caught by more than one family member holding hands or snatching quick kisses. No one disapproved; although Colton was once heard to say that he was totally grossed out, causing Carson to fall into fits of giggles.

Corbin got his new leg. It hurt a lot to begin with, but he had the support of his family and eventually learned to walk with it. He improved daily and began talking about getting some newfangled leg that bends naturally at the ankle and in the foot. Everyone hoped this would happen for him.

Rusty and Colton returned to school. Carson and Rusty wrote at least weekly, sometimes more often. Rusty and Colton had some of the same classes so were able to spend more time together cementing their old friendship.

During the Christmas break, Rusty went home and after a wonderful holiday, he went to Philadelphia to see the Jenkins family. He had brought small gifts for everyone and found that they had bought for him also. After everyone had opened their presents, it became obvious that Rusty had not given Carson anything. She never said a word, but Corbin asked "What's up Rusty? Did you forget to get Carson something?"

Carson blushed from ear to ear and sputtered, "Corbin, shut up, it's okay."

Rusty looked horribly confused and said, "No, I got her something, it must be under the tree still. Come help me look for it, Carson."

They both got down on their hands and knees and searched under the tree but came up empty-handed. Carson stood up and said that it was fine and that Rusty shouldn't worry about it. But Rusty, after cunningly reaching into his pocket, said, "Wait a minute, I found it."

Carson, who had started to turn away so he wouldn't see the tears forming in her eyes, turned back. Rusty rose to one knee and held out a ring box. He opened it and said, "Carson, will you be my wife?"

The whole room fell quiet. Carson was incredulous and stood with mouth agape. Finally she regained her composure and breathlessly said, "Yes," and then louder, "Yes, Yes, YES."

Rusty slipped the ring onto her finger, stood, grabbed her around the waist and twirled her in a circle, laughing joyously.

Carson turned to her family and said, "Did you all know about this?"

Corbin and Colton pled innocence, but her mom and step-dad just beamed. "The boys didn't, but of course we knew," her mom said, waving a hand at Carson's step-father, a gesture of inclusion. "Rusty asked your dad for your hand and then asked us too. We all accepted his offer at once. Your dad was thrilled to see Rusty again after all these years."

Carson was amazed at the extent of Rusty's proposal and the way he had included all of her parents. Tears sprang to her eyes and she suddenly found herself crying. Rusty rushed forward. "What's wrong? Are you okay?" he asked with concern.

Carson laughed and assured him that not only was she fine but that she was fantastic.

"But," Rusty began while touching a tear that trickled down her cheek, "Why the tears?"

Carson just shook her head and then explained, "They're tears of joy, goofball!"

"Goofball," Rusty exclaimed, faking outrage. "Goofball? Maybe I'll take back my proposal!"

"Not in this lifetime," Carson laughed, giving him a big kiss which he returned with gusto.

The wedding was planned for the spring after Rusty would graduate. That would be in three years, but with Rusty studying most of the time and visiting when possible, and Carson continuing with her modeling career, the time flew by. Graduation came and suddenly it was spring.

After much ado, Rusty was standing at the church altar looking with adoration into the eyes of his soon-to-be wife, the eyes he had fallen in love with fifteen years before....

Adjectivity

Or: The Lurking Evil of Circular Black Things

On my old brown antique wooden desk sits a small round black modern fan, right next to and beside the short green-shaded table lamp with the gold-plated base. It stares at me, its dark circular center a Cyclops's single-eyed ogling gape, but flat and black as a jet obsidian orb, like a shark's unwavering and unfeeling gaze. A squat diminutive thing, it poses no obvious threat, but is still threatening nonetheless. It simultaneously intimidates without being intimidating and presents a hazard while being completely benign, in a dangerous sort of harmless way. It radiates nonlethal lethality.

The snide little fan rests on a black hollow metal tube, twisted into a stand with three tiny black rubber grips, one at each of its two equidistant outer points and the other at the rear for sturdy balance. The fan hunkers in a hulky little crouch and waits with its hulky little attitude, strangely silent at the moment, perhaps brooding, possibly scheming, and most definitely glowering.

How could a small personal fan be so sinister? This is a good, reasonable, and logical question for which I have no sane and practical answer. None. It just is what it is and that happens to be pure unadulterated unexplainable evil. The fan takes on a dark and predatory character, its watchful posture creating a niggling and disturbing presence, like some new and heretofore unheard of form of vermin. Vermin are small, yet unsettling, even if their unsettling quality is mainly due to their power to disturb rather than any actual power for direct damage or aggression. That's it. My little desk fan is like a small diabolical electronic version of vermin. I consider giving it a derogatory nickname such as The Rat, The Cockroach, or The Bacteria. But, I reject the idea even as I embrace it. Therefore, I disagree with myself and after spirited deliberation, bordering on violence at times, I win the internal debate. I decide firmly and categorically not to name the fan, even as I immediately regret the decision.

I realize, recognize, admit to myself, and concede that I am only lucky and fortunate that it cannot reproduce or replicate itself. Or can it? My unnerved and apprehensive mind has traveled down a bizarre rambling nonsensical path, one filled with chaotic, absurd, irrational notions that can only just lead to incoherent misguided frightening conclusions. The ridiculous but dreadful idea that my small fan may give birth to even smaller fans is troublesome, taxing, and persistent. It is relentless, continual, ongoing, and generally constant. In fact, the crazy notion leaves my thoughts immediately, which is converse to, opposite of, and in direct contradiction to what I so steadfastly claimed earlier. I can't explain this apparent discrepancy; I can only report it. Still, my observations continue.

On the other side of my innocuous green table lamp squats a petite black Logitech speaker with a screened front and a round volume knob on the right-hand side above a dark hole that represents itself as a headphone jack. The speaker is narrow and sleek, sitting upon a short round pedestal. It, too, lurks. Barely visible behind its many-holed screen is a circular image, which is probably and in all likelihood the actual speaker itself, although I do not intend to prove it. This theme of circularity cannot be mere coincidence or happenstance, not by chance or twist of fate. In fact, it is deliberate, intentional, fully planned, completely premeditated, and I would say and still contend to this day, on purpose, even if it was accidental, which it was not. Again, the impression is that of a flat black eye fixed in unmoving inexorable patient scrutiny directly on me.

Beside the speaker, a pair of modest sized headphones lies. The black cord twists in repose over the glassy surface of my desk like a coiled serpent at uneasy rest. At rest, but not sleeping. No, this snake is merely in a sly pretense of slumber, not genuine, real, true, or authentic repose. Therefore,. I am not convinced. The ear pads of the black headphones are round, lined with black foam for comfort (or so it could be assumed, but I doubt it), and carrying forth the menacing circular theme that has already been so firmly established.

My white glass mug-style coffee cup, again circular, is situated atop a round lime green coaster which has a black backing. Black as the fan that haunts my desk, black as the accusatory stare of the speaker watching me with its veiled eye, black as the small round emblem on my computer mouse.

Somewhat surprised, mildly astonished, and only marginally interested at this point, I note there are actually two themes in play. The color black and the shape of a circle; double dismay. Glancing with nervous trepidation at my black keyboard, I must express further alarming and perturbing observations. My keyboard typing surface is rife with circular symbols ranging from the letter "O" to round punctuation marks and zeros. In fact, the keyboard is crawling with spherical round circular shapes printed upon a black background. A vile conspiracy is in the works; there is no other alternative additional option that might explain this disquieting distressing unwholesome trend.

Now that I am aware of the dangerous situation happening on my desk, I see sign after morbid hazardous sign of this ominous and upsetting state of affairs. The dangling dull flat black metal pulls on the seven desk drawers are round. The black pocket-sized notebook perched with faux fake contrived virtue and insidious sly guile on the sharp corner of my perilous desk features a small incongruous circular logo. The handy carrying strap of my small black digital camera is a loop, just another wicked circle, disguised as a harmless innocuous oval. The short shallow black container holding my assorted silver paperclips is round as a minted coin. A closer discerning look at my green desk lamp reveals a glaring circular base and a black round switch beneath a suspicious spherical bulb that itself contains noxious black writing, some of it circular, within a circle.

No more can I return to my prior and previous innocent state of unaware ignorance. I have now perceived the outrageous subterfuge, although I know not its secret hidden unrevealed purpose. I must be watchful and wary when I enter the enemy camp, otherwise known as My Desk; for I am watched, scrutinized, and observed. Foul malevolent devious forces are pitted against me. Fortunately, I am onto their underhanded sneaky malicious game and will remain ever vigilant while at my computer, the computer that I just noticed sits upon a round black base.

From now on, I am attuned to and in line with the reality of My Desk. I'll not be fooled again. Besides, I am growing sick of adjectives.

Climbing Out

What people can get used to, it's amazing. Filth, rats, dangerous characters, and other unpleasant and unsavory things.

There was a time when I had a home and family. I went through ordinary problems, like irritation over the hole in the screen door that made our house look tacky. Or the rings of sticky residue left by half-emptied glasses on the table. Sour milk in the bottom of the cereal bowls piled unwashed in the sink. Too much noise from the television or radio filling the air with annoyance. Then Vince disappeared in his Lincoln, just drove away never to return, and I was on my own. He didn't really give me a chance to work things out. He took the boys with him, without my knowledge. The town sheriff turned a deaf ear to my pleading.

"He has a right," he said. "They's his boys, too. He's probably just going to take them on a little vacation. They'll be back before long. You'll see."

But I knew they would never be back. I was alone.

I had no money. And, although I took a job waitressing at the café, I didn't make enough to pay the mortgage. As I fell further and further behind on the bills, I took more than a drink or two for the stress. None of it was my fault.

By the time they took the house from me, I had given up. The linoleum hadn't seen a good coat of wax in months; in fact, it hadn't even been mopped. Dust had collected in the corners, and a sour smell lived in the bathroom like an unwanted pest.

There was shame involved in the foreclosure.

Houses somehow know when love has fled. They break down faster. Paint peels and cracks with lightning speed. Dirt creeps in. Spiders become more industrious and spin their webs with renewed vigor. Weeds move into the lawn and bring their families with them. Hinges droop, boards loosen, and steps shift out of kilter. Everyone knows love doesn't hold a house together, but tell that to the house. Houses don't know it.

The last paycheck bought me a bus ticket. I was about to be fired anyway; I could feel it. With few dollars in my fake leather purse, I boarded with a sigh. I wanted a drink badly at that time, but I didn't give in to the craving. I had a small bottle in my bag that I was saving for later. I didn't even look at the dusty streets as the bus pulled away. Nothing in that town meant a thing to me anymore. I was on my way to a metropolis, a place where I could lose myself.

The city is an animal with a great beating heart, but no love. My money didn't last long. The first job I found was in a Laundromat, making change and keeping the machines cleaned out. Basically, I had to babysit the patrons. I was fired when caught sleeping in the back room one night. This wasn't my fault; I slept there because I had nowhere else to go.

Then, there I was, wandering the streets, hoping for a halfway decent place to sleep and any kind of work. I applied for lots of jobs. At least my clothes were clean; I had seen to that on my last job. I even found work here and there. But for one reason or another, none of those jobs had lasted and I got so I preferred not to think about them.

I became used to sleeping under bridges and in alleys, inside parked cars that people forgot to lock up, and beneath bushes. Even, for a short and frightening time, in the tunnels beneath the city. My meals came from a variety of places. Garbage bins, discarded fast food sacks, soup kitchens, and charitable strangers who would duck into a store and come out with something for me, a sandwich or carton of milk. Deeply ashamed and eternally grateful, I mumbled my thanks without raising my eyes.

The best thing I was ever given was a used backpack. It came from a church giveaway. It came in handy. The next best thing was the wagon I happened across. It was a lucky find, abandoned perhaps, in a yard. Abandoned or not, it became mine. It was rusty, but it held my possessions just fine. I couldn't say how many months I dragged that thing behind me, advertising my homeless condition. I felt the stares, some of pity, others of disgust, but I ignored them all. When a person sinks to a certain level, the only thing left to do is to take no notice of people and hope they leave you alone.

With everything in my soul, I longed to see my children. But by this time, I hoped with equal fervor they would never see me. Not then. Not the person I had become. So, while I scanned every crowd for their familiar little faces, I also dreaded the thought that I might actually find them.

One chilly day, I pulled my wagon behind me down the windswept street of a residential neighborhood well past its prime. *God bless the housing market crash*, I thought as I passed several foreclosed properties. Their windows held that same old vacant stare my own house had had when it was taken from me, that same forsaken look you might see in the eyes of mental patients whose families had long since forgotten to visit. Glancing around me and seeing no one, I hurried around the back of one of the places. It took some doing, but I got inside and hauled my wagon in after me. The house was an old Victorian, but fixed up some, not falling apart just yet.

I hoped someone had forgotten to turn off the electricity and water, but I had no such luck. Still, this house provided walls around me for safety and shelter from the elements. I settled in. I had to haul water in empty milk jugs from the park a few blocks down. And since I was new to the area, I had to scope out the best places to find discarded food and other items which I needed. At first, I was careful to hide my comings and goings. I never knew what watchful neighbor might take an interest. But, it seemed the people left in the neighborhood weren't concerned, or were too busy to care. They were mostly gone during the day. I grew braver and began using the front door. What I did was criminal and I knew it, but I did it anyway. It wasn't my fault.

Down on Matin Avenue I could panhandle if I watched for the cops. Some days I cleared as much as thirty dollars. Tucking my wagon into a bedroom closet, I set out on foot in the cleanest outfit I had. I earned twenty dollars that day, and someone gave me a bag of donuts. When I got back 'home', I pulled the realtor sign from the front yard and hid it under the house.

That first night in the house, I had done a lot of thinking. I figured now that I had an actual address, I could start my climb back up in the world. For three long years, I had been wandering the streets, but I had not forgotten what it felt like to have a home.

Neither had I forgotten my sons. Like grief when a loved one dies, losing my boys was an agony that would never truly pass. I had dwelt on it for so long, it was a part of me. It had dug around and eaten a big hole inside me, a scooped-out hollow place that was almost comfortable to settle down into with my bottle. But, that night I decided I would not curl up in that hole again. I would avoid it, even if it meant forcibly taking my thoughts by the shoulders and jerking them the other way. No, I would not even stand at the edge and look at it. Not for a long time. Not until I could see it without giving in to the urge to climb into it and wait for death. This took more strength than I knew I had.

My brain was fuddled, but it was clear I had to stop drowning myself in alcohol. I was not an alcoholic; I knew that. In fact, there were times in my downward spiral when I wondered how alcoholics did it. No, I knew I was not one of them. But my body didn't know it and when I tried to stop drinking, I became grievously ill. It finally occurred to me to wean myself away. This I could do. And I did. But it took several weeks and massive amounts of willpower. Every time the faces of my boys popped up in my mind, I pushed them out. I knew the guilt I felt from rejecting them like this would continue my whole life long, but I was desperate.

A visit to a food bank stocked my kitchen. A trip to a church charity group netted me some tattered blankets, a few changes of clothes, and a pair of shoes. A trip to the welfare office gave me some emergency cash. I bought supplies, including candles so I could have some light, and soap so I could wash. My excitement began to grow once the worst of the sickness had passed. Confidence bloomed weakly in me at first, and I responded by collecting my nerve. I walked into the electric company like I had a right to be there and paid a deposit to have the lights turned on in the house. I did the same at the gas and water companies. The gas company even sent a man out to light my pilot lights for me. I pretended to be a new renter who hadn't gotten my furniture moved in yet, and he was very nice to me. Just in time for winter, I had a home again.

But I had to face facts. Someday the house would sell. Just because I took the sign down didn't mean the house wasn't still on the active list at the realtor's office, or with the bank that had foreclosed on it. The thought made me quake inside.

In addition to that fear was the very real worry of how I would pay these utility bills when they came. I had no job and very little money, just what I earned begging, and that barely sustained me. I had to find work.

I luxuriated in the shower. Then I took a hot bath. It was a glorious feeling. I had nothing to dry off with other than my blanket, but it felt wonderful to be so clean again. I ate a cold can of soup and tried to not to fret. Now that I had the house, I feared losing it.

That night, as I tossed and turned on the floor near the heater vent, an outrageous idea came to me. The very next morning, I put on one of the outfits I had gotten from the church, walked to that real estate office, and applied for a job. I gave them a slightly different address so they wouldn't suspect I was living in one of their properties. They had no openings, the nice lady told me. I then practically begged. I said I would do anything, even part-time. File papers, answer the phone, even clean up properties. Anything. She told me to wait and disappeared behind a door.

Soon, a friendly man in a white shirt with rolled up sleeves came out. He shook my hand and introduced himself as the manager. I followed him back to his office.

"We don't really have any openings right now," he said as he sat behind his desk. He gestured toward a chair to the side. I sat.

"I understand," I said. I felt defeated, but tried not to show it.

He seemed to relent, looking thoughtfully at me. "I couldn't afford to pay much, but I suppose I could get you in here a few hours a day to answer the phones while my agents are showing houses. Things are really slow right now. We couldn't keep our full-time secretary busy, and she took another job."

"That's ok," I said, excitement bubbling through me. "Part-time is fine."

"You don't really have much experience," he said, looking over my application. "Kind of a spotty work history. But, these are hard times. I'll tell you what. You come in tomorrow and we'll do this on a trial basis. Give it a shot for a week or so, and see what happens. That okay with you?"

"Yes, oh yes," I said. We agreed on hours and pay, which was barely above minimum wage.

My scheme shouldn't have worked. I know that now. But it did work.

My first day on the job, I found the file on my house and got the name of the bank that foreclosed on it. I went to see them and offered to take over the payments, if they would just let me move in. I didn't, of course, tell them I already had moved in. At first, they flat out said no. But I reminded them they were making nothing on it now. I cajoled. I pressed. I was ready to resort to begging. They could find no credit report on me, as Vince had always done things in his name only. The whole affair ended with them taking a chance on me. So, like I said, it shouldn't have worked, but it did. The bank pulled the listing from the realtor, and I signed papers. The house was mine.

A part-time job was not enough to maintain a house; within a week, I had found a second job in a nursing home, cleaning rooms. I worked there in the mornings and at the realtor's office in the afternoons. After a couple of weeks, I was even able to purchase some second-hand furniture. Over the next few months, I painted and did some minor repairs. My house was starting to look like a home.

I had sunk into the depths of despair and pulled myself out again. When I began to evaluate my past instead of avoiding it, I eventually reached a point where I had to admit that at least some of my misery *was* my fault. Not all of it for sure, but some of it. Maybe Vince was not totally to blame for his decision to leave me. It was hard facing up to that, but I had to admit to myself that I was far from the perfect wife and mother. I had done some things I shouldn't have. I was finally ready to be accountable for my mistakes. It was a big step for me.

I am no longer ashamed to look for the faces of my sons in every crowd. I visit the library most weekends and do internet searches. And, I'm saving what I can toward hiring a private investigator. I will find my boys someday. The mother I could be now is a much better person than the one they knew. The choice will be up to them. I hope they'll give me a chance.

The Deconstruction of Dennis

This is the story of my demise. It is also the truth of my demise.

For some, the downward slide into madness starts as the result of a crushing emotional blow, or a cataclysmic lurch in some homeostatic process deep within the organism. No one expects it to be gradual and insidious. Conventional thought embraces the idea of a sudden trauma, a happening that we can point to and say, "Ah, so that's what did it." But despair can creep in slowly, an evil seed taking root in the depths of the psyche, watered by indifference, fertilized by caustic comments. It grows unseen in the head and heart, blocking out the light and taking over like a noxious weed, crowding joy out of its way like a rude stranger on a bus pushing other travelers aside. It settles in and spreads, becoming a thing unto itself. It grows into a smothering, nervous dictator, constantly harping, weighing down the soul, and pulling toward the dark bottom of life where hope has died.

The day I choose to die dawns with a merciless heat, yet my house is cold as always. When we had this house built, it was an ego boost. Set in a nice new neighborhood with prefab precision, it looked almost, but not quite exactly, like every other house on the block. But I have been proud of this house. It is an achievement for me, having a house built. It is a visible manifestation of years of education, hard work and planning. Who could have predicted within its walls would lay the coldest realm on the face of this earth? The warmth of real love is absent, leaving an empty chill inside.

This July morning I rise from the sofa where I have spent part of another sleepless night. I wonder if my family is still slumbering in my daughter's room, door locked against me. I want to go to them; I don't because there is an invisible barrier. Their indifference is a strong wall, and I am too weak to hurl myself against it anymore. The low-level buzz of sleep deprivation hums continually in my brain. I try to tune it out and go again to the mirror to check my hair. More of it is gone! A sickening lump of dismay slides down inside me, leaving a trail of disgust. I gently part my hair and check my scalp, tilting my head this way and that, carefully examining each area. To my rising horror, I find several more spots where my hair is sparse and thinning, and when I take my hands away, I see that several hairs cling to my fingers. I would weep if I weren't so damn tired. This is at least the thousandth time I have checked my hair since midnight. My long vigils have drained me and I feel the fatigue deep in my bones and my soul. I can almost hear the persistent thoughts out loud now, just on the periphery of my awareness, like a low icy voice in the next room...I look terrible, I am worthless, I will never get past this, I can't go out in public looking like this.....on and on until I think my spirit will crumble to dust and my body fall away in a puff of smoke. I pace the kitchen, then the living room, then go back to the mirror to check again, hoping that I am wrong. Sure enough, more hair is gone. Little pieces of me. Missing. They must lay scattered here and there tucked within the fibers of the carpet, or hidden among the rumpled clothes in the hamper, or evaporated into thin air for all I know. But they are not on my head where they belong, and I am turning into a freakish caricature of my former self. It is agonizing for me to watch my disfigurement grow each passing day, each hour, each moment. What will I do? How can I function? How could I present myself to the world looking like I do? I am weary beyond measure from the worry of it.

I am driving my family crazy with this. My wife says my hair looks fine; this *thing* is all in my head. She believes it is a delusion to which I am stubbornly and deliberately clinging. She has pointed out many times that I am selfish, possibly even lazy. My daughter tells me I am *acting like a retard*. "Maybe he is even faking it," she speculates aloud. They no longer want to hear my concerns. I have worn them down and they have distanced themselves from me emotionally. Now at night they retreat to my daughter's room and lock the door to get away from me. If I bring up the subject of my hair, they grow angry and cold, and roll their eyes in annoyance. They have become desensitized to my pain. I am losing my family. Maybe I have already lost them. I know this is my fault, but I can't seem to keep my fears to myself.

I am lonely. One night I ask my wife if she will please just hold me. I tell her we don't have to do anything or talk about anything, but would she please just hold me. I long for some connection to reel me back in, away from the free-floating aloneness that threatens to devour me. She gazes at me with that flat look in her eyes and turns away, closing the door softly behind her. I hang my head, accepting my punishment. We have reached a point where she can barely tolerate the sight of me. This is my fault...I have done this to us. I have done this to myself. I have become *inconvenient*.

In January, I was fine. By May of this year, I no longer have a job. When I became too distressed to work, my wife's attention turns to issues of money. I am no longer contributing financially, not shouldering my share of family responsibilities. The arguments replay themselves in my mind. I tell her to take my retirement to pay the bills. She tells me that would be fine in the short term, but she is looking at the big picture. She is bitter. She tells me I will never get better. She predicts I will never work again. She says she will end up carrying the whole financial load by herself. She talks of divorce. Conversely, she says knowing her luck she would divorce me and then I would get well and find some other woman. I realize how badly I have hurt this woman, but it seems that my fixation has more power over me than even she does. I dread a divorce; still I cannot stop, cannot 'grow up and snap out of it' as she insists I could do if I wanted to. And my hair continues falling out by the handfuls.

I defend myself the best I can, but my defense is timid for I know I am to blame for this crisis. We are not poor, I quietly remind my wife. We have savings. I have my retirement account. Our house is paid for.

My twenty-year-old daughter says to her mother, "Why don't you just get rid of him? Why are you fooling around with him anyway? I had a vacation planned and he's ruining it! And now he won't work! What good is he?" Each word is a blow to me. What have I done to my child? I have turned her against me. That's what I have done.

I have loved being a father. Every part of it. Tears of joy at the birth of my children. Tender love overflowing. Heart full, memories flow over me. Sitting at the kitchen table with my daughter, my angel, gazing at the shiny cap of curly dark hair as she bent over her homework, the curve of her cheek delicately and sweetly cupped in her pudgy hand, and her asking me, "Is this right, Dad? Is this right?" I remember the swim meets, spelling bees, cozy bedtime stories, giggling slumber parties, fierce tennis matches, family vacations, and the feel of her little hand in mine when we crossed the street. She no longer calls me Dad. Now she calls me by my first name, which causes some people to wrongly assume I am her stepfather. She used to look up at me with adoring eyes. But now she looks at me with scorn. I have alienated her and I see that she despises me. My first response is disbelief, but it turns gradually to acceptance. Of course, she would feel this way. I have let her down, too. I tell her I am sorry. I am so sorry.

My confidence is somehow linked to my hair and it begins to diminish with each small loss. I experience decimating self-doubt. Niggling fears skitter relentlessly around in me like furtive mice in a dark room. I am driven to check and recheck my hair continually. This started as a secret worry years ago, but it lived in the background for the most part. It stayed in its place. But it hides no longer.

I am fifty years old. I have fathered two children. I am a faithful husband. I have won weight training competitions. I am tall and correctly proportioned. I am a business major, a CPA, a master of numbers. But, I am not good with words. I see this is a failure to communicate. If I could only do a better job of explaining myself …

I plead my case to my wife on many occasions. I say if I could just get hair transplant surgery, I would be myself again. It worked before and it could work again, I tell her. I have lost my confidence, but I can get it back if I could just fix the way I look. She says it won't do any good. She says it costs money we can't afford to spend. We have a son and daughter in college, she reminds me. She says I am thinking only of myself. She says I have no income now. I am ruining her life, she says. I hear these things and I don't blame her. I know frustration is speaking for her. I also know her accusations are true. I *am* thinking of myself....I can't *stop* thinking of myself and my affliction. That's the problem.

I am ashamed. Ashamed of the way I look, ashamed that I cannot work, ashamed of what I am putting my wife through. She looks at me now and her gaze no longer holds any warmth or respect. She looks at me now like the useless piece of shit I have become. My shame grows and folds over itself inside me, expanding and pushing outward to make room. Will it extend beyond me someday when my body can no longer contain it? My breathing becomes shallower to accommodate its painful presence. Shame, with its leaking acidic drip, rolls inside me like a malformed fetus turning over in the womb. Shame, my new constant companion. Shame, my new best friend. I feel sorry for my wife, shackled by Catholic marriage to a man like me.

She pushes me to change. She pushes with condemnation, scorn, and threats of divorce. I feel the sharp fear of being alone, the sick apprehension of losing her. I will do anything to hang on. Anything, but stop worrying about my hair. That I cannot do. Contrary to popular opinion in my house, this obsession controls me, not the other way around.

I wonder how we ever could have thought we were superior, that we had the perfect family, that we didn't have *these* kinds of problems. Is this some kind of karmic retribution for our snobbery? A divine dressing down? My wife has done no wrong that I can see. My children have done no wrong. Is it then a lesson meant only for me to suffer with and learn from? Will I emerge a better man? I fear it is permanent. I also fear it is a curse, but not a real one put on me by some evil magician or anything. More an accident of fate, I think. I am targeted for this affliction like some people are assigned MS or cancer or brittle bone disease. I won't find a reason for this before I die.

"There's nothing wrong with your hair," my wife says yet again. "Listen," she says, "you need to shape up and you need to do it quickly."

But I so clearly can see the problem. Could it really just be my perception? Is it my perception that is wrong? Is it? I feel my head carefully, fingers flying over the surface of my scalp with intimate familiarity. I go to the mirror. *No, it's not just my perception*, I cry out silently. *Look! Look at it! My hair is falling out.* God. It is falling out more and more each day. I think my implants are shriveling, dying. Something is badly wrong. I look like a radiation victim. I don't say these things to my wife, however. Not yet.

At the end of June, my former boss offers me a lesser position (since mine has been filled) and my wife wants me to accept the job. I tell her I did not spend all those years in school to become a bean counter. She misinterprets these words as combative, although I did not mean them to be. "You are going to do this," she tells me, "You are going to drive to that job and work it and you are going to keep on working it until you retire."

But when the day comes for me to start that job, I find I can't do it. My nervous hands keep seeking my hair of their own volition, checking and checking. It is a compelling force I can no longer resist. I call my boss and tell him I am struggling with my nerves. He is a compassionate man, and he gives me a week to try and feel better. A week doesn't make a difference. In a week, I am actually worse. I have to let the job go. I am too sick to function, too sleep-deprived to think clearly, too fearful to face people.

My parents keep saying, "Go to the doctor; go to the doctor." Finally one morning I feel inside me a small hard nugget of self-preservation. I go to my mother's house and ask my parents to take me to the hospital. They jump up immediately and rush me out to the car before I can change my mind. I sit up front with my dad and pull the sun visor down so I can check my hair in the mirror. I feel a strange sense of relief at noting the ugly condition of my head has not changed. I am not crazy. My hair really is falling out. I really am deformed. How can no one else see this?

We have to wait quite a long time in the emergency room. I am extremely nervous, afraid I will see someone I know. They will know why I have come. They would think ill of me and perhaps even discuss me with other people, talk about my decline, talk about me behind my back, perhaps even joke about me as my wife and daughter sometimes do. Only when I am finally taken back to a room and I can close the curtains do I feel a measure of relief.

The ER doctor is unhelpful. It is a fruitless exercise. I do not tell him I think more and more about dying. I do not tell him about my hair problem, which I find so deeply shameful. I only tell him I cannot sleep anymore. And I tell him I am depressed. He doesn't ask the right questions. And I don't volunteer much. He prescribes an antidepressant and a sleeping pill, and tells me to follow up with my regular doctor. He is brusque and hurried. After all my anxiety and apprehension, it is over with in a few minutes, an anticlimax.

"Why didn't you tell him the truth?" my mom asks me as we are leaving.

"You don't want them to lock me up do you?" I respond.

"Of course not," she says, "but how can the doctor help you if he doesn't know the whole story?"

"I don't know," I say.

"Well, son, you take the pills like he said and maybe they will help you."

When I get home, my wife goes with me to the pharmacy. I can tell she disapproves in some way, but she remains silent on the subject.

But, the pills don't help. In fact, they make me feel worse than ever. I feel sorry for anyone who has to take this kind of medicine on a daily basis. I hate the way it makes me feel, the bright hard edges to the world, the dry taste in my mouth, the increased agitation, the uneasy sensation that things are moving around in my brain. After only a few days, I know this is not the answer for me. I stop taking the medicine; it's the only thing I can do. Still, I can't pass a mirror without looking. My hair continues to fall out, my bald patches enlarge noticeably each day, and I know it is only a matter of time before my whole head will be a big disgusting orb with patchy sick-looking hair. I am turning into a clown, a troll, a sideshow freak. And I can't stop it from happening to me.

The days have started to run together. The nights are long and tortuous. I am beyond tired from my pacing and my slavish devotion to the mirror. My son comes home from college for a visit and I tell him I am not doing well. He utters kind reassuring words. He does not belittle me, but he can't wait to leave again. I don't blame him. For just a moment in my memory, there is a flash of the boy he used to be, his little blond head bobbing in the car seat, tiny hands patting my face, baby talk, big hugs for Dad. And later, the basketball games, the weight lifting, the cars, motorcycles and debate club. I love him so much I ache inside. I wish he would stay longer.

My son is smart. He has changed his major several times. I used to joke that he is a career student. He spends a lot of money. It's expensive keeping him in school.

I tell my wife I think I may need to see a doctor. A small part of me fervently hopes she would say, "Yes, let's get you to a doctor. I will go with you, and I will stand by you. Don't worry anymore. Help is near." I want her to put her arms around me and tell me we can work this out together. I want her to tell me I matter to her, matter more even than the good life we have built. But that is an unreasonable hope. What really happens is that she reminds me that doctors are expensive and tells me our insurance has a $5,000.00 deductible. *So high!* I think.

"It didn't work very well last time, did it?" she asks pointedly. I look at the floor for a moment and then raise my eyes to eyes to her. She is standing with arms crossed, glaring at me. "But, by all means, go to the doctor," she says, "and use up your son's college money. Be selfish."

"No," I say, "I am talking about a psychiatrist, not our family doctor."

"A shrink," she says flatly. "That kind of doctor? Like a crazy person?"

I feel defeated as I realize she is right. The humiliation will not only attach itself to me, but spill over to her and my children as well. Her father was sick in the head, I know. And she is repulsed by mental illness. But, she is strong because she never had a childhood; she had to grow up fast; she did what she had to do. The implication is there that I could be strong too, if I wanted to be. She believes I don't want it.

But, I *do* want to be strong. I envy her that strength. Physical strength (which I have) in no way compensates for emotional weakness. Such weakness is unacceptable. How long can I hide this weakness from the world? But even more important to me, how long can I hide my hair loss from the world? Already I know I am being stared at and whispered about when we go out in public. How can I keep my disfiguring deformity from being noticed?

My wife says I call her too often now. I call her at work. If I keep going, she says she will have no choice but to tell her boss what's going on. "You know how embarrassing this is?" she asks.

"Yes," I respond.

I know what embarrassment is. I live it every day.

Another hot day rolls around after another sleepless night. Outside the oppressive heat presses its steamy hand over the wilting landscape.

"I want to go to the mall," my daughter announces.

"Come on," says my wife, "we're going to the mall."

I tell her I'm not up to it. She levels me with that look.

"Why not?" she asks, her tone dangerous with the promise of trouble.

"People will look at me," I whisper.

My daughter snorts. "Nobody's going to look at you," she scoffs. "You're an old man. Believe me; no one is interested in you."

So, I go.

I wish I could wait in the car. My wife turns to look at me, and I realize I have spoken my wish out loud.

"You are NOT waiting in the car," she says. "You are coming in with us, and you're going to act like a normal person."

She opens the door and waits expectantly for me to get out. I step out of the car in full view of the world…and hesitate. I am twisting in the wind. My daughter sighs with irritation. My wife is exasperated, her mouth set in firm lines and her posture squared for battle. I don't want to fight. I trail behind them toward the entrance, trying to see my reflection in the glass doors ahead of us.

I am aiming for a surreptitious look at my hair when something in the reflection catches my eye. It is heat rising in little waves off the parking lot behind me. It shimmers delicately. *Funny*, I think, *I only see the heat in its reflection.* I wonder if the same principle applies to my hair. Maybe my flaw only shows in a reflection. I ponder this concept as we drag from store to store, wondering how I can ever see myself from the outside to test this theory. Then I notice the people staring as they pass by, and I know what they see when they look at me. I know they shake their heads and wonder about me. I am intensely uncomfortable but there is no place to hide.

I am disjointed. The real me is transposed over the man I ought to be and the two do not mesh. I don't mesh anymore. But

I can't explain this to anyone.

Days stretch out, one after another. Nights are more awful than I can describe. I work on a secret plan. But, where would I do it? What would happen to my body? Who would find me? The first problem is how to do it. A gun, of course, is the best way. Quick, absolute and irrevocable. I do not own a gun. However, luck is with me as my son does own a shotgun for skeet shooting. Only recently, my wife told him to bring it home from college because she was afraid he would get in trouble if he was caught with it in his dorm. He did so one weekend and stored it in the closet of his old room. So there it is now, standing like a patient soldier in the corner. Problem number one is solved with the knowing or unknowing collusion of my wife. I will never learn if she deliberately placed the gun within my reach to make it easier for me or if she just forgot the danger. Nonetheless, it is there if I need it. Maybe it is her subconscious gift to me and to our family. Such an appropriate tool it is. It can not only end my suffering, but also destroy the part of me that I hate…the top of my head. I think about this for awhile. Mull it over. Taste of it until I became comfortable with the idea. At least in death my disfigurement will not be seen.

I take to visiting my parents. They are very worried about me. My wife doesn't like these visits because she is convinced I tell them things that might alter our image in their eyes. I visit them anyway, but it's just a small defiance. I tell them about my problem. I describe to them my agony, the repetition, the joyless cycle in which I am trapped. I ask them over and over, "What am I going to do?" They have only the same old answer for me….see a doctor.

In their home, I feel an acceptance that I do not feel any other place, but I do not feel relief. They are kind to me. But kindnesses have become ineffectual little arrows of warmth that bounce uselessly off the hard armor of my self-loathing. Compassion cannot penetrate the unyielding layers of my misery. I make my mother cry and I regret it. It is not my intention to hurt her, but my suffering does just that. It is hard for her to watch and know she is helpless to change it. I pay a price for these visits. "What did you tell you mother today?" my wife asks.

I now often call my mother just to talk. I have to keep my voice down so my wife won't hear. I am now afraid of making her even angrier with me. I whisper into the phone and my mother strains to hear me. I try not to do any more damage to my home life, but these are some wretched days. I ache for the comfort of my mother's voice. A mother's love is unconditional and permanent. I need that now. I know I have pretty much destroyed any love in my own home.

I am not refusing to be normal; I have just lost my grip on the definition of the term. I can't find my way back to myself. I am not mentally ill. I have a hair problem. But for the sake of argument, let's say I am sick in the head. What is my motivation to get well, to make that long hard upward climb? What would I be going back to? A grown man, living with his parents. No job. No wife. No children. No home. No life.

I tell Mom my new idea. "I should just shave my head," I say.

My mother is noncommittal. My wife, however, doesn't think I would like it and advises against it. I try to think this through. Frenzied thoughts run through my brain like rats in the timbers. If I shave my head, my old hair implants will show, I realize. I need to either get more transplants or have the old ones removed. But what if the removal leaves scars? That would be ugly. Could I get a hairpiece? No, because I would have to shave my head to wear one. And my old implants are there. My idea is a dead end. I am trapped. Mom just listens.

I need a consult with a specialist. I know this is the answer. However, my wife will not relent on this point. She has already moved our money around in the accounts so I can't access it. She suspects I might be desperate enough to go against her wishes and have some sort of hair treatment.

"I have to protect our savings," she explains patiently, as if she were addressing a dull-witted child. I can't imagine I would do anything that drastic without her approval, but she doesn't believe me. And I don't believe her when she tells me my hair looks fine. No one will admit the truth to me.

This dis-integrating, dis-assembling, dis-ordering of my life continues. I am an anguished shadow of my former self, hopelessly chasing one bad thought after another around in my tired brain, compelled to go to the mirror time and time again. Each day is worse. Each night is longer.

I have a plan, a plan hatched in dark hours of desperation over many sleepless nights. The gun is already in the trunk of the car, fully loaded and waiting to deliver me from my tortured existence. I am always hoping that somehow this problem will magically reverse itself. But, every time I see the disgusting ugly bald patches, my hope dissolves. The answer is so obvious. If I could just cease to live, problems would be solved. My family wouldn't have to put up with me anymore. I wouldn't have to put up with me anymore. But most importantly, my wife would have my insurance money. I have paid into that policy for years and now that I need it, it is there like an old friend telling me comfortingly to go ahead and let it take care of my family. Lord knows I can't do it anymore.

There is a hand held infrared device that stimulates hair growth. It looks like a robot's hairbrush. It costs a staggering $600. I would order one from the internet, but my wife has taken my credit cards.

My parents offer to take me out of town to a psychologist *and* pay for it. That way nobody will know. Also, it will not cost me a cent. My wife is welcome to come along too, they say. "We will go as a family."

For a minute, I feel a tiny upward tug on my spirits. I start thinking maybe this is the answer; maybe it will work. My wife, however, regards this offer as interference. Her response is quick and scathing. "Go ahead and go, but don't bother to come home."

She is simply fed up with my weakness. She is appalled that my parents indulge it. I am barely clinging to my marriage. Divorce is no longer a mere threat but now a distinct possibility. I have no choice but to decline the offer if I want to keep my family. We continue our new unnatural routine, me pacing, her sleeping apart from me, her going to work each day, me wandering about the house from mirror to mirror measuring and assessing my deformity.

My daughter still has her friends over, but she insists that I hide in the bedroom until her company leaves. I do this for her. I don't want anyone to see me anyway; I look so ghoulish.

Without my confidence, everything is difficult. I had never before realized how every little thing a person accomplishes depends entirely on self-image. My life is narrowing to an existence that is truly unbearable and I can see no way out. My job is gone, all those years of schooling and struggle for nothing now. My wife despises me. My daughter loathes me. My son stays away either because he just doesn't know how to handle the situation or because perhaps he too finds me repulsive.

There is no help for me. Every avenue is blocked. Hair replacement...blocked. Medical doctor or specialist...blocked. Psychiatrist...blocked. Anyway, I am afraid of mental hospitals. I have images of myself as a drugged-up zombie, imprisoned in the state hospital, shuffling senselessly from hallway to day room, my incarceration an embarrassment to my family, and my hope for recovery remote. I could never piece my life back together after that, and I could not bear knowing I had robbed my son of his future and my wife of her security and my daughter of her place at the center of attention. "Look what I am doing to my family," I tell myself. *How can I do this when I love them so much?*

But the love I feel for my family can't compete with the darkness into which I have fallen. How powerful this obsession is, I marvel. If I could go around the house collecting up my fallen hairs and glue them back onto my head, I would do it. My looks offend me, I admit to myself. They shame and frighten me. I hate them as badly as my family hates my failures. The loneliest place in the world is inside your own mind sometimes.

My mother-in-law suffers from a disease of the mind. She is in a nursing home, her memories erased by Alzheimer's. My wife suggests that I go stay in her mother's old house at night and come back home during the day. My daughter quickly agrees with this idea.

"You keep me awake at night," my wife says in her reasonable voice. "I need to get my sleep. After all, *I* have to *work* for a living."

My mother hates the idea. "There isn't even a stick of furniture in that house," she says. "I won't have you over there in that empty house every night." She says to pack my clothes and come home. She says there is always a place for me at her house. I tell her I will think about it. What no one seems to understand is that I don't want to leave my home at all. I want to be with my wife and daughter, even if it seems they no longer want me.

I tell my wife that I could go stay with my parents for a couple of weeks and give her a break. She says no; it won't look right. I suspect the real reason she opposes the idea is that she can't keep tabs on me as well. And she resents it that my parents know about our situation. It violates our privacy. So I am allowed to stay in my own house.

The brush of my anguish paints distorted pictures. Once I make the mistake of telling my mother that my wife is very disappointed in me. To my surprise, my mother says, "Well, you can tell her for me that I am very disappointed in *her*. She could try being a little kinder to you. I don't like the way she treats you." This bothers me a lot.

The rift between my family and my parents becomes a gorge. My mother believes with all her heart that I am being mistreated. My parents have lost respect for my wife. My wife and daughter resent my parents. I am torn by conflicting family loyalties. The confusion over right and wrong renders me helpless. But still above all, it is my hair loss that plagues me the most. It is paramount. My flaw, my defect, my shame.

I need to see a professional about my hair loss. I need it so badly. Selfish or not, I am desperate to have this. I can't solve this problem myself. It is the answer to everything. I know this for certain. If only my head looked normal, everything else would be alright again. My wife will not hear of it. In fact, she becomes very angry when I mention it. But my parents are willing to try anything at this point.

A few days ago, my mother was trying to reach me. She has good news for me, she says. My parents decided to cash in an IRA and use the money to take me to a hair specialist out of state for a consultation. They will pay for it all and they will drive me there. They will do anything they can to help me; they are nearly as desperate for me to feel better as I am. Hope blooms a tiny blossom inside me.

But my daughter is onto us. Tattletale. She can hardly wait to get my wife on the line and report that Grandma has been calling me. Shortly after, my cell phone rings and it is my wife. My daughter has contacted her and told her something is up with Grandma.

"What's going on now?" my wife asks, her voice weary with longsuffering. I tell her of my parents' offer.

"Get. Home. Now." Her voice is terse, clipped.

"What did I do wrong, honey?" I ask her. "What did I do wrong?" The last thing on earth I want is to give her more reasons to be angry with me. I rush home dreading the confrontation I know is waiting for me. I am hardly in the door when it hits like a storm. She is livid.

"What do you think you're doing?" she rails. She is furious with me, and with my parents. They are babying this sickness of mine. They are trying to circumvent her right out of the picture. They are doing the worst thing they could do, sympathizing. Sympathy does not solve a problem like this. It just makes it worse. I have stabbed her in the back. I have gone behind her back. I have betrayed her. She absolutely forbids this. She tells me once again that if I go to this doctor, not to bother coming home. And she means it. She is at the end of her patience with me. It doesn't actually matter that we won't have to pay for it. That's not the point. What matters is that my parents interfered in our personal business. That's the point. What matters is that we made a decision that she opposed, knowing full well that she opposed it.

I try, but I can't convince her that I need this; and I know if I do it now that I will be going against her wishes. I briefly consider self-surgery. I can see myself at the mirror with a sharp little knife and a pair of tweezers.

She winds down and the guilt rises up to choke me. I am so worn out and ground down. I don't know how to manage my own despair let alone the unhappiness I am causing her. She is a good woman and does not deserve this. I know I have destroyed her dream of a perfect family. It seems that no matter which way I turn, I am always causing sorrow for someone. I am a disgrace and the penalty is rejection. I am expelled from the circle of love that used to surround me.

"Have you seen my cell phone charger?" I ask my wife.

"I put it up," she says. "We don't need you running up the bill."

"Where is it?" I ask.

"You don't need it." She is stern.

My phone is dead. I can't call anyone. A few days later, however, she relents and gives it back to me. I don't know why.

My wife and I are standing in the driveway. She is looking at me with barely contained rage.

"That's it," she says, "give me your keys."

"But why?" I ask her.

She says we can't afford to insure the car anymore now that I won't work a job. If I want to go somewhere, I will need to ride my bike or walk. Part of me wonders if this is really a punishment for talking to my parents about our private business. But I dismiss that thought.

"How will I get into the house without my keys?" I ask her.

"You can wait in the garage until we get home from work and we will let you in."

I don't want to give up my keys and my fingers tighten

around them.

"Come on," she says quietly but firmly, "you don't want to make a scene out here in front of the neighbors."

I hand her my keys.

"If you want to drive the car, then you will need to go down and get some insurance on it," she tells me.

"But I have no money," I say.

"Well, I guess you should have considered that before you quit your job."

She is right. This is a situation of my own making. I don't make a fuss or embarrass us in front of the neighbors. I worry that my bald spots are showing. She puts my keys in her purse and we go inside. My daughter smirks as I head for the mirror.

I call my mother and ask her to come get me. She says of course but what's wrong with my car? I tell her I no longer have the key. I tell her about the insurance. Later, sitting around their dining room table, I confess to them that I am destroying my family. I don't know what to do. My dad keeps repeating go to the doctor, go to the doctor. I know he means well, but I am tired of hearing it. We have tried that, and I am afraid. What if they hospitalize me? What if my son's college fund is eaten up by my medical expenses? What if my wife leaves me and I am alone? What if my children hate me?

Hot windy day. My eyes have dried out and I need my contact solution. I can't get into the house to get it. I have my parents drop me off at home and I wait in the garage until my wife and daughter get home. It feels like my contacts are adhered to my eyeballs. It feels like a long wait.

My appetite is poor now. I am losing weight. I am at my

mother's house, and she wants me to eat something.

"Don't you think I should wait and eat with my family?" I ask her.

I try to call my daughter, but she doesn't answer. I try to call my wife, but she doesn't answer either. I think perhaps I *will* eat something with my parents. Then my cell phone rings and it's my daughter calling me back. She says if I will walk down to the corner, they will come by and pick me up. My wife will not drive up to my parents' house.

I set off down the dusty street, hands in my pockets. I look back to see my mother standing in the door, watching me walk away. It looks like she is crying.

"You need to mow the lawn today," my wife says. "Now remember, you don't have a house key, so don't lock yourself out. I can't be leaving work to let you in the house." I am careful to do as she says.

Morning dawns with a soft rain that breaks up the persistent summer heat, granting a reprieve in more ways than one. The rain has given me back my car. My daughter doesn't like to drive. She had a close call, a near miss, and now her mother and I drive her where she wants to go. That morning my wife hands me back my car keys because my daughter wants to go to the Y. We can't bike there in the rain. I don't know what happened with the insurance matter. I don't ask. It turns out I will now keep my car until the day I die.

After the Y, my daughter is hungry. "I want a taco," she states.

"But I have no money," I say.

"I want a taco," she repeats, "and I'm not spending my own money on it. You're the dad; you're supposed to feed me. In fact, you still haven't reimbursed me for that sweater I bought myself last week."

I pull the car over and we search the floorboards, glove compartment, and cracks of the seats. We find enough change to buy her taco, but not enough to buy a drink. She sullenly eats her meal, refusing to look at me. I've let her down again. I realize my hands are trembling slightly. I grasp the steering wheel harder to steady them. The rain throws a hazy gray coat over the world. I drive her home, the car filled with her accusatory silence as the heavens weep.

It is July 18, my anniversary. For twenty-seven years I have been married to this good woman, and now it is all reduced to nothing by the last six months. My mother convinces me to see her hairdresser today. I don't want to go, but I do it for my mother. She thinks it will help. The hairdresser takes me into a back room so I don't have to wait among all the other patrons. Her name is Vicki, and she is warm and kind. She doesn't feel like a stranger. She looks at my hair.

"Why, honey," she says, "you have a beautiful head of hair!"

I am too numb to respond to this.

"Yes, I see the implants and maybe just a little bit of thinning, but you have gorgeous hair," she says. "There's really very little hair loss, but I have a product that will take care of this. Your scalp just needs a thorough cleansing. I guarantee you that if you use this shampoo you will notice a difference in a week. I promise your hair will grow back."

I ask her the cost, remembering that I have no money, checkbook, or credit cards anymore.

"Now, you don't worry about that," she says. "You try it and if it works for you, you can pay me later."

Out of the blue I tell her I think my wife is going to leave me. "Oh honey, I have been married thirty-seven years. I know how marriage is sometimes. I bet things will work out with your wife. But if they don't, my goodness, you will have women all over you. You are such a handsome man!" she says. "You just try these products now, and before you know it your hair will be thicker and fuller. You'll see."

"Oh my god, look what he's got now!" my daughter says to my wife, rolling her eyes. "Special Shampoooooooo!"

"Oh, lord," my wife groans.

I am humiliated. They have a bit of fun at my expense.

"How much did that shit cost?" my wife asks.

"Nothing," I say, and step outside to throw it in the trash.

This anniversary is not a happy one. I accept their disdain and allow it to settle like a vulture on my slumped shoulder where it makes a fitting companion to my own self-loathing. I finally realize I am not loved. I really am not loved. This will be the longest night of my life.

When my wife and daughter lock themselves in the bedroom for sleep that night, I face my demons alone in the quiet darkness. The powers of the night are ever watchful that I not slip up and find some peace where certainly none is deserved. I take stock of where my life has led and all that I have lost, but thinking is hard to do. Clarity of thought has deserted me and only one neural pathway seems to fire at full capacity. That's the one that cycles me through my repetitive motions, the irresistible compulsion to feel my head and nervously inspect my hair over and over again for hours. And each time I check, my suspicions are again confirmed. And each time that old familiar shame and panic washes over me, sending waves of disgust and despair down into my gut.

The morning of July 19 finds me wide-eyed, nerves sizzling from lack of sleep, stomach churning, and heart racing inexplicably. I feel such heaviness of spirit that breathing is an effort and each step is like walking through a deep layer of heavy sand. I check my hair again, but still it is the same and defeat overwhelms me.

I thirst for peace. I am so tired. This is the day I will escape my personal hell on earth. It has to be today. Tomorrow is my mother's birthday, and I just can't do that to her. Not on her birthday. It has to be today. But where can I do the deed? I will go where I am loved, I decide. I will go where I know that my crumpled body will be lovingly cared for. I will go *home*, where I grew up. I will step out of this body like stepping out of a confining suit of clothes. I will be free. I can't do this at my house. It would be the final insult to my marriage to leave such a mess for my wife. And I do not want my daughter to see her father's shattered body dead on the floor, just in case some part of her still loves me. I don't want to hurt her any more than I already have.

It is only here at the very end my life that I have failed my family. I am sure of that.

There was a time when I had a good life. I am an educated man. For many years, I was successful. My wife was the single point of light in my life, from which radiated all the parameters of my world. I have a son who makes me proud, a bright assertive young man who pulls the good grades and goes around with all the right people. He writes brilliant papers. He studies. He drinks too, but I don't want to think about that. My daughter was, until recently, the center of our family. She is a cherished diamond, sharp-edged and fierce. A unique jewel sparkling with cold light and mysterious facets. I had vowed to give her everything she ever desired and deny her nothing. Until this condition took me, I held true to that promise.

But no longer can I find consolation in any of my past accomplishments because my true defective nature has now emerged and taken over. I have no one to blame but myself, but life as I knew it is over for me.

So here it is, July 19, the day before my mother's birthday, and the day after my anniversary. My wife and daughter leave for work. I call my mother. She says they are going to the grocery store, but for me to come on over. *Perfect timing*, I think.

However, when I arrive at my parents' home, I am surprised to find my parents still at home. They've had a change in plans and decided to go to the store later. So I must bide my time. They notice I am in poor shape. I know I can't hide it even if I try. I have seen my haggard face in the mirror with its deep lines, sunken eyes, and sagging skin. Mom comments that I am wearing the same clothes as yesterday, something I never do. Her eyes reflect her fear for me. I can't comfort her because I know her fear is justified. I am sorry when I see the pain in her eyes. She looks so sad.

I tell her, "I am so tired of worrying about my hair, so tired. I wish I could just fly away."

Her eyes fill with tears. "Honey, didn't you try your new shampoo?" she asks.

"No," I answer.

"Why not?" she asks.

"I don't know," I say.

I decide to make one last effort for living, and I call my wife. I tell her I am at Mom's.

"I'm feeling really low, very bad," I say. "Will you please talk to Mom?"

She hangs up on me.

I am stunned for only a moment and then think, well, this is the way I expected it would turn out. But this time it's ok because I am ready. Soon we will both be free.

I must soften the blow for my mother. It seems wrong to not at least try to prepare her for what is to come, so I ask her what she would tell people if I ever decide to take my life. She gasps and begins to sob. She tells me it would just kill her. She begs me not to talk that way. She says she is so sorry that she did this to me, that it must be some genetic or hereditary factor that caused this. She tells me she had wanted a son so badly and she never dreamed she would be passing on this awful sickness. I tell her she hasn't done anything wrong and this is not her fault.

My dad flies angry and tells me suicide is a coward's way out. His older brother had done it when my dad was just a boy, and it had devastated him.

This meeting is going badly and I am not sure how to smooth it back into place. My dad starts out the door, shakes his head, then turns around and comes back. He apologizes for losing his temper and tells me the following Tuesday he will take me to the hair doctor, the specialist, and we will get some professional answers. He is a fixer. He has always fixed things. But he can't fix this.

He is trying so hard, but he doesn't know I have already found my solution. I don't have the heart to tell him. Besides, I don't want him to stop me.

So, I humor him. I let him believe we will make this trip and I can see he is relieved. Then I ask my mother for a hug. I can't tell her this is goodbye, but it is. Then I tell them to go ahead, go to the store. They ask me to come with them. Of course, I decline. They don't want to leave me, but I convince them I am fine.

"I'm good," I say. "I'm good."

I tell them to go and I will be waiting right here for them when they return. They believe when they get back we will finalize the plans for our trip to the doctor. They believe I am ready to buck the system, ignore my wife's wishes, and follow through with this appointment. They walk out the door believing the cure for my suffering is in sight. It is, but not in the way they think.

Once they are safely gone, I sit in my boyhood home for a short time, absorbing the particular comfort that is my mother's house. I remove my shoes and one of my socks. I have researched how to do this.

I take a final look around my mother's home, feel again the misery pressing down upon me, and step outside.

I raise the garage door and drive my car inside; then

close the garage door behind me so no one will see. I open the trunk of my car and gaze at the gun. Now that the moment is upon me, I am strangely calm. I call my wife one more time, but she doesn't take my call. I had wanted to tell her goodbye, but I guess that is not to be. I speak privately with God instead.

I remove the gun from the trunk. I sit on the cement floor, lean back, and place the double barrels in my mouth, carefully aiming back and upward. I cup my fingers against my lips and press them tightly around the gun. It is uncomfortable against my teeth. I place my toe on the trigger. I realize suddenly that I have forgotten to tell my brother and sister goodbye. But, it's too late now. I am surprised to notice tears streaming involuntarily from my eyes.

How fast is a shot? Speed of sound? Speed of light? I don't know. But I never even hear the blast before I am flying home, propelled into the arms of Jesus.

I am ended.

Forbidden Fruit

I met her on the job when I was forty-six and she was forty-one. Something happened between us. We clicked. It seemed like we knew a lot of the same people; she had an older sister that made my friends accessible to her even though she was five years younger than they were.

She'd have a problem with an account and since I was the one with the answers, and also her direct supervisor, I spent a lot of time in her cubby. And while we fixed the problem, we'd talk. She was married, been so for twenty-two years. Happily, too. She had three children, two boys and a girl. I had been married for twenty-eight years, had four girls, and was not so happy in my marriage.

I became fascinated with her family. Learned the kids' names and the order they came into her life. Learned her birth date, what she liked to eat, all that good stuff. In only a short time, I had become attached to her, and it seemed as if she returned my feelings. But, how I could be sure? I had to think on that one.

As we spent more time together, in her cubby, in my office, at breaks and lunch, I worked on how to get her closer, much closer, right up close. I started loosening my collar before we met. I'd run my hand over my chest at the opening of my shirt, slowly, languidly, as if thinking. It wasn't long before her eyes began to follow my movements; and then, one afternoon I worked up my courage to ask her if she wanted to try it.

She grinned and to my surprise said yes. We both looked around quickly, and seeing no one, she reached her hand into my shirt and gently ran it over my chest, softly touching. I moaned a little and she self-consciously pulled her hand away as she blushed.

I apologized for not having any chest hair and she said she found it sexy; her husband was a really hairy guy and she sometimes hated the feel of all that hair, she liked touching skin.

We progressed along these lines, her touching my chest and me longing to touch hers. One day, she came to work in a button-up blouse. I knew immediately that she was bra-less; her nipples fought to poke through the silky material holding them in its slinky embrace. I followed those breasts around like a horse following a carrot. At last, she stopped in my doorway and said she needed help on an account. I invited her in and she pushed the door nearly closed behind her. She moved to the chair I had pulled over beside me and sank into it like syrup sliding from a bottle. She ran her hand over the opening in her blouse and asked if I wanted to try. Oh yes, I wanted to try alright. I couldn't believe how much my hand trembled as I placed it on her satiny skin. Timidly, I stayed near the opening, but she took my hand and guided it deeper, down, until my hand enclosed a perfect peach. Her nipple rubbed tantalizingly over the palm of my hand, filling my head with fireworks. We were both squirming when we heard footsteps approaching in the hallway. Back to business, as if that were possible, I could hardly sit in the condition I was now in, near exploding in my shorts like a teen-aged boy.

We managed to present a couple of hard-working employees by the time the knock came and the door opened. Another newly-hired person entered with a question. I found myself annoyed when his gaze lingered over the front of the blouse under which I had just been fondling. I made quick work of him, but by then she said she needed to get busy. We both threw promising looks at each other as she exited the room.

Things kind of slowed down for a while after that. I think

she was shocked at her brazenness, and I wasn't sure if I should pursue her or not. Things had progressed much further than the playful stage; things were leaning towards the forbidden stage. I wondered how she could be doing what she was doing if she was so happy in her marriage, and I asked her one day. She didn't know. Just that. She still loved her husband, completely, but she found me, well, *interesting*.

Then she asked how I could do it. My answer was more complicated. I wasn't at all happy in my marriage but I had always been faithful. I had children, and soon would have grandchildren. Half the time, I couldn't even remember the names of my own kids, only hers. The other day I struggled to remember how to spell my wife's name, but only *hers* came to mind. I was infatuated beyond hope. I said I found her interesting, too. We left it at that.

A week later, she transferred to another branch. I never knew why, I never saw her again, and I was never tempted by another woman.

The Erotic
Adventure of
Dick Speed

I am Dick Speed.

I am a very handsome man. I know this for two reasons. Women have told me so, and I can see it in the mirror. My body is properly proportioned, and I have a fine bronze tan, the best money can buy. My legs are not bowed, my rear is neither flat nor fat, and I have a trim waistline. I also am blessed with rich brown eyes, the appearance of which I have learned to manipulate according to mood. I have dark hair which is not thinning, and I am neither too tall nor too short. Yes, overall, I give the impression of a virile healthy male. One hundred percent man.

My personality includes a variety of killer components like mystery, sensitivity, strength, and confidence. My charisma is undeniable. Another irresistible feature is my razor sharp wit with which I often amuse even myself. My intellect is perfectly balanced. I am not so smart as to be intimidating, and not so dumb as to be pitiable. Women love my personality. All women love it. Without exception. The few who claim not to love it are liars. It's sad when a woman has to lie, but I fault their own in-securities and carry no grudges, which happens to be another of my favorable traits.

I am quite a sexy man. I know this for two reasons. I get looks from women all the time. Also, I am attracted to myself, and I feel I am a good judge of desirability. If I were a woman, I would date me. As it is, I feel fortunate that I can be with me all the time. This next part actually belongs in the previous paragraph, but I will say it here. I am also humble. Even though I know I am a sexy man, modesty prevents me from bragging.

My work brings me into frequent contact with beautiful dames. This is what women were called before they became equal to men and I find the term still fits. I am an interior designer. In fact, I have a very successful career as an interior decorator, and it's not due to my skill with décor. I know this profession conjures up images of fussy men with delicate clipboards and fabric swatches. But it is exactly that prejudice which gives me the element of surprise when dealing with female clients. I use this to my advantage all the time. I am a self-educated designer believing that true style comes from an inner conviction and not a college degree or training of any kind. And, *my* clipboard is manly.

One of the secrets of my business success is that I only offer a handful of packages and I stick with them because they work. They include the following décor choices: African Safari, Oriental Zen, and Futuristic Modern. That's it. I keep things simple. Besides, I've found that once my clients lay eyes on me, décor is the furthest thing from their minds.

I'll never forget my first client, Mrs. England. I walked into her impressive French-eclectic style home on a Monday morning carrying my masculine manly clipboard...

She meets me at the door with surprise on her face. Her lips swell at the sight of me. She's so affected by my presence, she looks as if she's been exposed to an allergen. It's a dead giveaway.

"What's a girl like you doing in a place like this?" I utter in a voice that is rife with undertone and hidden meaning.

"I live here." Droll.

"Let's discuss your redecorating ideas," I say, keeping my voice warm and intimate.

"Are you sure you are really a decorator?" she asks dubiously, lighting a cigarette.

"Why do you ask? Am I perhaps manlier than you were expecting?"

A sneer. "Yes, that's it exactly. You nailed me."

"Not yet," I smile.

"Indeed," she replies, arching a heavily penciled brow. "Now, answer my question."

"Yes, I am really a decorator. I have a tape measure and color swatches to prove it." I am not defensive. I expect this kind of reaction.

"Fine, then, I will tell you what I'm looking for." She turns and swishes over to the fireplace. "I am thinking something classical."

"That's not on my list."

"What?"

"You'll have to choose from my list. Didn't you peruse my brochure?" I throw a critical look her way.

"Refresh my memory."

"Safari, Zen, or Modern," I say patiently, turning slightly so she can appreciate my strong yet sensitive profile.

"What if I want classical?" she asks. Her stubbornness is very cute for a woman older than my grandmother.

"Then you would be making a grave mistake," I answer wisely. "Classical will go out of style soon."

"Classical never goes out of style."

"Who is the decorator here?" I ask sternly.

"I was wondering that myself." Hmmm. Sassy. She squares her shoulders, cleverly drawing my attention to her chest. My temperature starts to rise and perspiration breaks in a light sheen on my brow. I know I present a tempting picture and she's not immune to my magnetism.

"If you were to choose one of the styles I offer, which

would it be?" I ask. I sit on her sofa and hike my pant leg to give her a look at my ankle. I am wishing I had worn matching socks. She looks down, feigning distaste, but I know I have her attention.

"I wouldn't select any of the styles you mentioned." She was haughty, which turns me on.

"What if you were forced to choose one?"

"That wouldn't happen." She looks up and blows a stream of smoke, her red lips in a perfect O. I see now how she plans to play the game. I'm hip to her vibe. I'm reading her nuance. I'm catching her drift, and riding her wave.

"Let's say it does. Just for the sake of argument. Let's say a band of ninjas breaks in and shoves one of my brochures under your nose. Let's say they tell you if you don't choose one of those styles, they will fling you around the room like a bag of dirty laundry."

"You're crazy." Her voice is calm, full of contrived disdain.

"Suppose a flock of vampires bursts through those pretty French doors and surrounds you, and you are at risk of becoming one of the undead unless you select one of my designs. Which one would you pick then?"

"I'm not afraid of vampires." She gives me a meaningful sideways glance. "Not even if they have big fangs."

"Oh, really? Well, maybe a troop of mercenaries dressed in camouflage jump suits will rappel down from a black helicopter, tie you up in razor wire, torture you with incessant drips of cold water on your forehead, and insert an electronic homing device into your skull unless you choose one of my designs. What do you think of that?"

"That happened last Saturday. I wasn't impressed. In fact, I fell asleep halfway through the incident out of sheer boredom." She is hard to rattle. I have to admire that.

"You keep avoiding the question. That's foxy of you, Mrs. England. Or can I call you Betty?"

"My name isn't Betty."

"That's not the point. If you don't pick one of the options from my brochure in the next thirty seconds, things are going to get dicey." She looks like a Betty to me.

"Really? What will you do?" Challenging.

"I'm afraid I will have to pick for you," I threaten.

"Fine, then." She provocatively crushes her cigarette in an ashtray. "I choose Zen."

"Wise choice," I tell her. "For a Zen look in your front room, we'll start by covering your walls in rice paper. We'll rip out your electric lighting and replace it with calming scented candles. Then we will install bamboo screens in strategic locations around the room to provide a sense of privacy. Your carpet will be replaced with woven mats and we will bring in several potted bamboo plants. We'll accessorize with oriental lanterns, Japanese pillows, Asian artwork, a gurgling waterfall, and hanging chimes. The furnishings will be low couches, wicker chairs, Chinese tables, and dragon statuettes. I think this plan covers the main features of oriental design as it is perceived by the majority of consumers."

"I'm not convinced." She leans over and straightens a pillow on the couch, merely an excuse to flaunt her backside. Oh, yea. She's sending out the signals.

"Convince you, eh?" I am surprised at this turn of events. Things are moving along even faster than I thought they would. I reach for my belt buckle. "Maybe you'd like to see my bamboo shoot."

"Maybe I would." Her voice is sultry now.

I amble over to her and take her in my arms. I'm glad I remembered to apply copious amounts of Hai Karate that morning, thankful for the supply I inherited from Uncle Vernon. She looks up at me and bats her eyelashes. I stroke her generous neck with my sensitive hands and she gasps. Leaning down, I plunder her mouth with my manly sensuous lips. Her sigh turns into a wheeze, which only provokes me further. We kiss long and deep, my tongue dancing the rumba on hers. I feel her dentures shift, and find it strangely alluring. I've never shifted anyone's dentures before.

"You have lovely bosoms," I whisper. "Are they real?"

"How dare you?" She jerks back from me, indignant.

"It's a legitimate question," I defend myself. She relents.

"I like your style, Speed. I sure hope you don't live up to your name." She chuckles low and breathy as she unbuttons her blouse.

"My first or my last?" I give her a steamy look.

She doesn't answer. She flings her blouse aside and steps out of her skirt.

Betty has the look of a rich matron, a society broad. She stands before me in her satin slip and support hose. She kicks off her sensible brown pumps and puts a hand on her hip, which happens to be the exact size and shape of a 1948 Buick. She's a classic for sure, and my blood is simmering like a kettle full of red hot jambalaya.

"I'd like to suck the diamonds right off your ears," I say.

"Those aren't my ears," she replies. "They're prosthetics. I had my ears removed a decade ago for personal reasons."

Well. This is unexpected.

"Let's slip out of that slip," I suggest, the clever play on words demonstrating my skill with a phrase.

"Let's? I'll slip out of mine if you slip out of yours," she says with a wink. I don't respond since I know she is toying with me. And I like it. She lifts the slip over her head revealing a chest like a steel shelf.

"What holds those up?" I ask.

"I had a surgical lift," she responds. "And I have industrial strength rebar in my bra." Oddly, this excites me. "Maybe you'd like to see my bedroom, give me some professional advice on its décor."

"Maybe I would," I tease. She responds with a growl which scares me enough that I momentarily lose my stride. She takes over and pilots our way into her bland boudoir. I follow like a pure-bred bloodhound on the scent of a wounded opossum.

"What would you recommend for this room?" She pins me with a suggestive gaze.

"I would have to go with African Safari," I say, my mouth drying up from the heat of my desire. My tongue sticks to my lip for a moment. It's awkward.

"Mmmm," she says, tactfully ignoring my predicament. "Describe it for me." She runs her hands over the blond dresser by the door.

"Okay," I say, un-sticking my dehydrated tongue from my lip. "Most of your furniture will have to go. The blond wood just screams upper middle class monotony. It'll be replaced with heavy Mediterranean stock. We'll hang faux zebra skin drapes over the windows, flank the bed with night tables made of camel bones, install torches for lamps, a tiger-striped bedspread, pocketed khaki pillows with epaulets, a bear skin rug, and potted palms in each corner."

"Does Africa have palm trees and bears?"

"Oh, sure, they're all over the place down there. In fact, a lot of their palm trees have bears *in* them," I assure her with an authoritative nod of my perfectly-shaped head. She stares at my chiseled jaw and I lift my chin to accentuate my manly features. She is fairly drooling by this point. I give her a smoldering stare, lowering my eyelids for a reptilian effect that most women find irresistible. I realize then that perhaps I have pushed her too far.

She is decisive in her movements, a real take-charge kind of gal. Sniffing the air with predatory zeal, she does a mock crouch and tells me I have unleashed the cat in her. Honing in on my skintight V-neck shirt, she tears it apart with her nails. My gold chain goes flying, too. I'll have to add the cost of these items to her bill. Soon she has her diamond studded fingers firmly buried in my expertly moussed hair, which she musses playfully. I can feel it standing on end, straight up like a stiff flame. Lowering her meaty arms to my torso, she pulls me against her in a Heimlich-like hug. She pumps my torso like a caffeine junkie with a plateful of French fries shaking a catsup bottle. It's rough, but I can handle it.

I see at once there will be no finer points to this seduction, no finesse, no gradual warming of the coals. No, this will be fast and dirty. I'm fine with this, although I had been looking forward to trying my skillful techniques on her. Now I can see this would be a wasted effort and something for which she would have no patience.

Once she has bounced me around to her satisfaction, she collapses to the bed and spreads out like five pounds of flour in a ten pound bag. I need no further encouragement. I fall into her vigorous embrace. She writhes under me, and snarls like a carnivore guarding a fresh kill. It is much like wrestling with a rabid cheetah. I don't mind it at all though I bear the scars to this day. I enthusiastically give myself over to the moment.

Decorum prevents me from detailing any more of this wild adventure. It wouldn't be polite. Let me just say if Mrs. England were an amusement park, I had an all-day pass. Let's just say if she were a boxcar, I hoeboed all the way to Albuquerque. Let's just say if she were a septic system, then I was Roto-Rooter. Well, you get the idea.

And that was the auspicious start of my very successful career as Dick Speed, Interior Decorator Extraordinaire, undisputed love king of the design world.

Now, have you made a choice from my brochure?

Found Guilty

Paul Astoria had a long and tedious day at work. If something could go wrong, it did. Paul was supposed to get off work at five o'clock, but it was a quarter 'til six before he could slip into his jacket and pull on his coat. He headed for the parking lot, taking the long way around to avoid being stopped and asked for additional help with this project or that. Paul decided to stop off and play a round of poker at his favorite club before going home. He deserved some down-time after the day he'd had, and he wasn't ready to be nagged by his wife for doing or not doing god only knows what.

It was late, after one o'clock in the morning, when Paul stumbled from the bar and staggered to the parking lot. Weaving slightly, he managed to get his key into the ignition and began his trek home. As he drove, he lamented about the evening.

He'd sat down to play a round of Texas-Hold'em, and had pulled a pair of aces on the third hand. He'd bet high and another guy went all-in. Paul knew he was going to win; he had the best hand possible. He called. The other player turned his cards over to reveal a five of hearts and a seven of diamonds. *Idiot,* Paul sniggered to himself. The flop was a four of clubs, six of clubs, and an ace. *Yes!* Paul thought, elated. His elation died when the turn was a nine of hearts, giving the other guy a straight. He had to match one of the cards on the table to win for a boat or another ace for quads. The river was a queen of diamonds. Paul threw his cards angrily onto the table and shoved his pile of chips towards the idiot who had beaten him. "Suck-out!" he pronounced, glaring at the winner. Everyone ignored him and he moved to the bar.

He tossed back a couple of drinks, still staring daggers at the guy who had beaten him. Finally, his attention was snagged by a blond who was holding down a stool at the bar in a most delicious way. Paul knew he presented a decent picture. He stood six foot, weighed one hundred seventy five pounds, and had sandy blond hair in a neat cut over a nice-looking face. He never had problems talking to women and now he introduced himself to Sheila, a long-legged, pretty woman, and her pudgy friend, Dana. Paul bought Sheila a couple of drinks while Dana pouted. Finally, Sheila said Dana was broke and they were gonna take off. Not wanting to lose out on an opportunity to get Sheila into his backseat, Paul offered to buy Dana drinks also. They had moved to the pool tables, and Paul took every opportunity to touch Sheila, to pat her bottom, to smooth her hair. She seemed to be enjoying the attention. He could almost taste those red painted lips and feel the silkiness of her tongue in his mouth.

Then, Paul went to the john, and when he came out, Sheila and her friend were gone. Not in the restroom, not at the bar, gone. *To hell with them!* Paul thought and decided he'd had enough. Now, here he was, driving out of town to his two-acre estate that sat on a dirt road. He squinted out the window. It was starting to snow. "Great, just what I need!" Paul grumbled aloud.

By the time Paul had made his way through town, twice turning onto side streets to avoid police cars, the snow was falling steadily and the ground was turning white. Paul missed his turn-off and had to go to the next road before he could make a u-turn, which turned out to be a five-point turn, and then back to the road he lived on.

It was dark under the trees, the moon obscured by clouds. Snow was falling in large flakes, and Paul was driving much too fast. In the blink of an eye, a deer appeared directly in front of the car. Paul slammed on the brakes. The car slewed to the left, then back to the right, and finally straight ahead. With a sickening crunch, the vehicle hit the deer and the car lurched to a stop.

Paul's head slammed forward into the steering wheel and for a minute or two he was confused, uncertain what had happened. He touched his forehead gingerly and then, with the aid of the dashboard light, he saw blood on his fingertips. Paul choked back the desire to vomit and peered through the windshield which was quickly becoming covered by snow.

Another damn deer. That's what had happened. The third one in a year. "Damn it! Are they all out to jack my insurance sky-high?" Paul voiced his complaint in a loud, gruff voice.

He tried starting the car. He had every intention of going around the deer and home. He'd be damned if he was going to stay here and wait for the cops. "Damn deer!" he repeated.

The car wouldn't start. "Oh, hell!" Paul climbed out of the vehicle and walked around to the front. The deer lay where it had fallen. Blood oozed from its mouth and nose. Paul felt no sympathy. He blamed the deer for this whole mess and felt the animal deserved to be dead.

Anger bellowed up and Paul reared back his leg, swung it forward, and kicked the deer in the ribs. The first kick seemed to release a black fury, and Paul responded to the rage. He battered the animal with kick after kick. Several minutes passed in this manner before Paul fell back against the front of the car, red in the face, and panting from exertion.

Silence fell over the snowy night. Paul noticed movement off the side of the road. He looked up. Surrounding the patch of light from the car's headlights were a dozen bucks, antlers rising regally above proud heads. Moving silently through the dark, like ghosts, they had appeared as if by magic. Paul watched as the deer looked upon their fallen companion. After appraising the deer lying in the snow, they looked at each other, communicating without sound, appearing to pass judgment.

Paul, sensing something bad was about to happen, had begun to back around the car towards the open door. He never stood a chance. First one deer, and then another, approached, reared on back legs, and brought their sharp hooves down on the murderer of their friend.

The next morning, Paul's body was found trampled to death next to the deer he had run down. All tracks from the dozen stags had been obliterated by the snowfall. It was decided that the fallen deer had lived long enough to attack the man after he left his vehicle. But you and I know the truth. Murder had been committed, and Paul Astoria had been found guilty. The fallen had been avenged.

Life of a Beat Cop

"Mom!" Toby's voice rose as he impatiently tugged on the sleeve of his mother's uniform. "Please! Can I go out and play on the sidewalk?"

"Shh, Toby. Don't bring attention to yourself." Abigail spoke softly to her son as she poked at her spiky red hair, trying to tame it into place. The babysitter hadn't shown and she'd had to bring Toby to work with her this afternoon, even though she knew she risked being fired. Now, Abigail glanced around with anxious eyes looking for Mr. Cafenator, the owner of the diner where Abigail waited tables. Not seeing the burly, unsociable man, Abigail leaned down to her seven-year-old son and smoothed back his jet black hair. "Okay. You can go outside. But," she admonished, "stay right in front where I can see you. Understand?"

Toby nodded seriously, his shaggy hair bobbing back around his face as he pushed his glasses up his nose. "I understand."

Abigail, love swelling in her heart, watched as the stick-thin body of her only child raced to the front entrance and exited onto the busy sidewalk. He turned and waved at her and then pulled some toys from his jeans pocket and began playing. Abigail moved to wait on a customer who had just been seated in her section.

"Hiya, Jake," she said as she slipped a glass of ice water in front of him.

"Hi, yourself," Jake drawled. His lips were swollen from the many hours he spent blowing tunes on his sax; jazz was the way he relaxed in the evenings. "Speaking of high, have you seen Pineapple Express yet?" Jake, a film critic for one of the local rags, always managed to slip something about movies into his conversations.

"No time," Abigail said, trying to sound disappointed; although, if the truth be known, she actually had no desire to go to a movie. She was way too tired after putting in long hours on her feet each day, and besides, she'd rather curl up with a good book. For a second, her thoughts turned to Half Bitten by PJ Hawkinson that was lying on her bedside table; she wished she could slip in between the sheets and find out what was going to happen now that Trudy had gone with her boyfriend to his parents' summer home. With an inward sigh, she dragged her attention back to her customer. "What can I get you, Jake?"

Jake, who reminded most people of a young Jack Nicholson, placed his order and leaned back to listen to the conversation in the booth next to his table. He plucked stray hairs of his cat, Satchmo, from his jacket sleeve and watched the traffic out the front window as he eavesdropped.

"You'll have to swing by the house sometime this week," a pretty, chocolate-skinned woman said to her companion. Her hair was worn in a natural afro and her clothes were simple but stylish. "I threw together an outfit that would look stunning on you."

"I couldn't possibly wear the beautiful clothes you design, Tamilia. You know they're way too flashy for my tastes."

Jake rolled his eyes. The woman who had spoken the words dressed like an old woman when she couldn't possibly be out of her twenties. Jake could see Mrs. Cleaver from the TV show 'Leave It To Beaver' wearing the same dress. He thought maybe the woman would do well to try wearing something flamboyant that would bring out her stunning green eyes. Maybe big gold earrings like the hoops the other woman was wearing.

As if she'd heard Jake's thoughts, Tamilia spoke, "I just designed a blouse that matches your green eyes. The material is soft and shimmery. Come off it, Carol Orion! Just stop by and check it out."

"I'll stop by," Carol said. "But, not to try on a blouse. I want to see the girls. It's been so long; how old are they now?" Carol poked at an unsightly blemish on her face, resisting the urge to squeeze.

Tamilia raised her fork to her mouth, her Indonesian bangles jingling on her wrist. After swallowing the bite of food, she replied with a sparkle in her almond-shaped, deep brown eyes, "Jamilia is eight and Carmon will be six next week. Let me tell you, those two girls are one biggg handful. I'm just glad their dad took a local position and is home every evening now. We love him not being away so much."

"I know you do." Carol glanced at her wristwatch. "Oops, I need to hurry. Gotta get back to work. You don't know how lucky you are, being able to stay home every day."

"Oh, I do know. Go ahead. Finish up and leave me the check. My treat."

Jake had turned his attention to the scene outside the window. A policeman was walking past, a small boy was playing with what Jake recognized as a Transformer, and a car was slowing beside the curb. Jake could see the man driving the vehicle speaking to the little boy. Jake frowned.

Out on the street, the car rolled to a stop and the driver leaned across his seat. "Hey, hurry over here, get in the car," the man called to the boy.

Toby looked in the window, trying to get his mother's attention. But Abigail was busy and didn't see what was happening outside the diner. Toby looked back at the car and then slowly walked to the vehicle.

The man reached over and opened the passenger door. Toby slid into the seat as the policeman turned to watch.

The officer took several steps towards the car as Jake, inside the diner, stood and shouted, "Someone is stealing that little boy!"

Forks clattered to plates as everyone stood to look out the plate-glass window. Abigail took in the scene in a glance. She ran to the door, jerked it open, and ran out onto the sidewalk. "Wait!" she shouted and ran after the car that was just pulling away.

The policeman was reaching for his revolver, but the car pulled back to the curb. "Toby," Abigail cried, opening the door and pulling the little boy into an embrace. "You didn't think you were leaving without giving me a kiss, did you?" She kissed the boy all over his face and neck, eliciting giggles of delight.

"Mom," he protested. "Stop. Everyone's looking."

Abigail gave him one more kiss and then let him climb back into the vehicle. She leaned down and spoke curtly to the driver.

As she closed the door, the policeman, who had came near enough to hear the conversation, heard the man ask the little boy, "Ready?"

Toby smiled broadly. "Ready, Dad."

The car pulled away and Abigail hurried back to work.

Jake and the other customers sat back down as they realized everything was okay. Carol bid her friend goodbye and exited the building. She moved past the policeman as he continued down the sidewalk, covering his beat.

Rick Stuckman had been a beat cop since he'd recovered from the injuries he'd received during his stint in the first Gulf War. The job was pretty boring for the most part. His heart had pumped faster when he thought he was going to see some action in front of the diner. Still, he was glad the little boy wasn't being kidnapped, that everything was okay on that front. Now, he glanced at his reflection in a shop window with his pale blue eyes and grimaced at the sight of the scars on the left side of his face. Red and jagged, they ranged down his cheek from below his eye to his chin. A second uneven line cut across his forehead and stopped just as it passed through his eyebrow. Rick frowned at his image, flexed his neck, and turned away in time to admire the sway of a woman's hips as she moved down the walk in front of him.

Carol noticed how attractive the policeman was when she passed him. She figured him to be in his mid-thirties and, by appearance, of Asian descent. As he gazed into the shop window, she gazed at him. She noticed he had the beginning of a beer-belly. She also noticed the scars on his face and thought it was a shame that they marred his otherwise good looks. Smiling a little, she added extra swing to her walk as she continued on down the sidewalk.

Rick watched the woman wiggle until she entered the Snyder Building Complex, his next stop on the beat. He enjoyed the way her straight, shoulder length brunette hair swayed back and forth with each hip twitch.

As Carol entered the building, Margery Newbert exited. Rick almost laughed, even though he had seen the woman many times before. Extremely tall, with a large head and long arms, Margery wore her usual turtleneck shirt, self defense against her clients. What made him want to chuckle was the bottom half of her body. Covered with fur and sporting a long tail, Margery was cat on the bottom and woman on the top. Over one arm was draped the upper half of her cat costume, including the whiskered head. Margery was a Cat Whisperer by trade.

Margery was in a hurry. She almost collided with the local policeman in her rush to hail a cab to get to her next appointment. Her mind whirled with the patient's problem. A beautifully coated, lilac Burmese, Kitty was acting contrary to her usual smart and playful norm. Margery had been working with Kitty for several days and thought that today was the day she would make a breakthrough; she had decided that Kitty didn't like her name. Her true name was Katherine the Great, but her owner had chosen to call the magnificent creature by the diminutive name. Margery was full of her plans to whisper Kitty into accepting her nickname by reminding her of her royal namesake. She slid into the rear seat of the taxi and continued laying out plans as the vehicle rolled down the road.

Inside the complex, seated behind a behemoth of a reception desk was Sara Smith, Administrative Assistant to all the businesses located within the building. As Rick entered through the revolving doors, Sara was thinking what a shame it was that Margery couldn't find a way to get her Webcam Cat Counseling site up and running on the internet. Sara enjoyed walking with Margery in the park on their lunch hour. Margery's bright clothing of gold and maroon always buoyed Sara's moods. And Margery didn't expect Sara to talk since she herself listened to disco on her ever present IPod. Sara, unlike most the other people within the building, didn't find Margery's career odd. Nor did she think it strange that the woman liked to build bird houses and break-dance in her spare time. Sara Smith simply liked people and would go out of her way to be helpful.

Rick smiled at Sara and stopped to chat for a minute before making his rounds through the many floors. Rick had considered asking Sara out on a date, but he never did because he always found his thoughts turning to another woman. "How you doing, Sara?"

"Great, Rick. Everything good on the streets?" This was Sara's usual question and Rick gave his usual answer.

"Everything's always great while I'm looking. Just let me turn my back and all hell breaks loose."

They both laughed and Sara turned her hazel eyes and sweet smile away from Rick to take an incoming call. Rick waved and moved towards the elevator. Normally an officer would not patrol inside a building during his beat, but his captain's wife had an office here, and Captain Jerarrfe wanted to be sure that everyone knew the building was protected. So up the elevator Rick rode.

As the elevator ascended, Rick felt icy fingers slide up his back. His breath blew cold in front of his face and he saw movement from the corner of his eye. He whipped around but no one was there. He hadn't felt this afraid since the time in the desert when he'd heard the snick right before an explosive blew half his face off. As he stood shaking, he saw an image in the mirrored wall, an image of a beautiful red-haired buxom woman wearing a deep-cut turquoise dress. Whipping around, Rick found himself totally alone. He turned back to the mirror but found it empty. The elevator doors slid open behind him and he stumbled out backwards and bumped into a body. With a yelp, Rick turned to find himself face-to-face with the woman he longed to hold in his arms.

Fantasia Muck towered over Rick as his eyes raked her stick-thin body with admiring eyes. Her maroon hair, tied back in a bright green ribbon, flowed down her skinny back in a thick braid. "What's wrong?"

Rick looked back at the elevator and shook his head. "I don't know. Nothing really. I just had a funny feeling in the elevator."

"Oh! You met Ruby, hunh?"

"Ruby?"

"Ruby used to come here to…well, to 'service' the corporate heads."

"Service? Do you mean what I think you mean?" Rick sounded shocked.

"Oh yes, but that was years ago. Things were different back then." Fantasia smiled softly. "Mr. Palmer had a big thing for Ruby. He hated that she visited other men; he wanted to marry her. But Ruby wasn't the marrying kind. Then, Ruby was found dead in her bed one morning. Turns out she didn't have any family; she lived alone and raised bees. Mr. Palmer paid for her cremation and she sits in an urn on the mantle in his office."

"No kidding. And she still hangs around the place? But why did I get so spooked? Was she mean? Is she mean now?"

"Oh! Gosh no. Ruby was supposed to be a great girl. But who knows. Maybe they can't help but be scary." Fantasia giggled.

Pete, the building cat, strolled from an office. He stretched. A long-haired, albino cat with large pink eyes, Pete ruled the offices throughout the building. Now, he rubbed up against Rick and Fantasia, trying to fulfill his goal of shedding on everyone's pant legs.

Fantasia leaned down to pet Pete, and Rick took the opportunity to sneak a peek at her skinny bottom. He looked away quickly as she stood back up. "I've heard rumors that Pete likes to urinate on Palmer's clothes. I actually think Pete's hated him since he first laid his lazy pink eyes on him. But Pete's been here longer than the janitor. If Palmer tried to get rid of the cat he'd have an uprising on his hands."

They were interrupted as Freddy Funk came out of the accounting office where he worked as a clerk. Freddy patted his Elvis-styled hair to be sure every hair was in place. Even with platform shoes, he only came up to Fantasia's shoulder. Now, due to a mishap with a firecracker in his youth, he turned one large brown eye on Rick and one small blue eye on Pete. "We talking about the cat?" he asked. "I got a story to tell you about Pete here." His voice squeaked after long sentences.

Rick and Fantasia looked askance and Freddy continued. "I had to go see Palmer the other day. You know how Ruby sits up on the mantle, right?" When his audience both nodded, he went on. "Well, did you know about the bee?"

"What bee?" Rick looked puzzled while Fantasia nodded knowingly.

"Tell him about the bee, Freddy," Fantasia said.

Freddy preened. He knew Fantasia longed to be with him. He couldn't wait to go home and write in his diary. He could see it now...*Today I am 28 years old. Fantasia Muck made eyes at me while we stood in the hallway. I know she wants me. Maybe tomorrow I'll ask her out...*He drew himself away from his reverie and began speaking. "See, ever since Palmer brought Ruby's ashes back here to the office, there has been a bee flying around the urn. Probably because Ruby loved bees so much. Anyway, Palmer's secretary named the dang thing Cannibal Nector. Says it's a worker bee during the day and a deranged psycho at night. A terror to the bee community." Freddy squeaked out a giggle.

"What's that got to do with the cat?" Rick asked.

"Oh, the other day, when I was in there, Pete was staring at the bee. His head was going back and forth so fast I thought it might turn in circles. He was about to leap when Palmer yelled at him to get the hell away. Then," Freddy bent over, holding his stomach in mirth, "Pete went over, jumped up on a table next to the coat rack, and took a leak on Palmer's cashmere coat." Tears leaked from the tiny man's eyes while Rick and Fantasia gave small laughs.

Rex Stanton, Sales Manager, moved to pass the trio in the hallway. Driven, narcissistic, charismatic, and unfulfilled, his athletic body seemed to glide past them while he kept his blue eyes averted. The smell of hairspray drifted back to them from his sandy-blonde hair.

"Well, that was a funny story," Fantasia said, sidling past Rick and into the elevator.

Rick watched unhappily as she pressed the button and disappeared behind the closing doors. He had missed another opportunity to ask her out. He'd longed for her ever since the day he had went to her for a massage and she had rubbed him with those long skinny fingers, pressing all the right spots. Turning from the elevator, Rick found Freddy still there. "Well, see you around," Rick said and moved on down the hall.

As he approached the office vending area he found a number of people crabbing about company policies. "What's the issue under discussion?" Rick asked. He was a well-known figure around the building and no one questioned him being there.

Steve Krushcek, the Shipping Manager, spoke angrily. "Promotions from within. I say all jobs should be filled by someone within a company. Why should an outsider get a job that someone currently employed knows inside and out?" Steve had recently been passed up for another promotion and was bitter.

Ford Onbeirg, a new employee in the call center, had recently arrived in town. He was quiet, exceptionally good looking, and quite tall. He had rather unruly black hair and gentle brown eyes. He usually stayed out of conversations and seemed to almost fade into the woodwork at times. In a melodic voice, he said, "Still, if there isn't a good match for a job from within, the company needs to go outside."

Steve glared at Ford. What a stupid name. And what was up with the dude anyway? He hardly ever spoke and Steve suspected he had a secret that kept him quiet. Plus, Steve had heard that he had been spotted by some talent people and would probably leave the company and make millions. He stared reproachfully, hunched over his coffee with his scalp shining through his thinning brown hair.

Iwanna Beleve, resident daycare worker, looked young enough to be one of her wards. She smeared an extra smattering of jam on the bagel she held and took a small nibble before voicing her thoughts. "I agree with Steve. No one should come in and take jobs from us. We work hard to move up the ladder and should be rewarded."

Steve smiled at Iwanna. He had seen her glaring at the charges she took care of daily and suspected she didn't really like children. But still, she continued to feed, herd, discipline, and play with the ankle-biters every day.

Iwanna frowned at Carmine LaRoche who had just taken a dollar from his pocket and slipped it into the soda machine. The wiry little man practically dripped Brylcream. Now he spoke over his shoulder in a fake French accent. "Ze coompanny cane hi-er anyboody zay wan. Et es up to zem." He wished he had his guitar so he could sing a song he knew about working. Maybe he'd sing it for his next client. She was due in his office to sign him on as her talent agent this afternoon. He would try to get her on in Nashville but doubted if she would make it since he couldn't and he was extremely talented. He wandered away from the discussion, nervously smoothing his thinning hair back.

Iwanna also turned to leave. Man, how she wished she could raise ferrets. But, she didn't have the funds to start a ferret farm and the daycare job paid the bills. She hated break being over and having to go back to work. The kids pulled her hair, stepped on her toes, and plus, they were short. Short and they smelled. She looked at Rick as she passed. He was a little too tall for her. People shouldn't be tall. They can't wear hats at the movie; they can't find dates 'cause they're all too short. She was glad she wasn't tall.

Ahead of her, Carmine reached out to shake hands with a woman who had just arrived at the door to his office. Iwanna shuddered at the thought of his greasy hand touching hers. She knew from Lettie, Carmine's secretary, that she had to constantly hide his guitar from him so he wouldn't torture his clients. But, Lettie said, he always found the thing. She thought he sniffed it out by scent. Iwanna shuddered once more as smoothed the hair she wore up on top her head.

"What do you think, Rick?" Steve asked.

"Hmm, I'm not sure I have an opinion. I've always been kind of the low man on the totem pole and haven't really tried to move up the ladder. Sorry I can't add anything." He quickly moved away. Hopping in the elevator, he nervously waited for Ruby to make an appearance, but she remained aloof.

Rick waved once more to Sara, thinking it was a shame that she had been assaulted when she was young. She could really make some man happy if only she weren't carrying around so much emotional baggage. Rick pushed through the revolving doors and stopped. Leaning against the building was Hercamer Fannylick. Hercamer held out a Virginia Slim in greeting. "You know," he began. "I really hate these things."

Rick smiled. He liked the bald hunchback. Hercamer always had a quick smile and his eyes were always kind. "Why do you smoke them then?"

"Oh, I guess it's because they remind me of my mother."

"How's business?" Rick asked as he rubbed his hand over his own head, deciding not to pursue the topic of Hercamer's mother.

"Slow. No one seems to believe in phrenology anymore. They don't believe the bumps on their heads can reflect their character." He paused, looking towards Rick's head. "Why don't you stop up sometime and get a reading?"

"I just might do that," Rick stated as he turned away. He was having dinner tonight with his mom and dad; a husky American soldier and a native girl who found love in Vietnam during the war. Rick understood well why his dad loved the little Vietnamese who was his mother; she was the best mom ever. Rick sped his steps as he hurried towards his family and a good hot meal.

Ruby, Pete, and Rex
the Cheat

Ruby held the pet taxi close to her side as she threaded her way through the busy coffee shop, hoping her trench coat would help hide it. Inside, Pete was making small anxious noises, peeps really, and Ruby shushed him.

"Just be a good cat for a few minutes," she pleaded as she found a corner table. "I just want to grab a bite to eat, and then I'll get you to the vet. Like that's a real treat for you anyway. You should be glad we're stopping here for a while." She placed the pet carrier behind her chair and draped her coat over it. Maybe the darkness would encourage Pete to take a nap. She could hear the swish of his fur as he turned circles within the small enclosure.

"What can I get for you?" A tall dark-skinned woman with flaming red hair stood by the table with pen and pad in hand. Ruby was startled; she hadn't heard her approach over the muffled conversation and other noise in the place. She looked up at the tag on the woman's brown blouse.

"Abigail," said Ruby.

"That's right," Abigail said slowly, "and I'm your waitress. You sure seem jumpy, miss."

"No, I'm not!" Ruby burst out. Then quieter, "No, I'm not jumpy at all." She sat her purse on the table, knocking over the cardboard menu. She and Abigail watched it flutter to the floor. Then Ruby burst into tears.

"I take it you're not crying over the menu falling down," Abigail said. She handed Ruby a napkin. "Want to tell me what's wrong?"

"Do you have any children, Abigail?" Ruby asked as she blotted tears from her eyes.

"Yes, I do, as a matter of fact. A son, Toby. Here, let me show you a picture." Abigail reached into her pocket and pulled out a wallet. She opened it and stuck it under Ruby's nose. A slender dark-haired boy of about seven stared at her from the photo. He looked nothing like his mother.

"Where is he right now?" Ruby's voice had a worried tone.

"He's at daycare. With his favorite daycare worker, Iwanna."

"Iwanna? Seriously? What's her last name?" Ruby pulled from her doldrums for a moment, pondering the unusual name.

"Beleve."

"You're pulling my leg now," Ruby said. She almost smiled. "Iwanna Beleve. Very funny."

Abigail chose to ignore this. "Anyway, Iwanna is really good with the kids, although I think she'd rather be raising ferrets. I think Toby likes her because she's short. I mean, really short."

Ruby seemed interested, but Abigail changed the subject. "What about you, honey? You got any kids?"

This brought fresh tears from Ruby. "No," she wailed. "And I never will have. Look over there across the room. See that couple?"

Abigail nodded.

"Well, that's Carol Orion. I work with her. And sitting next to her is Rex Stanton, our sales manager. He was also my boyfriend up until this morning. And I thought Carol was so shy and conservative. She dresses like a librarian. How can he stand her? She's cute but her face breaks out all the time, and Rex is a perfectionist. Still, he's sitting awfully close to her." Ruby's voice trembled as she dried her eyes again with the napkin.

"They do look pretty cozy," Abigail observed. "But honey, there's more than one fish in the sea. You can find someone else."

"I'm too old to go fishing any more! My bait is drying up and my biological clock is just about to wind down. Rex was my last hope. Look at him. Wouldn't he have produced a gorgeous baby?"

"Well, he thinks so, obviously," Abigail said dryly as she watched Rex admiring his reflection in the back of a spoon, brushing at his sandy hair with one hand, and widening his china blue eyes as he preened. In fact, despite sitting too near her to be merely casual, he seemed to be ignoring his date.

"You're right about that," Ruby agreed. "He does appreciate himself quite a bit."

"I've got to get back to work," Abigail said. "Can I bring you something? A Danish and some coffee, maybe?"

Ruby nodded.

"Okay, honey," Abigail patted her shoulder. "I'll try to squeeze in a few minutes to chat with you when things slow down. I'd like to offer you some advice, just give you my perspective on things."

As she walked away, Pete meowed softly and Ruby murmured to him while she looked around. She noticed Hercamer Fannylick, the company phrenologist, standing at the counter next to Freddy Funk, the accounting clerk. It seemed everyone from her floor was there to witness her humiliation. She could probably get a date with Hercamer if she wanted, she thought. At forty-six years of age, bald, and carrying his long 5'8" frame in a hunched posture, he was hardly the office catch. She reminded herself he was quick with a smile and had the kindest soft gray eyes. He lit a Virginia Slims cigarette and blew the smoke toward Freddy, who wheezed.

"You can't smoke in here!" cried the cashier.

"I'm sorry," Hercamer said contritely as he ground the cigarette on his heel. "I forget."

Sara Smith, his administrative assistant, rushed to his aid. "Don't yell at him," she said in her sweet voice. "He didn't mean to break any rules. He only smokes those because they remind him of his mother." She patted Hercamer on the arm and held out a Styrofoam cup for him to discard his butt.

"Let him speak for himself, sister," the cashier said gruffly, crossing his beefy arms over his chest. Sara cringed. She still responded automatically to aggression with a defensive posture, even though years had passed since she was assaulted. Ruby shook her head. She was familiar with Sara's past and sympathetic to her struggles. There wasn't a nicer person in the entire company than Sara, but her timidity and anxious helpfulness often made her a victim. People took advantage of her. This time, however, Freddy stepped in. He was successful in defusing the situation, largely due to his high squeaky voice, obvious Elvis-inspired hairstyle, and two differently colored eyes. The cashier couldn't stop staring at him, seemingly intrigued by his eyes which were not only different colors, but different sizes, due to a mishap with fireworks as a youth. Freddy carried himself with confidence, however, thinking he was sought after by all women. He had no idea he presented such a comical picture. The cashier shrugged and turned his attention to the next customer in line, and the tension drained from the moment.

Just as Abigail returned with her order, Ruby overheard Hercamer say, "I was just about to offer to feel his head for free."

"Somehow I don't think he would have appreciated that," Sara said as the three of them took their drinks to a booth. Ruby hoped they wouldn't see her. She didn't want company. They did fix their eyes on Rex and Carol. Hercamer shook his head and she knew he was feeling sorry for her. Ruby wanted to crawl under the table. She busied herself with her Danish and coffee, looking around the room as if expecting someone.

She turned toward the door in time to see Jumping Jake stroll in, his skinny tie swinging and his briefcase tapping against his leg. She recognized him from the jazz club where he played sax every Friday night. He had a day job as a freelance film critic, but he loved to play. It was obvious in the way he caressed his instrument on stage. Ruby had stared at him many times through the smoky haze. She thought he was sexy, but too young for her. She watched him glide to a window table and take a seat, drizzling into the chair like melting wax.

Later on, Ruby would remember this moment because Jake was soon joined by Ford Onbeirg, a nobody then, but a man who would soon take the box office by storm. Ruby couldn't help but admire his striking looks. Nearly six feet tall with unruly black hair and rich deep brown eyes, his melodic voice carried to her table. She couldn't make out the words, but the tone nearly mesmerized her. He had gentle but sensuous mannerisms and she felt a strong attraction. *There's somebody who could make me forget all about Rex*, she thought, *but he'd never give me a second glance.* (Other women over the past few years had shared that thought. And they were dead now. Ford's gentle ways hid an evil side that even he did not know existed.)

Ruby glanced over at Rex and Carol again. She felt a jolt when Carol's eyes met hers, and her face set in hard lines. At least Carol had the decency to blush and duck her head. Rex, on the other hand, seemed not to even recognize her as his gaze flitted impatiently around the room. He suddenly lifted his hand and waved to someone near the door. Steve Krushcek, the shipping manager, marched over to Rex's table. He seemed angry as usual. Jerking a chair out, he flopped down and snatched the menu from the center of the table. Abigail went to his side to take his order. As soon as she left, Ruby could hear his voice booming over the café noise.

"I guess you heard about Peterson getting that promotion," he practically shouted. Rex shrugged, and Sara looked down as if embarrassed. "Shoulda been mine, you know." He ran a hand through his thinning hair and sighed in a put-out way as he slid forward in his chair, his poor posture turning him into a question mark. "One of these days, I'm just gonna snap. Snap, I tell you!"

A cop sitting at the counter turned to stare at Steve. He looked like he almost would invite trouble to relieve the boredom. Ruby tilted her head and watched him. He was close to her age, mid-thirties or so, had a rugged visage, but handsome. She wondered where he had gotten the scars, one on his left cheek and a smaller one above his right eye. In spite of these blemishes, he was a good-looking man. Perhaps he was not in the shape he once was, his muscular build was trending toward fat, but still he radiated strength and confidence. His bearing revealed a military background. She felt her heart rate pick up. His light blue eyes swept the room, almost as if he had felt her gaze. When they stopped on her, she felt a slow swirl inside her belly. He gave her a quick smile before turning away. He had felt the connection, too. She just knew it.

She pulled her cell phone from her purse and called her best friend.

"Tamilia," she said. "I hope you're not busy. I mean, that's a dumb thing to say to someone who homeschools her three kids and is starting her own design studio on the side."

Tamilia responded with her low velvety laugh. "I've got a few minutes. What's up?"

Ruby pictured her friend, leaning against the breakfast bar, her curvaceous figure hidden in her signature flowing skirt, loose blouse, and long jacket. She knew Tamilia dressed for comfort, but had a flair for fashion that managed to shine through anyway. Whatever Tamilia wore seemed to compliment her warm chocolate skin and deep brown eyes. The natural afro she wore to embrace her heritage gave her a regal appearance, like an African princess. Ruby thought Tamilia was the most beautiful person she knew, and that's why she wanted her advice at this moment. The clicking in her ear told Ruby that her friend was turning her head to check on the children as she spoke, causing her gold hoop earrings to tap the phone.

"I'll talk fast," Ruby began. "Originally I was going to call to whine about Rex dumping me. But, Tamilia, I just saw the most delicious man! And I don't know what to do!"

"Well, I have no idea where you are, but I would say just go up and talk to him," Tamilia said.

"I will, I will," Ruby whispered. "But if he's interested and if he asks me out, will you help me dress for the date? I want to knock his socks off."

"Oh, of course I will," Tamilia assured her. "In fact, I already have an outfit in mind for you. You are gonna be gorgeous when I get done with you!"

"Oh, he's coming over here," Ruby said. "Talk later. Bye."

She slid the cell phone back into her purse as Officer Rick Stuckman approached. At that very moment, Pete decided he could take no more of his confinement. A howl erupted from behind Ruby's chair and increased in volume until everyone in the place turned to look at her. Rick looked surprised and tried to see around Ruby's chair to find the source of the noise.

"Oh, my," Ruby muttered.

As if sensing he had everyone's attention, Pete ramped up his efforts and screeched at the top of his lungs, flinging himself against the side of his pet taxi at the same time.

"What the hell is that? You got a cougar back there?" Rick asked, reaching for his gun.

"Oh no! It's just a cat," Ruby said, as she got to her feet. "It's just the office cat. I was taking him to the vet."

"We don't allow animals in here!" bellowed the beefy cashier as he strode toward the table.

Pete yowled again and rocked his cage so hard it fell over with a thump.

"Everyone just calm down!" a voice cried. All eyes turned to the woman standing on a table near the center of the room. "I'm a professional. I'll handle this!"

She leaped from the table to the floor like a giant fairy, her wispy pink skirts swirling around bony stilt-like legs. Knob-

Knobby wrists protruded from a purple turtleneck whose sleeves were too short for her exceptionally long arms. Thin pale skin stretched over an abnormally large cranium topped by frizzled platinum hair. Thanks to her skill as a break dancer, her awkward-looking body touched the floor with unexpected grace and she bowed to the gaping crowd.

"Who are you?" Ruby gasped.

"I am Margery Newbert, cat whisperer," the female scarecrow announced. "And this is my calling. Out of my way, everyone!"

Seventies disco music blared from the earphones now dangling round her neck as she busted several moves over to Ruby's table. Bending low, exposing her bouncing rear end encased in its crepey pink wrapper, she put her garish red mouth close to the pet taxi and whispered.

"Mmm. Mmmm-hmmm," she said after a fashion. She stood to give her decree. Everyone paused to listen.

"This cat does not like being in this pet taxi," she stated authoritatively. "And he says there is a bee inside the office that plagues him at night. An evil bee named Cannibal Nector! Something must be done about this at once if you want your cat to find his center and be as one with the natural world. I have spoken!"

Everyone applauded and Margery bowed again. A man broke from the crowd and made his way to her side.

"Carmine LaRoche, here," he said, shaking Margery's hand. She pulled away and looked at her hand with disdain, wiping it on her pink skirt, leaving a greasy trail. He nervously smoothed back his thinning hair which was thick with Brylcream. "I'm an agent. I'd like to represent you."

Margery's face broke into a smile, transformed by the prospect of fame. Taking his elbow, she led him away. "You know, I have lots of ideas about my career. I someday want to conduct webcam counseling sessions with my feline friends. Maybe we could do something with youtube? Anyway, I have lots of talents. I even assemble bird feeders, and paint them myself. Usually gold and maroon. Those are my colors, don't you know…" She bent over Carmine's wiry little form like a praying mantis over a succulent mate.

"I play guitar, when it doesn't slide out of my hands," he said. "I could come up with a jingle for you." They disappeared into a booth.

Ruby glanced down at Pete, now sleeping peacefully in his pet taxi and then up at Rick. A smile broke out on her face. Rick returned her smile. The meaty cashier stood a few feet away, tapping his feet and giving her a dirty look.

"How about I drive you and your cat to the vet?" Rick asked, glancing at the cashier who fumed nearby.

"That would be lovely," Ruby answered as she slipped on her coat, threw her purse over her shoulder, and hoisted the pet taxi.

Rain

Twenty-five years ago, I fell, not onto the ground, but under the influence of a seductress and under the weight of my own sorrow.

I bowed under the stabbing knives of truth when Vada walked away, glancing back at me over her soft white shoulder, dark hair sinuously swinging with a small shake of her head, escorted on the arm of a man I had thought of as a friend. Acid poured into my center and turned me weak as it ran red down the walls of my insides. I stood frozen, unmoving, but a part of me wanted to beg her, prove to her she was making a mistake, convince her it wasn't really happening. Turn her around, crush her to my broad chest, and squeeze her small frame until she realized it had to be undone. Somehow undone. Not forgiven, not explained, not cleared up, but undone.

She had given me no advance notice, no hint of things to come. Strolling into the bar where I worked, her luscious hips rolled under a clinging red skirt, and her dark eyes slowly traveled the room. I thought she was there to sit and drink at the bar, as usual, where she could watch me until the end of my shift. At first, I didn't even see Deez trailing behind her. His lizard eyes were fixed hungrily on the tail of this illusive beast, one that would make a meal of him someday. He was still stupid then, like I had been before that night.

Vada sidled up to the bar, lighting up my world with her presence. But, she did not return my smile, which was uncharacteristic for her. The Dark Horse was playing that night, a cool trio whose music was heavy on the bass, but soft on volume, relying on finesse to modulate the sound. Their songs were velvet daggers, hurting you before you even realized it. People didn't have to yell to be heard, yet my woman crooked her finger at me, called me over. I leaned down so she could whisper in my ear.

"I owe it to you, I guess, to tell you."

"Tell me what, angel?" I still held the glass, drying it with a white cloth. A moment later, it shattered in my hand.

"I'm taking up with Deez. We'll be leaving the city tonight."

My large size made me slow, and the shock made me indecisive. Good thing or I might have killed them both, and then regretted half of it later. Deez stepped forward and took Vada's hand possessively. He tucked it inside his elbow and guided her through the milling crowd toward the door. He looked nervous and defiant, and yet proud too. That's how Vada slid away from me, easy, like a dollop of rich butter down a hot griddle. That backwards look she gave me, the small shake of her head, the slight frown; I didn't know what those gestures meant. Pity? Remorse? Disgust? Or just a wordless request that I let her go?

Mac approached me. He leaned his broom against the cooler and laid the dustpan on the counter. Gently, he unwrapped my hand from the base of the broken glass still clutched inside a now-bloody towel. He tossed the mess into the trash and led me like a stunned blast victim to the small bar sink where he ran water over my fingers, and then wrapped them in a clean cloth. Without a word, he swept up the shards and tipped them into the trash.

"Why don't you take five in the back room?" His tired gray eyes were almost misty. He'd seen it all before, but had never grown jaded.

I stumbled toward the back, but didn't stop at the small storage room. I continued on, outside into the cool spring night. Lights over the alley were smeared by a misty rain, or maybe by the water in my eyes, I don't know. Dropping to my knees on the wet bricks, I took one shaking deep breath, and then bellowed out my pain, sobbing like a child. I should have known. A woman like Vada could never really love a man like me. But for almost a year, I had believed she did. My brain still played with me, throwing me thoughts I could cling to like life preservers in a raging river: It was a joke; they'll come back in laughing and saying how they really got me. Or, she didn't mean it; she was just trying to get my attention. Or, she won't really do it; she'll get to the edge of town and turn around, race back to me crying and begging me to take her back. And I will!

But, of course, none of those things were real. When I threw off my initial dumbfounded stupor, I rushed to our apartment, hoping to catch her. But she had cleared out before she even came to the bar. There, I found empty spaces where her things had been. Her clothes were missing, along with my stash of tips and the little I had been able to put back from my pay. I had been giving Vada most of the money left after paying our rent and taking her out to eat almost nightly. It had nearly broke me, but I loved the twinkle in her eye when I used to say, "Get dolled up, sweetheart. We're going out."

So, she took my money. She took my dignity. She and Deez also apparently helped themselves to my supply of Vodka and the dark ale that I always kept on hand for Vada. None was left. It's good that Deez was sizes smaller than me, or they would likely have stolen my clothing too. I noticed they also made off with my small black and white television, my stereo, and my collection of albums, a collection that had taken me years to accumulate. I most hated to lose the blues records and those by Old Blue Eyes. I had met him once in Vegas, but that's another story for another time.

I sunk to my bed, the bed upon which Vada and I had so eagerly romped, entangled in cheap sheets that smelled of Downy, her perfume, and our love. The bed upon which I left her sleeping late each day, blankets wrapped round her succulent form and shades drawn against the daylight. I remembered creeping out and softly closing the door behind me, careful to preserve her slumber. I was in the habit of making life as easy as possible for Vada, so she would want to stay with me. I spoiled her. I doubted Deez would do the same, but you never know about a man once he has within his grasp a woman like none other, a woman whose mere presence sets a champagne sun in the sky, and fills each night with sweet hot embraces, like molten caramel. A man does a lot of changing for a woman like that.

I clenched my fists at the thought of his skinny arms around her, with their ugly black hairs curled like tiny parasites against his pasty white skin. *How could she prefer him to me?* I wondered. I am not a handsome man, but at least I have a healthy complexion and size to my credit. Size and strength. I recalled Deez emerging from the lake where we swam sometimes, looking drowned and diminutive. At the time I felt sorry for him. He was a ferret of a man, his greasy hair slicked back over his sloping head, a head that lacked only two round ears atop it to thoroughly resemble that of a rodent. How could she prefer him to me? He must have come into some money or talked a good line.

Looking around, I saw a shabby room with tall ceilings and old stained wallpaper. Beneath me was a tattered bedspread, hotel issue, gotten at a bargain price from the thrift store. A beat-up dresser and chair that looked like it had gone rounds with Mohammed Ali completed the furnishings. With shame, I remembered that I had seen this room with different eyes not so many hours ago. I had seen it as our love nest, cozy and inviting. Now, the stark bulb overhead cast things in a different harsher light. What did she expect? How could I have done better when I spent most of my money on her? I shook my head, trying to crawl out from under the cloying self-pity, the choking despair.

The least they could have done was left me one bottle of comfort, one bottle of blessed oblivion. I felt I had earned at least that. Grabbing my jacket, I rose from the bed and stumbled through the tacky living room/kitchen combo. At the front door, I turned to sweep my critical gaze over my apartment. I found it as lacking in charm and warmth as the bedroom. I almost decided not to even lock the door as I left. What was left to steal?

Thumping down the wide staircase, I couldn't help but notice the soiled threadbare carpet and small piles of dust in the corners of each step. I conceded to myself it wasn't a very nice place to live.

Over the entrance to the building, a ragged canvas awning leaked rain onto my shoulders. Shoving my hands into my pockets, I trudged to the liquor store at the end of the block. Good thing I had twenty bucks tucked away in my wallet.

Drops ran down the glass front of the shop and a bell clanged as I entered. Old Emory was manning the counter, his rheumy eyes lighting with recognition as I approached.

"You seen your woman tonight?" he asked in his raspy Louie Armstrong voice, incongruent with his toothpick-slender frame. He should never have said those words. My face grew tense. Emory's hands trembled slightly as he fiddled with the pile of brown sacks next to the register. His black skin glistened under the artificial lights like the moisture on a glass of Vada's dark ale. He looked hot and uncomfortable, in spite of the coolness of the weather. A soft sympathy for him bloomed inside me because I realized that he knew my shame. If he spoke of it, I wouldn't handle it well.

"Uh-huh," I answered. "Why?"

"Well, then, I guess you know what's going on." Emory nodded his head as if he had just dispensed sage advice.

"Did you see her?" I asked, dreading the answer.

"They was in."

"Don't say any more." My voice held a warning. Emory looked down, nervous now. Probably he had only wanted to offer me some sympathy, or perhaps a hint of where they were heading, a snippet of overheard conversation. No matter. I wouldn't go after them now. Maybe in the first fiery moments of agony, I might have. But not now. Now, I didn't care who paid the price for their betrayal. Anyone would do, and I think that fact had dawned on Emory just a few seconds too late.

I glared at him, but he wouldn't meet my eyes. Smart man he was, he didn't say another word about Vada and Deez. I waited for my anger and hurt to subside, for there was a big part of me that truly didn't want to hurt him. *None of it is his fault*, I told myself. Still, he had seen my woman with my best friend. And obviously they had confided something in him, perhaps even mocked me.

"Walk into the back room with me." I pinned my gaze on him. I felt heat coming from my eyes like x-ray vision, a strange sensation. It mingled with the pain rising from my gut into my throat, and my voice had grown hoarse.

"I don't believe I care to do that, Ray." He was swaying a little now, and fidgeting around the counter with his hands.

"What are you doing? Let me see your hands." I wondered if there was an emergency button or some such thing he was seeking.

"Nothing, Ray. I ain't doing nothing." He seemed furtive to me then, although he raised his arms above his waist so I could see them.

"Come on," I said, and moved toward him. He cringed and turned to scurry down the narrow dark hall. I could tell it was in his mind to escape out the rear door, so I laid a meaty hand on his shoulder. It felt like an assembly of bird bones under my flesh. Again I felt sympathy for him wash through me, for I knew then what I was going to do.

"Ray, now I want you to remember I've always been good to you." His voice didn't shake, which earned my respect. Likewise, he didn't plead or whine. "I ain't got nothing to do with what happened to you. Nothing at all. I don't even like that Deez fella. I ain't *never* liked him."

I said nothing. When we reached the back room, I guided him through the door with a small push. He lost his balance but quickly regained it. Old as he was, he still retained a natural grace.

"Sit." I indicated a chair in front of an old metal desk. He sunk onto it as if his legs were about to give out. I strode the small space in front of him, back and forth a few times. Then I stopped and leaned down to speak to him.

"I'm sorry as hell about this," I told him, closing my fist.

"Why, Ray? Why me?" It was a simple question, spoke quietly, with dignity.

"I can't say," I answered. "But it's not personal. You know that, right?"

"I know it, Ray. But, you don't have to do whatever it is you're thinking about. It won't help. In fact, it'll make matters worse, son. Much worse." Emory still used the quiet voice, didn't beg.

"Just stop." I didn't want to hear another word. The pain churning in the pit of my stomach had become a living thing now with a personality all its own. It hurt so much. I never knew heartache could hurt so damn much!

"It was raining the night I met her, just like it is tonight. Did you know that, Emory?"

"No, Ray. I didn't know that." The relief on his face made me sad. I could see he was thinking about keeping me busy, talking his way out of this awful predicament. Of course, it wouldn't work. Emory didn't realize it yet, so I let him have this false reprieve for the moment. It was my gift to an old man who was about to suffer for actions not his own.

"Yep," I said. "She came in with a jerk, a right bastard of a man. She caught my eye right away, beautiful as she was. I kind of kept track of her throughout the evening. About halfway through the night, he got rough with her. Pushed her around, smacked her. I was over that bar like a caged animal finding its freedom, and I pounded his ass. Then I threw him out. She looked at me like I was some kind of hero. It filled me up, that look did. And she went home with me that night, and stayed." My face felt wet and I was surprised to feel tears on my skin when I reached up to touch my cheek. Everything was just so sad. Vada leaving me, Deez betraying me, the shabby apartment that was all I could afford, poor Emory, in the wrong place at the wrong time.

Emory had stood and began to edge toward the door. "That's right, Ray," he said. "Vada loved you, man. She loved you until that smooth talking Deez turned her head."

I think the first blow shocked me as much as it did him. His eyes opened wide before he collapsed to his knees, blood streaming from his mouth. A couple of teeth skittered across the floor with a light clacking sound. It made me think of dice tumbling on the kitchen table when Deez and I would play, Vada leaning against the counter in her slip with a glass of dark amber liquid in her hand. She would watch us with eyes half-closed in that alluring animal way of hers.

"I was good to her, Emory," I muttered as I grabbed his collar and yanked him to his feet for another punch. "I treated her like gold. Like pure gold."

This time his head snapped back so hard, I thought I might have broken his neck. He couldn't have stood had I not been holding him up. A deep moan gurgled its way up through the blood in his throat. The tears continued to stream down my face. I reached for his shoulder with my other hand, bent him forward slightly, and kneed him as hard as I could in the gut. It was unsatisfying, even though he vomited. A sour smell filled the room as Emory lost control of his bodily functions. I was embarrassed for him.

"I used to love rainy nights," I said softly. "Now, they're ruined for me. From now on, I'll hate them. I'll hate every single one."

Emory didn't answer. Releasing him, I let his body drop heavily to the floor. A well-placed kick from my huge boot snapped some ribs. There was little satisfaction in this either. I needed more. I knelt beside his convulsing form and pounded on his face, crushing his nose and pummeling his eyes. This produced wet-sounding smacks and thuds which finally seemed to ease my anguish, but only a little. So intent was I on my task, I did not hear the men enter until they announced their presence. "Police. Stand up slowly and put your hands on your head. Step away from that man."

Confused, I twisted my torso to look at them over my shoulder. Their words didn't register initially, but they had weapons drawn. Looking down the barrels of their guns, I blinked and mumbled, "What?"

Somehow a great misunderstanding was taking place. I felt a need to explain. I was certain that's all that was necessary. We needed to exchange information, them and me. I was unclear what specific information might be required, though. My thoughts had become jumbled.

"Wait," I said.

"Stand up slowly. Put your hands on your head. Don't make any quick moves." The officer speaking was almost as large as me and had short red hair, a red face, and hard gray eyes. Gray like the rain outside. The other man, a lithe dark-skinned fellow, was calling for an ambulance. He was dexterous, keeping his weapon on me at all times. A multi-talented person multi-tasking, as only those types can do. It was impressive in a distant impersonal sort of way. I would mull it over later.

"Now!" There was no denying the authority in the voice. Even in my pain-riddled fog, I could appreciate it. I rose to standing, glancing down at the bloody pile of rags on the floor. It made no sense. I couldn't remember for a moment exactly what I had been doing. I should have been at work; it was my shift. Why wasn't I at work? I stepped toward the officers with my hands outstretched, imploring them.

"What's going on?" I asked, and then noticed my hands were covered with blood. "I think I've been hurt. I'm bleeding." I stared at my hands in wonder.

The officers were quick, had me down on the floor before I knew what hit me. As my wrists were bound, I found my face resting in a puddle of noxious fluids. I gradually recognized Emory as I stared at his wrecked face a mere twenty inches or so from mine. I could hear his labored breathing. Someone had attacked him too, I concluded.

"Emory's hurt." I announced.

As the large red-haired officer pulled me to my feet, I mentally traversed my body to figure out where I was injured. I could detect no wounds other than a dull ache in my knuckles, like arthritis.

"What happened to Emory?" I asked, baffled.

"Shut up, you piece of shit," the dark-haired officer said.

"I just want to know," I said, ashamed of the pleading tone of my voice. I'd known Emory for years, thought a lot of him. The larger officer read me my rights and escorted me to the waiting police car. Rain drenched my head and shoulders as he ushered me into the back seat and shut the door on my questions.

The rain reminded me of Vada. The evening I met her. The long sultry nights under the covers in our bed. And then, in flashes, I recalled the evening and its preceding events; Deez and Vada sauntering out of the bar, my fists and their gratifying connections with Emory's frail flesh, my subsequent confusion. Each recollection slammed me like a body blow, causing me to jerk against the seat and recoil with dread.

"Oh, god!" I cried. I stared out the rain-streaked window of the car as a scene of horror unfolded before me. The ambulance workers rushed Emory out on a stretcher. Static from the officers' radio broke the sweeping sound of the storm into fragments. Another police car pulled up and two more officers emerged.

"Emory!" I yelled, straining against the restraints cutting into my wrists. "Emory! Emory!"

He did not raise his head, nor did he stir, as his mangled form was loaded into the waiting ambulance. A sense of unreality flowed over me in a numbing wave as my mind struggled to catch up. It was me that did it. I hurt Emory. The ambulance sped away, siren wailing. And the rain fell.

In fact, it's falling again now, outside the barred window of the small cell I call home.

Overheard

Three nicely dressed people were sitting around a cloth covered table in a respectable restaurant eating a chicken dinner one Sunday afternoon. On one side of the table sat an older woman; on the other, a young man who was her son and a young woman who was his wife. They were catching up on news. Flowered wallpaper adorned the walls, and the oak woodwork gleamed in the soft lighting. A small candle burned on each table. Several other diners sat scattered around the room. Waitresses in dresses and caps moved quietly among the tables.

"Has your neighbor still been 'helping' you?" asked the older woman.

"Oh, yes! He took the trash out the other day. Of course, he always adds his own trash to our dumpster. I guess he thinks of it as his pay for hauling it to the curb," said the young man.

"Even though we never ask him to," inserted the young woman. "He scared me the other day when you were at work."

"Did he? You didn't tell me that. What did he do?"

"Yes, what did he do?" repeated the older woman.

"Oh, just a little thing really."

The young man pressed for answers, "What? Do I need to speak to him?"

"No, of course not. He came and filled a bucket with water. I just didn't realize he was there and stepped out the back door. I almost ran right into him. It startled me, that's all."

"He shouldn't do that," said the older woman. "You need to be careful."

"No, he shouldn't do that. He shouldn't be at the house when I'm not home."

"But, he didn't do anything wrong. All he did was to get a bucket of water."

"Still! I wish he wouldn't come around while I'm gone."

"Doesn't he have water?" asked the older woman.

"Sometimes," said the young woman. "I think that he has to decide between water and electricity some months."

"Water *or* electricity? Why can't he have *both*?"

"Well, water can be gotten elsewhere, but electricity heats the house and warms his food. Although, I don't think he has much food or warms his house too well," said the young woman.

"But why not?" the older woman asked.

"His wife died last year. Remember me telling you?" the young man asked.

"Yes."

"Well, when she died, he must have lost part of his income. He doesn't have enough money to have both electricity and water. Sometimes I don't even think he eats."

"Doesn't eat? Why doesn't anyone help him?"

"We've tried," said the young woman. "But he's a proud old goat. He doesn't like to accept charity."

"He has this little dog," the young man said. "He loves that little rag-mop. I think, at times, he feeds the dog while he himself goes without food. We've started leaving a bag of dog food in the trash every week or two. We try to make it look like we're throwing it away; you know, put it in but leave it sticking out so he can see it when he hauls the can to the road."

"That's very nice of you," the older woman said. "Why can't you leave him food the same way?"

"It would never work," said the young woman. "He'd catch onto that right away. Of course, he knows we are giving him the dog food; but, like we said, he loves that little dog, so he takes the food."

"Sometimes I wonder if he eats some of it too. I would if I got hungry enough," said the young man.

"Why don't you pay him for helping out? Didn't you say that he tries to help shovel the sidewalk and driveway?"

"He does try. I fear that he is going to give himself a heart attack, but he seems to want to help and I hate to hurt his feelings. He's really a nice old coot," the young man said.

"Doesn't he have family?"

"A daughter, I think. We see a young woman stop by every couple of months. She always leaves quickly. She looks as if she is embarrassed to be seen at the old guy's trailer house. We've never talked to her. She always looks angry and avoids looking our way," said the young woman.

"What about the mail?" the older woman asked.

"What about it?" asked the young man.

"Can't you send him food? Or gift certificates for the local grocery store? He would never have to know where they came from."

"Hmmm," said the young man as he exchanged looks with his wife. "We've never thought about that. The store is in walking distance of the house and there would be no way for him to know we sent them."

"Oh, he'd probably know it was us, but who cares. Let's do it."

"See," the older woman said. "All you had to do was ask me and I came up with the solution. That's what mothers are for."

Laughter pealed and the conversation turned to other subjects as a waitress quietly removed plates and served ice cream in small white dishes.

Party Time

Hot! So hot! Sweat drips off my face and trickles between my breasts. *Where are they!* My eyes probe the darkness. *Where are they?*

A light at the corner is giving off a little illumination but it is not enough to reach into the gloom where I'm crouched. *Where are they?*

A sound to my left, very small, barely discernable over the distant city sounds. *Is that them*? I shrink down into the shadows. There's nowhere to hide.

I scan the area, looking for the cause of the sound. Nothing! Too dark! Tears mix with the sweat and burn my eyes. Why is this happening? How did I get into this?

Five hours earlier...

"Mel," my younger sister barged into my room.

"Did you knock?" I asked pointedly. Callie is a year younger than me, seventeen to my eighteen. I'm no stick in the mud, but Callie? Callie is the rose in our family's garden while I am the daisy. She is easily outgoing, drawing people to her like bees to a rose garden. I'm totally the opposite; I have to work hard to make friends.

"Sorry." Callie backed out of the room, pulling the door closed behind her. She knocked loudly.

I sighed. "Come in."

Callie's eyes roamed over my room. She managed to contain the sneer as she looked over the posters on my walls. Her walls are covered with rock band posters and current hot actors; mine are plastered with kickboxing posters. Boxing gloves hang from my dresser mirror. Dragging her attention back to me, Callie began again, "Mel, Tina just called and she knows where there's a party tonight."

"And that's new how?" I asked. Callie's friend always knew where the parties were.

Callie laughed, "Well, anyway, she wants me to go, and I want you to go."

"Uh, hunh," I nod. "In other words you guys need a driver."

"Don't be that way," Callie soothed. "We want *you* to come. Not just for your *car*. Come on Melody, please."

"I don't think so," I said, registering Callie's disappointment. "I have to study for the final in trig this weekend if I'm going to get a passing grade."

"Mel! Come on! You can study tomorrow."

"No!" I said flatly, holding the door for her. "Go!"

Callie stormed from my room. I heard her door slam down the hall, and then silence.

I dragged out everything I'd need to study and tossed it on my desk. Looking around, I added pencil and paper, turned on my desktop lamp, and started to sit but stopped. I left the room, headed for the kitchen to get a soda.

As I passed, I could hear sobbing coming from behind Callie's closed door. I sighed. Callie, though extremely popular, had just suffered a breakup with her long-time boyfriend. They had been going steady for four years, during which time Callie had retained her sexual innocence. Then, boys being boys, Bane had started pushing Callie to do things she wasn't willing to do. She finally broke up with him. It had been a month and Bane had not tried to get Callie back. She was brokenhearted.

Looking at the door, I hesitated. Callie and I didn't get along well. Being totally different, we were constantly rubbing each other the wrong way. Callie could use some fun, I thought. At last I knocked. "Go away," she said.

"Okay. But if you're not ready when I leave, then I'm

going to the party with Tina and you can stay home." I turned and started down the hallway.

I made it three steps before Callie's door opened and she rushed into the hall. She threw her arms around me from behind, gave me a bear-hug, and headed back to her room. Over her shoulder she announced, "You're the best sister ever."

I shook my head as I reentered my room. Now I'm the best. Now that I'm giving in. But usually I don't get that title. Usually I'm the reason for Callie's disappointments. I stopped being critical and started flipping through the clothes in my closet. "Where is the party?" I hollered.

From down the hall, "I'm not sure. Somebody's house, I think."

Okay. That means casual. I grabbed a pair of jeans and a raggedy red t-shirt with a black stick figure kick boxer above the thin black words, 'Kick It'. I ran a brush through my shoulder-length, dishwater blond hair and left it hanging free. I slipped on tennis shoes and went to Callie's door. I knocked and waited for permission to enter. "Aren't you ready?" I asked.

Callie turned and looked at me, "Is that what you're wearing?" She looked at my ensemble with scorn.

"I don't have to go," I said, turning to leave.

"No," Callie said quickly. "It's okay, I guess. Whatever you're comfortable in." Callie was wearing a pair of skillfully torn jeans; ones she had paid a hundred bucks for. Now she pulled on a tight t-shirt with some kind of Mexican design done in brown metallic. She added a pair of sandals. Her platinum blond hair was pulled back in a ponytail and held in place with a ribbon, and her make-up, though subtle, was done to perfection. She looked gorgeous, as usual.

I shook my head in awe over the way she managed to make everything she wore look good. "Let's go get Tina."

After picking up Tina and stopping for a six-pack of soda, we headed for the party. Tina's directions led us to the edge of town and into an area where the houses were few and far between. Most of the ones still standing appeared to be abandoned.

"Are you sure this is the right street?" I asked skeptically.

"I'm sure," Tina stated firmly. "Gregg said the address was 16202." She squinted into the darkness, "This one is 16555; it should be a couple blocks yet."

Finding the right address, we pulled up to the curb. Loud music was blasting from the open windows and doors. Several cars were parked out front. "This must be it," I stated the obvious. I peered unhappily at the house. "The place is a dump. Who did you say told you about the party?" I asked, with a trace of concern.

"Gregg," Tina said.

"Who's Gregg?"

"Oh, a guy I met at the Stop-and-Go," Tina commented nonchalantly.

"You don't even know the guy?"

"He's so cute," Tina giggled.

"I don't know," I started to say but Callie and Tina opened the doors and got out. I hurried to catch up with them as they cut across the grassless yard to the front door. Through the screen, I could see people dancing and just hanging out. At least the music was good.

Callie walked in without knocking; just like home, I thought.

"Well, well, well," a man's voice said. "Who do we have here?"

"Hey," said a second man's voice. "You came. Cool!"

"Gregg," Tina said as she crossed the room to stand next to him. "This is my best friend, Callie." She didn't introduce me.

Gregg put his arm over Tina's shoulders and pulled her close. "Umm, Callie's a cute one, ain't she? Who's the other chick?"

Tina looked at me and said, "Oh, that's Mel. She drove us here."

"My sister," Callie added.

"Mel? Ain't that a boy's name?" He transferred his gaze

from Callie to me, "Are you a boy? You dress kinda like a boy."

"Whatever." I turned to scan the room. Behind me, I heard Callie say that my real name was Melody and the guy responded with 'whatever'.

Looking around, I grew more concerned. The people here were all older than us, probably in their mid-to-late twenties. And they looked rough, mean. Several of the guys were wearing black leather, even though it was a warm night. The girls were all skimpily dressed; tank tops and short-shorts seemed to be the clothes of choice. A lot of dirty-dancing and making-out was going on. Booze and pot was being passed around openly. I wanted to leave. I turned to voice my concerns to Callie, but she and Tina were deep in conversation with Gregg and a friend.

Not wanting to seem like a nagging big sister, I decided to try to be cool, but to keep an eye open. I moved to the couch and sat on the arm, tapping my foot to the music and attempting to act nonchalant.

"Hey," a man's voice said from the couch beside me.

I turned to look and found a nice-looking guy sitting on the sofa. He had shaggy brown hair that grazed the back of his neck. A crooked smile lit up a cute face, and his big brown eyes smiled along with his mouth. He was wearing pretty much the same outfit as me, except his t-shirt was gray and didn't feature kick boxers.

"Hey," I returned.

"I've never seen you here," he continued. "My name's Jeff." He stuck his hand out and I shook it.

"I'm Melody," I told him.

Jeff and I turned out to have a lot in common, and soon I was lost in conversation with him. I hadn't noticed that the crowd had thinned out until Jeff stood. "As much as I hate to, I gotta go. I have to work tomorrow," he told me.

"Wow," I said. "Almost everyone's gone. We probably ought to be heading out too."

"Can I call you sometime?"

I gave him my phone number, and after giving my arm a friendly squeeze Jeff went out the front door.

Looking around, I noticed that Callie and Tina were dancing way too closely with a couple of guys. Gregg watched with a look on his face that I didn't like at all. He seemed to be enjoying the dance more than he should have; so were his buddies. In fact, several guys were watching, and a couple of girls. They all wore leers on their faces.

I jumped up. "Time to go, Callie." She ignored me. I went up and took hold of her arm to get her attention. "Come on Callie, it's time to go."

The guy dancing with Callie rounded on me and gave me a shove. "Leave the little lady alone. She and I are happy right where we are."

Callie smirked at me and returned to the guy's arms.

I was furious. How dare he touch me! "Callie," I said firmly. "Now!" I started to the door but one of the girls stepped in front of me.

She reached out and ran her hand down one of my arms, "You don't really want to go now, do you cutie? We're just getting ready to really party." She licked her lips seductively. I shuddered.

"Yes, I *really do* want to leave."

Callie had seen this exchange, and had noticed a change in the way her dance partner was holding her. He pulled her way too tight and was nuzzling her neck roughly. She tried to push away and aimed for a lighthearted tone. "Well, you heard my sister, it's time to go. Sorry!"

"Oh, I don't think you're going anywhere," the guy told her and kissed her roughly.

Callie shoved the man and he slapped her.

Tina stopped dancing and looked aghast at the man. Shock replaced the smirk that had sat on her face a second before. Had he just hit her friend?

I started across the room to go to Callie's defense, but Gregg stepped between us.

"Let's party," he leered and grabbed for me.

I dodged his arm and saw the man with Tina start to pull her into one of the back rooms. She was struggling to get away. Then Gregg grabbed me and pressed his sloppy lips to mine.

Kick-boxing! I really enjoy kick-boxing. Now, I planted my foot in Gregg's solar plexus. "Run!" I yelled.

Hands reached for me, trying to get a hold, but I dodged. I saw Callie and Tina struggling to get loose from two men as I threw myself out one of the windows, busting through the rusted screen like it was crepe paper. I hit the ground, rolling with the fall and jumping to my feet. As I turned to run, I saw Tina and Callie pushed into a closet and a chair shoved under the doorknob. "Get her!" Gregg hollered, pointing to the window I had exited through.

I ran! My purse was sitting on the couch and my car keys were inside, as was my cell phone. I ran!

The door of the house crashed open behind me, and I heard muffled complaints as too many people tried to exit at once.

Nowhere to hide. The houses around here appeared unsafe to enter, even if I were brave enough to go in one. Bushes and cars were going to be the first places they searched. I crouched into open darkness and tried to make myself small. I needed to get my sister and her friend out of that house.

Voices called tauntingly, "Come out, little mouse. Come play."

Other voices held menace. "Where are you? I'm gonna make you pay for kicking me!"

"Oh where, oh where, can the little girl be?"

Men and women were searching. Sweat beaded up on my forehead. I was shaking so hard I was surprised they couldn't feel the ground move.

Suddenly, Gregg's voice rose above the calls, "Okay, everyone be quiet. I can't hear. If we shut up, we'll hear her."

Silence.

Where are they?

A shadow passed close by and I dropped flat on the ground, trying to blend in to the dark. The shadow passed on by. *Where are they?*

I made my way slowly, ever so slowly, towards the rear of the house. I had to get my sister. I had to get Callie and Tina. I had to get them out. A crack sounded nearby. I froze. I tried to pierce the darkness with my eyes. Nothing. *Where are they?*

Slowly, I began moving again. Soon I could see the back porch. Someone was standing there, waiting for me. Watching.

I watched. I listened.

"I think she's in here," a voice sounded from across the road and down a bit. "Hey, Gregg! I think she's in the old Anderson place." I could hear many sets of feet hear pounding in that direction, and I could see people flitting through the shadows.

Up on the porch, the watcher turned in the direction of the hunt. "To hell with this," I heard a girl's voice say. She leaped from the porch and took off to join the search.

Are they all gone? Did they all go? I watched and listened for several more minutes. Finally, I crept to the porch. Climbing cautiously up the steps, I opened the screen door and entered the silent house. No, not silent. I could hear muffled shouting and banging coming from the living room; Callie and Tina.

I wanted to run to their rescue but I forced myself to move slowly, listening, looking. Finally, deciding there was no one left in the house but us, I ran for the closet. Pulling it open, I grabbed Callie and we hugged each other. "Shhhhh," I cautioned. "Keep quiet. We have to get out of here."

Tina was crying. So was Callie. I felt tears on my own cheeks. I grabbed my purse from the couch and they grabbed theirs from the table. "Put the chair back under the door," I told Callie. "We have to make them think you're still in there."

Callie shoved the chair back in place and stared around frantically. "Now what?"

"Now we hide." I pulled both girls after me into the

kitchen. Pulling open one door I found a pantry. The second door revealed the basement stairs. "Go!" I pointed down.

Tina started to back up. "I'm not going down there. "Unh, un, no way."

"You are," I told her, giving her a shove. "Now. Before they come back." I was pulling my cell phone out as I pushed her towards the steps. Reluctantly, she followed Callie into the dark.

Quietly, I called 911. I gave them the address and told them we were hiding in the basement. Then we huddled together under the stairs, back in the farthest reaches, brushing spider webs out of our hair and resisting the urge to run screaming up the stairs as we felt little legs crawling over our arms and faces.

Soon, footsteps entered the house above us. "I can't believe we couldn't find her," Gregg's voice came clearly through the floor above us. "How did you let her get away?"

"Me?" a man's voice answered. "You're the one she kicked."

Grumbling, and then, "Well, at least we still have the tasty little morsels in the closet."

We could hear the chair pulled away and dropped to the floor. "What the..." sounded a voice. "They're gone. Search the house."

I couldn't believe the words. No! They can't find us. Not now. The police are on the way. I held Callie and Tina's hands tightly. "Shhhh," I reminded them as we all pushed back against the wall, trying to burrow into the cold concrete.

Footsteps pounded through the house and then came the sound we didn't want to hear; the basement door opened. A foot came down on the top step at the same time a pounding came on the front door. "Police!" boomed a voice. The foot disappeared back into the kitchen.

We huddled, clinging to each other. We heard exclamations and denials issued from the lips of the men and women above. Finally, we heard one voice of authority say, "Hold on! I can settle this right now."

Footsteps once again moved across the floor and the basement door opened. A flashlight beam preceded the man as he came down the stairs.

Who is it? Is it help? We stayed still, unsure who carried the light.

The light moved around the room and finally sought out our hiding place, revealing three tear-streaked, scared faces.

"Girls," the man said. "It's okay now. I'm Officer McDaniel. You're safe."

I put the last box in the car as Callie stood by watching. "I don't want you to go," she said, softly.

"I know," I told her. "But, college beckons."

We hugged fiercely, close since our encounter with danger. Oh, we still have our tiffs, but what sisters don't?

I watched in the rearview mirror as I drove away. Callie moved to hold hands with Clark, her new boyfriend. A nice guy; not pushy like Bane.

I smiled as I thought about Jeff. He and I would be in many of the same classes this semester.

The Rustling Dark Shadows of Autumn

I turned quickly, and my shadow moved also. But there was another shadow beside mine and it did not move. Looking around, I could see the shadow of a tree, extending from its base. I could see the shadow of a streetlamp, its long skinny form folding over the curb and up onto the sidewalk. But the other shadow, the peculiar one, seemed connected to nothing. Disconcerted, I took a few steps and looked back. Again I saw my shadow and right beside it another, darker than mine, denser. Ominous.

A chill crept over my skin that had nothing to do with the crisp fall weather. All around me, the autumn sun shone, casting its honeyed light onto the red, golden and brown leaves that skittered past like mischievous rats. The breeze died suddenly, leaving behind an empty stillness. Yet, just beneath the hum of distant traffic on the boulevard, I detected a rustling sound as the mysterious shadow shifted. My heart beat so hard against my chest, I could feel it in my throat. I ran.

A few blocks away, my house beckoned. Home. Safe and warm and familiar. Glancing over my shoulder as I ran, I could see the odd shadow was staying with me, dogging my steps. Slamming my way inside, I leaned against the door, breathless and thrumming with adrenaline.

My parents were still at work and my younger brother, Alex, would be at his friend's house for after school games and snacks. With dread, I lowered my eyes to the floor but saw no shadow. Relief made me weak.

Was I losing my mind? I half convinced myself I had imagined the incident, given in to unreasonable fear. Panicked. When my breathing slowed, I tossed my books onto the table and dug in the refrigerator for a snack.

As I crunched my veggies and dip in front of the TV, I recalled the previous weekend. It was just a harmless little experiment with the Ouija board at a pre-Halloween slumber party. Could that have anything to do with the shadow? Had I inadvertently opened a gateway to another dimension? I would have to call my friend, Carrie, and see if she noticed anything odd. As I determined to do this, I thought I heard a rustling sound in the house with me. I stopped chewing and listened. The sound stopped also, but just a fraction of a second after my crunching. The hair raised on the back of my head with a tingle, like bony fingers trailing over my scalp. The television suddenly switched off. Without moving my head, I cast my eyes downward. A thick black shadow lay across the carpet at my feet like the yawning portal to some dark underworld.

Shrieking, I tossed my plate in the air and ran from the room. As my feet pounded on the stairs, I thought I heard a sibilant rustling behind me. Too afraid to stop, I dashed into my bedroom and slammed the door behind me. Looking down, I saw the shadow creep under the door, entering my room like an ink stain spreading at my feet.

"What do you want?" I screamed, standing on my toes to avoid the dark smudge on the floor. I backed away and crawled onto my bed. Pulling the covers over my head, I huddled with eyes closed, shaking from fright. I stayed that way until I heard my mom and dad come home.

When my parents' voices, mingled with that of my younger brother, filtered up the stairs, I threw off the blankets and ran as if pursued down to the kitchen.

"Angie, what's wrong? You're pale as a sheet!" My mom put her hand to my forehead, and I wrapped my arms around her. This was unusual behavior on my part as I felt myself too grown up for hugs anymore.

"Something followed me home!" I cried into my mother's lilac-scented shoulder.

"Who was it?" my father demanded. He took a step toward the door.

"Not a who," I whispered. "A thing! A shadow!"

"Oh, honey," Mother soothed. "Shadows are nothing to be afraid of."

"You're afraid of a shadow?" Alex mocked, a grin plastered on his freckled face. "What a chicken!"

His smile faded as a dark shape stepped into the doorway, blocking the light from the dining room. Cold malice radiated from its rustling form. "Oh, no," Alex said, his voice shaky. He backed into my father's legs and leaned against them for comfort.

"What?" Dad asked, looking around. Mom appeared to be equally baffled.

My brother's eyes met mine and we knew. Without words, understanding passed between us. Whatever this was, only he and I could discern it. And it meant to do us harm.

Outside, ragged autumn clouds suddenly obscured the late afternoon sun and gusts of icy wind slithered around the house, whistling against the kitchen window like passing ghosts. Spidery naked fingers of leafless trees rubbed against each other with diabolical delight. In the doorway, the malevolent shadow trembled and rustled in response. The moment stretched out as Alex and I stood frozen with trepidation.

Evil had come to visit. And it intended to stay.

Mahoomba

Janet Norman glared at one of her assistants over her half-glasses, obviously angry. "Why did you subpoena these witnesses?"

Karl was stunned for a moment. *Had she forgotten?* "Because you told me to."

"Well, that's not what I wanted." Jan blew out her breath in annoyance. A garlicky smell drifted through the small office space.

Well, then, maybe you shouldn't have told me to do it, Karl thought. "Um, I just followed your instructions."

"Next time, check with me!" She spun on her heel and stormed off, her pumps clicking on the tile.

Karl looked at Andy and shrugged his shoulders. "Check with her before I follow her instructions? That'll go over like a lead balloon. She gives me orders and five minutes later I pop into her office to make sure she really wants me to do what she said. Yea, right. She would chew me a new asshole. Just two weeks ago, she was mad when I *didn't* subpoena the witnesses."

"Did you forget?" Andy asked with sympathy.

"No, I didn't forget. She told me *not* to subpoena anyone, so I didn't. Then when she got back from court, she was furious. 'Where were my witnesses?' she demanded in that snotty voice. 'Why weren't they subpoenaed?'"

"Did you remind her that she had told you not to?" Andy asked.

"Sure," Karl replied. "But she denied it. She just repeated that I should have subpoenaed them and that I ought to know that by now. She told me she was making it very clear right then and there; I was to *always* subpoena the witnesses listed on the information sheet. Always."

"So, you did, and now this…" Andy shook his head. "I think she expects people to read her mind, because you sure as hell can't go by what she says. I tell you, Karl, I don't know about that woman."

"Me either. I wish I could figure out a way to do what she wants instead of what she says. Guess I forgot to take ESP 101 in college. " He chuckled, and then turned grim. " Seriously, I can't decide if she has ADD or Alzheimer's, or some such disorder. Or, maybe she's just wacko and likes to find reasons to argue with the staff. Whatever it is, I wish she'd get on some fucking medication." Karl turned back to his computer. "I don't like scheduling her appointments, either. She tells me one thing, and then when I do what she says, she changes her mind and blames *me* for the confusion. Makes me cancel or reschedule her appointments all the time. She's very hard to work with."

"For." Andy's look was grim.

"What?"

"A boss like her, you don't work with; you work *for*. And she never lets a person forget it. She could make things really miserable for you or me, or any of us here. She's a regular fruit loop."

"True that." Karl smiled. Then his look turned pensive. "But if she really does have some sort of dementia, then she honestly won't realize how she contradicts herself. She probably thinks I'm being insubordinate or just plain stupid."

"She thinks everyone is stupid." Andy winked, trying to lighten the mood. "Crazy, isn't it? She's certainly not the queen of linear thinking herself. One time she had me make three copies of a shitload of papers; then she went through them and eliminated a bunch of them. *Then* she asked me to go through all of copies and take out the papers that weren't needed. Why she didn't just go through them first and then have me copy the ones she wanted, I'll never know. She wasted hours of time and tons of copy paper and ink. She can't think logically. I swear, I'm amazed she gets to work with her underwear on the inside of her clothes instead of the outside."

Karl chuckled. "Maybe she tried putting her shoes on first but couldn't get her pantyhose over the heels."

"For a supposedly intelligent woman, she has some real flaws in her thinking," Andy said. "Maybe she did lot of drugs in college, damaged her brain. I don't know how she ever graduated law school. Someone else must have done her assignments for her."

"Maybe she was tutored extensively," Karl suggested.

"Maybe." Andy tapped a pencil against his leg. "And maybe we're being too generous, giving her the benefit of the doubt."

"What do you mean?"

"I mean, maybe she doesn't have some kind of brain dysfunction. Maybe she's just a hateful bitch. Ever thought of that?"

"Ah, hell," Karl sighed. "I don't like my life very much right now, Andy. I ought to run away to a tropical island."

"What would you do there? Live in a hut? Change your name to Mahoomba and wear a grass skirt?" Andy snickered, amused by his own wit.

"What would be wrong with that?" Karl looked dreamy.

"Nothing at all," Andy mocked gently. "Except for everything. Like how would you live? What would you eat?"

"I'd fish. Maybe pick coconuts. I don't know. One thing's for sure. I'd eat when I got hungry, sleep when I got tired, and use my time for enjoyable pursuits. Like doing something to make my own life better instead of selling my precious time to help other people make money. Do you know how precious time is, Andy? Do you ever think about it? And none of us knows how much we get. And here we are, stuck inside this office without any windows, as our time dribbles away." He punched a few keys on his keyboard. "Well, anyway, break's over. I'd better get back to work. The Fruit Loop wants me to draft some interrogatories, which she will probably tell me she doesn't need after I've spent three hours on them."

"It's likely. That's what she did with that petition I drafted yesterday. I guess it slipped her mind to tell me she didn't need it after all. She let me spend hours working on it. Never told me until I was done that she had changed her mind. Good thing we're not that busy around here right now. Damned economy."

They worked the rest of the afternoon in relative silence. Around 4:30, Karl stood and stretched. As luck would have it, Jan marched into the office at that exact moment and saw him. Her frown made it obvious she thought he had been slacking off. "Do you have those interrogatories done yet?" she demanded.

"Yes, they're finished." Karl sat back down.

"Well, why haven't you emailed them to me yet?" she pushed her glasses to the bottom of her nose and studied him over the rims.

"I did."

"Well, then why haven't I received them?" she asked, raising her eyebrows.

"I don't know. I emailed them." Karl wasn't sure how to answer her question. Perhaps she really thought he had control over Yahoo Mail, or the internet in general. "I can send them again if you like."

"Never mind," she snapped. "Just print them out and bring them in to my office."

She swept out of the room, leaving a sour smell in her wake.

"Doesn't that woman ever shower?" Andy whispered, waving his hand in front of his face.

"Well, she's a professional woman. I would think she knows about personal hygiene." Karl's smile was wry. "She does smell a lot like my Aunt Joni before we got her into that nursing home. She had trouble remembering to bathe. Man, it was a deadly combination of body odor and bad kitty."

"That's gross, dude. Accurate, but fucking gross." Andy turned to answer the phone. While he talked, Karl printed out the document and took it to Jan's office. Since she was away from her desk, he placed it on her chair so she would be sure to see it. Then went to the break room and cracked open a Coke before returning to tidy his desk and get ready to clock out. He planned to do some filing until it was time to leave.

By quitting time, he was more than ready. He couldn't wait to shed his business clothes, get into his shorts, and work on his boat. He'd named her *Paperback Writer*, and getting her seaworthy was his obsession. Just a little more work, and she'd be ready.

The next morning, Karl went to work well-rested and in a good mood. He booted up his computer, checked for phone messages, and poured a cup of coffee. The peace didn't last long. Jan was her usual distracted chaotic self. She buzzed into his office, interrogatories in hand, and announced, "These are wrong. I told you to use the form I gave you."

Karl was astonished. "I did use your form, Jan."

"You used my *old* form. I have a new one. You should have a copy of it." She tapped her fingernails impatiently on the top of the desk. "Check your computer. I emailed it to all the staff."

Karl opened his email and scanned the inbox, then the spam folder. He checked his various folders, all the while Jan was breathing down his neck.

"I'm sorry, Jan, it's not here. All I have is the email you just sent this morning. When did you send it?"

"I don't know, days ago. It's got to be there. Check again." She crossed her arms under her chest, her irritation invading the room like an odor.

"It's just not here," Karl said after checking again. His head was beginning to ache and he felt the familiar strain of tension gathering between his shoulder blades.

"Well, I know I sent it; you had to have deleted it. Anyway, fix these. I've made corrections and emailed them back to you. I'll go to my office right now and email you the *right* form to use on interrogatories from now on." Jan tossed the papers on Karl's desk and left the room just as Andy was coming in.

"What now?" he asked.

"She doesn't like my interrogatories. Says I used the wrong form. The interesting thing, though, is that she said she emailed them back to me with corrections. How did she do that? I mean, yesterday she said she never got them when I emailed them to her." Karl scratched his head. "She doesn't have a scanner and there is no way she would have typed them all into her computer herself. And even if she had, wouldn't she have caught it while she was typing that I had used the wrong form?"

"You'd think. Let me see those." Andy took the interrogatories and perused them. "This is the same form I have."

"What the hell is she talking about then?" Karl's frustration began to mount.

"It is puzzling, but just another day in the world of Janet Norman." Andy turned on his computer and left to put his lunch in the fridge.

Karl opened the most recent email from Jan, found the interrogatories with corrections, and saved them to a folder. He noticed a new email come in from her and opened it. There in front of him was the very form he had used in the first place. The message Jan sent with it said, "Here is the correct form. Use it from now on. We can't keep reinventing the wheel around here."

"Something is seriously wrong with that woman," he muttered to himself. He made the required corrections on the interrogatories and emailed them back to her. He then started on a stack of dictation and immersed himself in the work. Andy came back into the room and did likewise. The day passed pleasantly as most of the attorneys, and especially Jan, had to be in court. Karl was able to get a lot done.

In the next few weeks, however, work was less than pleasant. Business was slow and at times the staff had little to do. Karl didn't understand why the partners didn't send some people, like him, home on slow days. It would save the company money, and Karl hated to be idle. It was torture to sit there all day and try to create busywork. The time crawled by, and he thought of all he could be accomplishing on *Paperback Writer* if only he wasn't tied to this desk.

Not only that, but Jan seemed determined to pick at Karl. He got to the point where he tried to avoid her because nothing he did pleased her. Even if he followed her requests to the letter, she was not happy. She changed her mind frequently about what she wanted, but failed to tell him. Yet, she expected him to know. There was no tactful way to reason with her. She thought any explanation he offered was nothing more than a bunch of excuses.

Things eventually came to a head. Jan stomped into his office one day, told Andy to leave, and closed the door behind him.

"I need to talk to you," she said. "For your information, I am one of the bosses around here. It isn't going to do you any good to try and circumvent things by going to the partners. You just don't get it. They're going to side with me, not you, on any issue."

"I haven't spoken to the partners about you."

"Well, Mitchell in accounting went over my head to talk to one of the partners and I want to know why he did it. I know you and Mitchell have had a few cozy little chats about me. Crissy out front told me so. I want you to explain to me why he did what he did."

Karl racked his brain but couldn't figure out a diplomatic way to answer her question. He decided to just be straightforward. "I have no idea. Maybe you should ask him."

"I did ask him," she barked. "Now I'm asking YOU."

She was prickling with aggression; Karl could sense it. He felt the blood rush to his face. "I don't know why he did it. I could only speculate on why Mitchell does anything he does. I can't read his mind."

"Well, why do you *think* he did it?" She was just not going to give up on the notion that Karl somehow had access to Mitchell's private thoughts.

"Again, I don't know. I could only guess, and I might guess wrong. I think you should take it up with him." Karl was on the verge of disbelief that someone in a position of authority could be this unreasonable and obtuse.

"I guess you and Mitchell think that somehow going to the partners will result in things going your way around here. I guess you think you can run and tattle to the partners like they are my parents or something. Well, it doesn't work that way. I don't know what you hoped to gain, but you made a big mistake."

"Jan," Karl reminded her. "I didn't go to the partners. It wasn't me. You're yelling at the wrong person."

She glared at him for a moment. "I don't know if I'm going to be able to work with you," she said flatly. "I don't like your attitude. You never do any of my work right. And it seems to me like you don't know much. Why don't you know more?"

"I know plenty," Karl said, his ire aroused. "The partners seem to be satisfied with my work." He was being set up, he realized. They were alone; she could say anything and it would be his word against hers. Quickly, he said, "I think I'd like to postpone this conversation until the partners can be present."

"No, we're not postponing anything. Do you think I'm not your boss? Do you think I don't have the power to hire and fire, just like the partners do? If that's what you think, then you are dead wrong. Now, I asked you a question and I want an answer. I can't believe you've worked here as long as you have and can't do the simplest thing right. Why don't you know more?"

"You know what?" Karl said, finally fed up. "What you said earlier? Well, the feeling is mutual. I don't think I can work with you anymore either." *And to think there was a time when I really did want to please her,* he thought. *I went out of my way to try and get a coherent response on how she wanted things done. She wasn't capable of producing one, and now I'm getting the blame for her mental problems.*

Royally pissed off now, Jan whirled and left the room with a head of steam. Karl was almost shaking from the effort it took not to point out to her why staff had such problems working for her. He knew if he did that, he'd be fired for sure. He walked straight from his office to one of the partners and asked for the rest of the day off.

The next day was Saturday. Karl had spent the night before deliberating on his situation. He knew he simply could not work in that environment anymore. He'd be damned if he'd tolerate being talked to like that. And he knew the partners would never fire Jan; she made them too much money. She cost them a lot of money too, with her rudeness to clients, refusal to return calls, and callous disregard for the problems of the people she was supposed to represent. She cost them money, too, in time and resources wasted due to her chaotic thinking process and memory problems. However, the partners didn't know about those things, and no one was about to tell them. The writing was definitely on the wall. He was either going to be fired or he was going to have to quit. He just didn't know which.

Karl drove to the office where he cleared his desk of all his personal belongings while the place was empty of people. He didn't want to have to gather up his things in front of everyone, like some kind of disgraced employee. Once he had his possessions out of the building, he was better prepared for whatever was to come.

Early Monday morning he received the call he was expecting. One of the partners, in his most regretful-sounding voice, told Karl he was being laid off. He said the conflict with Jan was not something that could be resolved.

"Ok," Karl said. So that was it. No more job. All those years down the drain because of one fruit loop in dire need of a Strattera - Ritalin cocktail.

At first, Karl was devastated. But as the reality grew clearer in his mind, he realized he was, for the first time in years, free. Free as a bird, free as the south wind, free as a prisoner let out of jail. A smile spread across his face.

Six months later, Karl's cell phone rang. It was Andy.

"Hey," Karl said.

"Hey yourself," Andy replied, his voice artificially cheery. "Haven't seen you in a long time. Thought I'd give you a call."

"I'm glad you did," Karl said. He stared out over the pristine beach to the aqua waves beyond, as they lazily rolled to shore, glinting prettily in the sunshine. He marked the page in his book and laid it aside to visit with his friend. "How've you been?"

"Not so great. After you left, Jan started targeting me just like she did you. The partners had to finally face the fact that if they didn't step in and do something, they'd lose all their help."

"Really?" Karl wasn't all that surprised.

"Yea, so they assigned Crissy to be her one and only personal secretary." Andy laughed.

"The receptionist?" Karl asked. "Well, that ought to work out pretty good. She and Jan are two of a kind."

"That they are. Birds of a feather. Turns out Crissy was working behind our backs anyway, going to Jan and telling her stuff staff members had said in confidence, trying to stir up trouble. Hell, for all I know, she was making shit up, too. Hard to say, but you know how much Crissy loves drama. So, in light of that, I guess she more or less deserves to be Jan's secretary. She's got all the drama she can handle now. It's poetic justice."

"Ah, office politics," Karl remarked dryly. "I feel your pain."

"So, Karl," Andy's voice became solicitous and kind. "How are *you* doing? Are you ok?"

Andy's tone took Karl by surprise. "I'm doing well, Andy."

"I bet you hate Jan right now."

"Nope. Not at all," Karl replied. "In fact, she inspired me in a way. If not for her, I wouldn't be where I am today."

Andy sounded puzzled. "And where's that?"

"Sitting on that island we talked about, looking out over the ocean."

"Really? You're not shitting me, are you?" Andy's voice rose in disbelief.

"White sand and blue water, my friend," Karl told him. "*Paperback Writer* docked nearby, rocking in the gentle waves. Palm trees and coconut oil. I eat when I'm hungry, sleep when I'm tired, and spend my time doing what I want. No grass skirt, though."

"How?" It was the only word Andy could form, he was so shocked. He had expected to hear Karl's unemployment woes and was ready to commiserate with the lousy hand he'd been dealt. This happy-sounding Karl was completely unexpected.

"Cashed in my retirement, sold my house and car, and came here where the scenery is gorgeous, and the living is cheap."

"You're kidding!" Andy was flabbergasted. "Karl, you're pulling my leg."

Karl smiled, leaned back in his deck chair, and took a long sip from a tall icy drink. "Just call me Mahoomba."

The Perfect Employee

Sam was a loyal employee. In fact, Sam was the only employee. She was a jack-of-all-trades; she made sales, she did the accounting, she cleaned the restrooms. But Sam had a flaw, a flaw buried deep inside, one she wasn't even aware of herself.

"Hey Sam, see you're bright and early." *As always*, Harold thought, as he greeted his employee upon arriving at the shop to open for the day.

"You know me; early to rise makes a person healthy, wealthy, and wise," Sam quipped, quoting her boss's favorite line. Sam had no idea what these words really meant. She had never had a runny nose, never had aching muscles. Her paycheck was direct deposited into an account that she never accessed. And, as far as being wise, Sam knew what she needed to know and nothing more.

"I hear you," Harold said, only half listening as he readied the cash register and unlocked the door so the first customers on the busy tourist strip could enter.

Harold often watched his employee. She was a real looker; curves in the right places, long wavy blond hair, and sparkling blue eyes. Her voice was neither high, nor low; it was a well-pitched voice, easy to listen to. Sam never got flustered. She never had a hair out of place. Always dressed nice and neat. Harold had asked her out to dinner a couple of times in the first year she had worked for him, but had been politely turned down. That was ten years ago and she hadn't changed at all; no gray hairs, no wrinkles. Harold found her 'sameness' disturbing at times. *But*, Sam was the perfect employee, so Harold would always push aside his concerns.

Each evening, at closing time, the same scenario played out. "Time to call it a day," Harold would state after collecting the till that Sam always had counted and ready. "Why don't you go ahead and take off?"

And, as every other evening, Sam would reply, "Go ahead, Harold. I have a few things to take care of here. I'll lock up."

Harold used to argue, saying he could handle it, she should go out and enjoy herself, go home and take it easy. But Harold had learned not to push the issue; he never won, and tonight would be no different. "Okay, then. I'll see you tomorrow."

"See you tomorrow, boss." Sam smiled her perfect smile and locked the door behind him.

Each evening, after closing time, Sam would clean the shop. She would straighten and dust the shelves. She would arrange clothing on the racks, nice and orderly. And each night she would choose something to wear for the next day. These clothes she would change into after her final chore of the evening, cleaning the restroom. When Sam was done, she would hang up the clothes she had worn for the day and place them on the rack she had gotten them from the night before. They would still be spotless, just like they had been when she had put them on the night before. And, the shop would be spotless. She would *sleep* until morning, until right before Harold arrived to open for the day.

One day, Harold didn't arrive for work. Nor did he come during the following days. Sam wandered aimlessly around the shop, tidying up the already neat store. She was surprised when, after several days, the rear door to the shop opened. Harold's son and daughter-in-law, whom Sam had met only once, entered.

"Oh," Kim said. "You startled me. We didn't know anyone was here."

"Where else would I be? This is my job." Sam was puzzled.

"Have you been coming in everyday since Harold passed?" Bernard asked.

"Passed?"

"Yes, of course. Didn't you know my father died?"

Sam looked blank.

"Well, I hope you won't want to be compensated for the time you've been spending here. You might as well pack your belongings and go; we have someone coming in to pick up all the stuff in here."

"Pick it up? Why?"

"They bought it to add to their own inventory. We don't have time to run the shop; don't even have the desire to." Bernard gave himself a mental shake. "Anyway, we no longer need you here. You may go."

Sam's mind reeled. Go where? She had always been here. She'd awakened one day and this was where she had been. She had stayed. Now, they wanted her to go. Go where? Sam wandered into the back room. She remembered the attic. No one ever went there. Sam pulled down the hinged ladder and climbed the stairs, pulling the steps up behind her. She moved into the darkest corner of the otherwise empty attic, stood in the shadows, and waited.

Once the activity down below died out, Sam crept from her hiding place. She walked in a daze around the empty shop, picking up hangers from the floor and placing them on built-in rods, gathering up discarded odds and ends, cleaning up. Time passed.

Officer Walker was getting ready to retire after twenty years on the force. As he worked with the new beat officer who would take his place, Walker paused in front of a shop window. "Here's something you'll find interesting, Peterson." He gestured towards the inside of the shop.

Peterson peered through the spotless windows. Inside

were empty shelves, clothes racks, and a counter. The only other thing in the room was a mannequin dressed in clothing styled from a decade before. She stood, posed by a shelf, with a feather duster inches above the dust free surface.

"Wow," Peterson declared. "Has she been there long?"

"Oh, she's not always *there,*." Walker said. When Peterson looked askance he continued. "She moves around."

"She *moves* around? Are you nuts?" Peterson spouted. "Oh, sorry, I didn't mean to be rude."

"Don't worry about it. I thought I *was* nuts to begin with, but it's true. Every night she is in a different spot. In fact, we'll come back by later and she'll have moved."

"Right." Peterson eyed his partner.

"You'll see." Walker smirked.

And see Peterson did. They passed the store about an hour later, and there was the mannequin, broom in hand, near the front window. "I'll be danged." Peterson quipped. He peered closer. "Who do you think is moving her around?"

Walker shrugged. "I don't have a clue. I've never caught anyone inside with her. She just moves."

Peterson stared for a few minutes. "She's a looker, ain't she?"

Walker agreed. He walked by this store many times each night; had been doing so since old Harold died three years ago. He didn't say it out loud, but on his last night with the force, Walker planned on entering the shop. He planned on removing the mannequin from the shop; taking it home. He'd see what happened then. Walker whistled happily as the two officers moved away from the window.

We Need to Talk

"We need to talk."

The words caused my heart to race. Sweat broke out on my brow and my palms. I shook from head to toe and my fingers felt numb. I had never said these words before, at least not to *him*, and I couldn't believe they had just left my mouth. But it was too late; I'd already spoken.

Slowly, I placed the phone receiver back in its cradle. Hopefully my voice wasn't recognizable over the answering machine, and I prayed there was no caller ID on the receiving end of my call. *Oh, what have I done?*

I buried my face in my hands. I pulled at my hair. I paced. It was twenty-five to eight in the morning and I had no idea when to expect a response to my call, or if I would even get a response. I could only hope there would be no response. I raised the receiver once more and called my secretary to explain that I wouldn't be in this morning, and possibly not this afternoon.

The day passed. I tried to watch television but the only shows were soap operas. I tried to read but couldn't focus on the words. A car door slammed out front. I snuck to the window, parted the shades, and peeked out furtively. It was only my lawn service. Finally, I took a hot shower and a nap.

When I awoke, the room was dim and I was disoriented, groggy. Something had interrupted my sleep, but in my confused state it took a few moments to collect my senses. A light rustling sound drew my attention to the corner of the bedroom where something tall and dark waited in the shadows. A low, breathy chuckle sent chills down my neck into my spine. At that moment, I knew my call had been received and my insides clenched with dread.

"So, you want to talk," the figure addressed me in a deep gravelly voice, made all the more ominous by its quiet mocking tone. "Our 'arrangement' is so uncomfortable for you that you would request a meeting? With me? That surprises me."

I was so overcome with fright I could only stutter, " S – s – s. . ."

"Now, now," he admonished with a wave of his long finger. "I hope you weren't going to speak that atrocious name some use when referring to me. *Never* call me by that name, little man, even when I am not present. The walls have ears, you know." To illustrate his point, the walls of my room sprouted hundreds of dark fleshy protuberances, all pointed my direction. The faint light from around my window shades reflected on them, painting them with a surreal luminosity. They expanded and contracted as if breathing, and then retracted into the plaster. My flesh crawled at the sight. There was a long pause, and then the walls became flat and ordinary again, awash with the shadows of drawing dusk.

"I'm sorry." My tongue was dry as powder and my words came out in a hoarse croak. I wished he would step from the corner so I could discern his face. At the same time, I fervently hoped he would stay hidden. "What then *should* I call you?"

"You may call me L...." He stopped and chuckled. I nearly expired from the mere prospect of hearing his true name. "Call me Master."

His whisper played along my arms and face with painful sensations as if my skin were being abraded. I was mute.

"So, brave soul," he said with great sarcasm. "What fleeting impulse of false courage drove you to contact me? Have you a complaint to register?"

I could not find words, hard as I tried.

"Cat got your tongue?" He laughed softly, and with his words an emaciated-looking gray cat leapt with feline grace upon the bed beside me and began chewing on a grisly pink morsel. With a visceral shock, I realized my mouth was empty of my tongue. I moaned as nausea played around the back of my throat. I endured a long moment of agony, a groan working its way up from deep inside me. Then, I swallowed hard, and realized with great relief that my tongue was once again in its proper place. Looking up at me with a hateful glare, the cat slowly vanished.

"Weren't you the one who said we *had* to talk?" The figure shifted in the corner and his cloak settled around him with a horrid sound, like the crackle of burning fat dripping from a spit over flames. A stench filled the room and I choked.

"What you really meant is you have to talk and I must listen. Surely you know I bend to the will of no man. And you? You're hardly even a man. You are nothing special. You are lower than a common snake beneath my heel."

A serpent slithered up my side. I looked with horrified eyes as it drew nearer. In place of its reptile's head, it had a likeness of me, a shrunken replica of my head and face atop its long scaly body. It grinned at me as it slid over my torso, a slender forked tongue flicking in and out of its mouth that looked oh so much like my own! Its oily weight atop my chest sickened me, but I was frozen in place; I could do nothing but watch it with wide eyes. It nestled into my neck and latched onto my skin, where it began sucking.

"No," I moaned, hating the feel of its mouth on me. I felt a sharp pain as it drove its tiny fangs into my tender flesh. Master gave a low chuckle and the snake vanished. Then he sighed as if weary.

"Look at me," he commanded. Cringing, I raised my head. Two burning spheres met my frightened gaze. In their red glow, I could make out the hard bridge of his nose and the hollows beneath his fearsome cheeks, cut like granite into sharp angles and planes. Quaking so hard my teeth clicked together, I was helplessly pinned, until he withdrew deeper into the shadows of the corner and the fire in his eyes receded, thus releasing me.

"So talk. Speak now, or regret it," he said with impatience.

I had no courage, but I feared what he might do if I refused to answer. Taking a deep ragged breath, I pushed the words past my vocal chords. "I can't do it anymore. I can't do the things you require of me. Master." Tears rolled down my cheeks.

"You have a problem preaching the word of the 'lord' to his minions?" The word of his rival rolled off his tongue with distaste, and he spat into the corner, leaving a pile of mucus that sizzled as it ate through the floor. "You find it irksome to lie to the earthly population, to deceive them into believing they will be saved if they only empty their bank accounts for the good of the kingdom? Is this what you wished to *talk* about? SPEAK!"

I rolled off my bed and groveled at his feet; even going as far as to kiss the hoary scales while trying to avoid the razor-sharp fungus-ridden nails. "No, Master. I mean, yes. I did wish to speak to you about this; but, I have changed my mind. I had convinced myself that taking money from these harmless souls was wrong, that posing as an evangelist was deceitful. But now I remember all you told me when I accepted the offer to walk in your path. Taking from these lowly beings is right; no, it is righteous. It is your wish and I will grant your wish, my Master."

The shadowy being in the corner stood silent for a moment, silent that is except for the deep wheeze that seemed to emanate from the depths of his soul, like the burning of a mighty fire in a deep pit. "Welll…we will see. If you continue to bring money to my campaign all will be fine; if not, *we need to talk.*"

Before I could respond, he was gone. I scrambled to my feet and made my way to the garage. I hastily drove my Mercedes to the stadium where I would perform this evening, preaching the word to thousands that would be present and to millions who would watch from in front of their televisions in the comfort of their homes.

At my cue, I walked quickly onto the stage, my gleaming white robes bellowing behind me. White hair surrounded my face and head like a halo. People stood, people dropped to their knees, people worshipped. Me, they worshipped me. Although they proclaimed to worship their lord, I knew the truth. As I preached the word from their good book, I added embellishments that were from my master. No one knew; they dwelt on my word, my master's words. And they reached deep into their pockets, drew out their checkbooks, drew out their cash, and gave it to me. Not to the church, to *me*. Oh, I used just the right phrases, just the correct nuance, to make them believe they were contributing to the path to *heaven*, but most of the money stayed with me. I distributed the amount agreed upon by the Master to many organizations and individuals across our country and even in other countries. To people who would aid my Master in his battle against good. To people who had no qualms about setting off weapons of mass destruction in highly populated areas; people who would give their own lives to fly airplanes into large buildings; people who would not flinch when releasing viral contaminants into water supplies. I gave this money knowing the consequences.

The problem was my conscience. Most of my life it was small and underdeveloped; it rarely gave me any trouble. At least, not so much trouble that I couldn't easily tune it out or squash it down inside me. Lately, however, it had been making its presence known, growing in strength. And it seemed, along with the stabs of guilt came an ever-growing fear that bordered on terror. I began to question what I was doing, and worry about the larger consequences. This was far out of character for me; it took me by surprise.

Questions began nagging at me. Was I contributing to the ruin of the world? Was I playing a part in the destruction of hapless souls who looked to me for guidance? Was I ensuring my exalted position beside an eternal fiery throne or dooming myself to never-ending torment in the scorching pits of Hell? After all, Master was a liar. My long reward might not be at his right hand, but under his heel.

I had wanted power, notoriety, fame, riches and adulation. True to his promise, Master had given me all that. And I loved it. The applause, the adoring looks from my 'sheep', the glory, the prestige, the moral authority, the money. Oh, the money! But then my conscience had worked at me and badgered me into making that phone call. I glanced over my shoulder and wondered if Master could read my mind; I half expected to see him hovering at the back of the stage. But no, my purple-robed choir was there as always, swaying as the organ music swelled in preparation for my first mighty words.

Tonight I had embedded a special message into my sermon, one that would drive hundreds of people to their ATMs, checkbooks, and hidden stashes. The coffers would be stuffed by tomorrow afternoon, with more to come in the mail. All because of my words. Mine!

Pride swelled in my chest and pushed aside my conscience, blanketed my fear of Master so that I didn't have to acknowledge it. A tiny thought, just miniscule really, tried to sneak in, tried to remind me my fear was misplaced. I crushed it like a giant stepping on a pesky squeaking mouse. Moving to the podium, I raised my arms. The music stopped and the audience held their breath. Anticipatory silence filled the auditorium; the air was charged with expectation.

"Brothers and sisters!" my voice boomed over the amplifiers. "Heed not the false prophets! Hear my voice and know the truth!"

Somewhere in the crowd in one of his usual disguises, Master smiled.

I preached, pouring forth a mixture of truth and lies. The words of my Master mingled unnoticed in the visions of golden streets and pearly gates that I called forth. But the gates that were truly waiting these star-struck audiences were anything but pearl; they burned with an unquenchable fire, rising high into the sulfurous air. The words suddenly dried up in my throat and refused to move past my lips. I held *The Book* in my hands. I looked at its brilliant white leather cover and remembered verses

I had read in preparation for adding my Master's message. Suddenly all the words I had studied over the years, the words I had used as a basis before adding my Master's, came back to me in magnitude. I stared into the unfathomable eyes of my Master as knowledge flowed over me. I was going to renounce my loyalty and I was going to die.

I remembered verses that had always seemed meaningless before; such as: *And let patience have its perfect work, that ye may be perfect and entire, lacking in nothing. James 1:4*

I knew I was lacking.

And then, there was: *I am the light of the world: he that followeth me shall not walk in darkness, but shall have the light of life. John 8:12*

I knew I walked in darkness.

Whoever loves money never has money enough; whoever loves wealth is never satisfied with his income. This too is meaningless. Ecclesiastes 5:10

I thought too much about money.

Do not fear, for I am with you; do not be dismayed, for I am your God. I will strengthen you, and help you; I will uphold you with my righteous right hand. Isaiah 41:10

He *would* uphold me. *Me.*

Suddenly buoyed up, carried away in exaltation, the evangelist began to pray. He dropped to his knees, raised his face to the heavens, and prayed for all he was worth. He begged for the forgiveness offered to him and claimed his gift of salvation. His audience of millions saw a change come over his face and felt the difference as well. As if a single entity, they all dropped to their knees. All but one. This one was infuriated. He raged. Demonic fire burned behind him as he strode to the stage in impossibly long steps.

On stage, the evangelist prayed to God.

The Lord is my Shepherd; I shall not want.
He maketh me to lie down in green pastures:
He leadeth me beside the still waters.
He restoreth my soul:
He leadeth me in the paths of righteousness for His name's sake.

The devil stormed among these people praying to their God, his fury sending twisting tendrils of flame and smoke about his hoary head. They did not notice his passing; their devotion was pure.

Yea, though I walk through the valley of the shadow of death,
I will fear no evil: For thou art with me;
Thy rod and thy staff, they comfort me.
Thou preparest a table before me in the presence of mine ene-
mies:
Thou annointest my head with oil; My cup runneth over.

With demonic pleasure, Satan wrapped his burly arms around the puny man who had turned against him. He began to apply pressure. His putrefying breath wafted around the man but seemed not to faze him.

Surely goodness and mercy shall follow me all the days of my
life: and I will dwell in the House of the Lord for ever. Psalms
23

Death, in the form of Lucifer, took the life of his long-time servant that day in sight of millions of viewers. They did not see this. They saw a golden light envelope their favorite preacher as his life left his body at the end of the prayer. They mourned his passing.

As for the disciple of Satan, he passed not into the bowels of hell but stands in line at the gates of Heaven. It is here that he will be judged and a decision as to whether he is worthy of passing through the gates will be made. Let us not forget the golden light that illuminated this man as he found his true God; and let us hope he was not too late.

Blue

I was sent to that god-awful house when I was eight years old. Deep in the Appalachian backcountry, bordered on one side by a desolate field, guarded on two sides by thick stands of sinister-looking trees, and butted up against the tangled foothills of wild mountains; it was the residence of a reclusive inbred clan. The efforts of my mama to keep me away from those people were all in vain, because she died and then they had me.

The woman in charge of this filthy house was full of mean bones. Her real name was Zelda, but everyone called her Meme. An ugly name for an ugly woman. She got the name Meme because that was what she said from the time she could speak as a toddler. Me, me, me. She bragged about this as if it were a proud accomplishment. But, the truth is that she was a selfish child who grew to be a selfish domineering woman. She was my grandmother by blood, on my daddy's side. Or so they all claimed. From the first fear-filled moment I stepped foot on the weathered gray boards of the porch, I denied it. Out loud and to anyone who listened, until the notion was smacked down. Then, I just denied it silently but with vehemence in my soul. *I can't possibly be part of this family.*

My mama loved all the colors in the world, and so she named me Blue. She named her still-born twins, her first babies, Violet and Lavender. And a little brother I barely remembered, who died when he was still an infant, had been called Baby Red.

Although she never liked to talk about it, I knew from overheard conversations that there had been another boy, born before me, whose death was shrouded in secrecy. His name was

169

Grey, and I knew he had died when he was only four years old, a year before I came along. I was the only child left to this woman, and she fled to protect me. For several years, she stayed on the run and kept me safe. But, death interfered with her best intentions, and I was sent by Social Services to the Clapper family to be raised.

The first day in that house destroyed any hopes I had been clinging to that they would be nice people who would look after me because I was blood kin. I would have been better off thrown into a pack of wolves or sent to an orphanage. From the start, I knew there was danger. It lurked around every corner of that trashy old house, in the lanky frames of the men folk, and in the coarse hands of the women. It hung like a ghost in the cracked plaster walls that had seen too many unspeakable acts, behind the doors that hung crooked and scraped the uneven floors, and simmered in the small close-set eyes of the cousins, aunts and uncles.

"Well, here she is," Meme crowed as she shoved me up the steps onto the front porch. It was crowded with lazing men and lolling women, guzzling Falstaff beer and drinking from Mason jars, smoking their hand-rolled cigarettes and spitting chew. They were a ragged bunch that radiated casual violence and dark, unrestrained proclivities.

A pack of undernourished grubby-looking children crawled like rats among the legs of the adults and played around the corners of the house. "This here is Blue, everyone."

One of the men snorted and tossed the flat yellowed butt of a cigarette into the dirt yard. It was immediately snatched up and puffed on by one of the children. "I got me a huntin' dog by that name," he said. "You some kinda dog?"

All of them laughed as my cheeks burned red. I froze, clutching my rag doll.

"Say, Blue, did you know we're foreigners here? That's right. We all got Roman hands and Russian fingers," another said with a wink. The group sniggered lethargically, as if it were an old family joke they'd heard many times. Meme snickered too, but her knobby hand propelled me forward the length of the porch, past all those similar sets of malformed eyes, toward the screen door. A dirty jean-clad leg lifted to block my progress.

"Let me have a look at ya," said a rail-thin man. He had a shock of dark hair above a deeply tanned face. Taking my chin in his hand, he raised my head. Then, he stroked my cheek in a nasty lingering way that reminded me of the slime on the sides of the fish tank in my old apartment, before Mama and I'd had to run again. I stared into those odd hazel eyes and trembled. His voice was like gravel in a bucket, deep and jagged-sounding. "I'm yer Uncle Jez, brother to yer daddy. Well, well, Blue. Looks like you done lost both a yer front teeth. Ain't you a right big girl? Did the tooth fairy leave you a quarter?" He tossed a significant look to the other men who each chuckled. "Uncle Jez'll give you a quarter, later on. I got some magic tricks to show you, too."

"Hehe!" a rat-faced man in overalls hooted. "Looks like Jez got himself a little crush on Blue."

The others laughed and one of the kids sang, "Jez and Blue, sitting in a tree…."

Everyone but me thought it was pretty funny.

"Aw, she's shy," Jez said. "Look at that face, boys. Just like a little scared mouse."

My so-called daddy sat there on the edge of the porch, sullen and half-drunk, staring at the hard packed dirt beneath his boots. He didn't stick up for me. Neither did Meme, but she did put a stop to the teasing.

"That's enough of that shit!" she bellowed. She kicked Jez's leg out of the way and pushed me past him. "You shut yer big mouth, Jez. Blue here has got real work to do. She ain't gonna have time to be playing with you. Gal's got a lot to learn, and she don't 'pear to be none too bright."

I stumbled forward, through the screen door. Jez called to my back, "I'll teach you some things, girly." His low laugh made my insides hurt, and tears ran down my cheeks. I couldn't have guessed then that Uncle Jez would turn out to be my favorite. But, given the alternatives, that wasn't saying much; and just because he was my favorite doesn't mean I liked him. It just meant I hated him the least.

"I don't want to stay here. I want my mama!" I wailed.

"Now look what ya done!" Meme turned to stare at Uncle Jez through the rusty screen. "You made her cry, you ass. You think I wanta listen to a bunch of bawling?" She turned to me and squeezed my chin hard, forcing me to look up at her. "You stop that sniveling right now, you little baby. Jez was just joking with you. You'd better grow a thick skin if you want to be part of this here family."

"I don't want to be." My voice shook, but I was naïve enough to think all I had to do was say it and I'd somehow be released.

"Want to be what?" Meme frowned at me, putting her face close to mine. I caught a whiff of alcohol and old tobacco on her breath.

"Part of this family. I'm not part of this family." I hugged my doll closer and tried to pull my face from Meme's grasp. Without warning, she let go of me with one hand and slapped me with the other. She didn't hold back, and my head snapped to the side. The shock and pain of the blow set me to crying harder, deep wrenching sobs. She took my shoulders in a claw-like grip and began shaking me back and forth.

"Let's get two things straight right now, you snotty little brat. You are a part of this family whether you like it or not. I don't care what kind of hoity-toity bullshit yer mother filled yer head with. And second, I don't tolerate crying. I like my peace and quiet, so you just shut yer ugly mouth or I'll slap it right off yer stupid little head. You got that?"

I'm going to die, I thought. *Just like my brothers and sisters did.*

I cut off the sobbing, panting from the effort, but couldn't keep the tears from flowing. Nodding, I hung my head before Meme.

"Well, good then. That's better." She seemed mollified. "I'll show you around a bit and then you need to get busy on yer chores. If you think yer just gonna mooch off of us, you got another think coming. Yer gonna carry yer weight, or regret it!"

We were standing in a cluttered living room that had an old pot-bellied stove for heat and a tattered sofa next to a wooden barrel that was being used as an end table. It held a lamp with no shade, a cut-off coffee can overflowing with cigarette butts, an oil lantern, and a dog-eared TV Guide. Brown paper sacks full of clothes were piled next to it. An old armchair slumped under the front window, its stuffing creeping out from under the bath towel spread over its seat cushion. A dirty braided rug covered the dusty floor and a couple of wood crates with boards over them served as a coffee table. On the opposite wall from the couch, a decrepit black and white television showed the news, its rabbit ears tipped with crumpled foil and its picture snowy, volume low. I looked up at the soot-covered paisley wallpaper, bordered near the ceiling with a stained lacy looking pattern that was very old. The light from the bare bulb did not reach far and the upper corners of the room were shadowy. Still, I could make out cobwebs drooping under the weight of sooty filth. Down lower, dust bunnies huddled around the perimeter of the room and empty beer cans and bottles crowded every surface. Several lopsided wooden chairs leaned tiredly next to the dining room doorway.

"You'll be cleaning up the living room every morning when you get up, Blue. It's one a yer chores." Meme batted ineffectually at some grunge on the back of the chair. "I hope yer not as lazy and no-account as yer mother was. Worthless as tits on a boar, that one." She yanked my arm, pulling me into the next room.

"This here's the *formal* dining room," she said proudly. "Just like all them rich Knoxville bastards have got. No different." I looked around at the battered table with its heavy wooden legs and scarred surface, and shuddered. I could see nothing to be proud of. I was pretty sure the rich folks in Knoxville didn't have a room like this one, but I knew better than to say so. There were cabinets built into the wall that were so crooked a marble placed on them would roll off. An unmatched set of filthy lace curtains hung unevenly over a large crooked window. More wooden chairs and a few crates stood around the table which still held remnants of the evening meal. Several flies buzzed angrily around the scraps. The corners of the room were stacked with junk. A woman in a baggy blue calico dress appeared next to the table, glared at me for a minute, then grabbed some dishes and went back into the kitchen.

"That's yer Aunt May-Belle, Blue. She and Jez is sweethearts. You mind her like as if she was me, you hear me?" She gave me another cold look and I swallowed hard before whispering assent.

The next room Meme took me into was the kitchen. The floor sloped and the door didn't close flush. It was hot as hellfire in the room. I stared wide-eyed at the old fashioned black cook stove, a barrel of dried corn cobs next to it, the hand pump over the deep sink, the peeling wallpaper, ancient refrigerator, and curling linoleum on the countertops. It was the worst place I had ever seen, worse even than the cheapest motel room or shabbiest apartment my mama and I had stayed in. A fat cockroach scurried from under the stove and squeezed beneath the peeling baseboard near the back door. The sight was repulsive; I felt as if it had crawled on my skin rather than the floor.

May-Belle was pouring hot water from a pan off the stove into an enamel basin in the sink. I had never seen a sink so old and deep, chipped and grimy. Steam curled above it and plastered May-Belle's wiry brown hair to her neck and forehead. Another woman sat at the rickety kitchen table playing solitaire with a tattered deck. She had pale skin, the same close-set eyes as the rest of the group, and a disproportionately large head covered in thin black curls. Her upper lip had enough hair to almost be called a moustache. She stared stupidly at me.

"This here's my daughter, Trinket. She's one of yer aunts, too." Meme smacked the side of Trinket's head. "Why ain't you helping yer sissy-in-law with the clean up?" Turning to me, she explained, "Trinket's slow in the head. I got to remind her all the time."

I felt a quick surge of sympathy for Trinket, but it left me when she punched me in the arm as she stomped over to the sink beside May-Belle. I massaged my arm pointedly, watching

Meme the whole time, but she didn't say a word about it.

"You'll meet the rest of the family later. Right now, you help May-Belle and Trinket get these dishes washed and the mess cleaned up." Meme left me standing in the middle of the kitchen, staring down at the worn linoleum. *An entire army of housekeepers couldn't clean this mess up*, I thought bitterly.

"You can dry this time," May-Belle said, tossing me a grayed flour sack towel. "Starting tomorrow night, you'll be doing the kitchen chores yerself. Meme said so." May-Belle turned and began scraping food into a metal bucket before sliding the melamine plates into the hot water. Trinket drifted over to the kitchen window and stared at the darkening yard on the other side of the bleary glass, a dreamy look on her moon face. She had no intention of helping. My fear and sorrow took a backseat to a momentary flash of irritation. She might be dim-witted, but that was no reason she should get out of doing any work.

"Well, what you waiting for? An engraved invitation? Get yer sorry ass over here and start wiping these dishes. Meme likes them dried and put away. Believe me; you don't want her mad at you." May-Belle's voice was hard like stone, and she washed and rinsed the dishes with jerky movements as if angry. Laying my doll on one of the chairs, I moved to the counter. I took the dishes as she handed them to me, dried them, and stacked them on the table.

"Put those dishes away, Trinket," May-Belle called over her shoulder. "And hurry the hell up. Don't make me tell you twice."

With an pouty huff, Trinket gathered up dishes in her arms and stormed into the dining room.

"I'm hungry," I said softly. "I didn't eat today."

"Oh, for god's sake," May-Belle grouched. "Fine time to tell me, just when we're cleaning up. Yer already a pain in the ass and you ain't been here five minutes. I suppose you can eat the rest of the gravy in the skillet. Here," she said as she handed me a biscuit. "Dip it out with that. I don't want you dirtying a spoon. I just got them washed. I'll be here all night, the rate you're going."

Taking the biscuit, I dipped gravy into my mouth. I felt like I was starving; I hadn't had a meal since the day before at the foster home. The biscuit was hard and the gravy was greasy and bland, but it was still warm from the stove. When the food hit my belly, exhaustion came over me in waves. After the past three days of fear and heartache, buckets of tears and sleepless nights, a little food just about put me out. May-Belle turned from her washing to stare at me. Her forehead tensed into a tight frown.

"Yer eyes is looking mighty damned heavy. Don't you even think about sleeping 'til we're done. Meme won't have it. Hurry up and chew that food. Damn it, girl, you are slowing me down! I want to get this shit done so's I can get outa this hot kitchen. Damn men; all sitting out on the porch where it's cool. Damn Meme sitting out there. It ain't fair. But that's what you get in this family."

"I'm not in this family," I murmured, to which May-Belle harrumphed.

"Yer just like yer damn mother. I knew you would be. I tried to tell 'em, but would they listen to me? Now, hurry up and eat that food. Yer getting on my last nerve."

I wanted to stick up for my mother, but couldn't summon the courage. Shame rolled inside me for my weakness. I chewed as fast and hard as I could, making my teeth ache. The mess stuck in my throat and I asked May-Belle for a drink of water.

She reached for a metal dipper, filled it with water from a bucket on the counter, and then handed it to me. She leaned against the counter and put a hand on her hip. "Anything else I can do for you?" she asked in a sarcastic voice. "Do you even know how to wipe yer own ass? Or do you expect me to do that for ya too?"

I didn't reply; I just drank quickly and handed back the dipper. Although I was still thirsty, I kept it to myself and rushed to finish drying the dishes. May-Belle didn't talk to me while we worked, and I was afraid to talk to her. When we were down to the black cast iron skillets, she told me to carry the pail out to the hogs. Glancing out the window, I shivered. It was twilight and I had no idea where to go.

"Trinket!" May-Belle yelled. "Show her where the hogs is."

Trinket slouched over to the pail and picked it up. She went out the back door, and I had to run to keep up. Off the ramshackle back porch, down steps made of old cracked cement blocks, I followed Trinket to a path barely visible in the fading light. Weeds brushed against my legs and lightening bugs flickered here and there over the shadowy yard. In the distance, I could just barely make out the rising hills studded with trees that led up into the mountains. Millions of insects filled the air with their raucous cacophony. Coyotes called to each other, their eerie voices sounding at first far away and then frighteningly close. Trinket ignored the sounds as she led me to a fence of boards and pointed.

"Them there's the hogs," she announced before dumping the pail of scraps into their trough. It made a wet sound which was followed by snorting and scuffling as the pigs crowded around to eat. Without another word, she headed back toward the house. I followed close behind her, afraid to be alone in the night. When we reached the porch, she turned and slapped me in the side of the head before slamming through the screen door into the house. It didn't hurt much; stunned me more than anything. I wondered if this girl was going to be after me every day from now on, and what I could do to avoid her.

The kitchen swallowed me in its oppressive heat once more. I noticed Trinket was back at the old banged-up Formica table, again playing with the tattered deck of cards. I watched her for a moment and shook my head. She wasn't doing it right. She was putting all the face cards on top of each other and all the numbered cards according to color in some random scheme that made sense only to her. I couldn't believe a grown woman didn't know how to play solitaire any better than that. May-Belle looked at Trinket with annoyance, and then turned to me. "She's hopeless, but she's yer problem now."

"What?" I asked as I stared with confusion at Trinket. I looked at May-Belle, sure she was joking. How could I be in charge of a grown-up?

"That's how it works around here; the newest does the chores and Trinket 'helps'. Now that yer here, I'll be sitting my ass out on the porch after meals with everyone else. *It's just how it works*. Bonnie-Lee was doing the kitchen work till I got here, then she was sitting outside with the others. Starting tomorrow night, I'll be a-sitting out there too. You and Trinket will be doing the chores."

"But, she doesn't like me." I sidled over to speak to May-Belle in a low voice. "She hits me."

"She hits everyone that don't hit her back. What do you expect? She's a moron. Meme told you she's slow in the head; don't you listen?" May-Belle wiped her hands on a rag and tossed it onto the worn countertop. "I'm going outside. You can come out or you can stay in here with Trinket."

"Where am I supposed to sleep?" I asked timidly, gathering my doll into my arms again and hugging her for comfort.

"You just don't stop, do you? I'm hungry, I'm thirsty, where do I sleep." She mocked me in a sing-song voice, rolling her eyes, and stomping her foot like a child having a tantrum. With an exasperated toss of her head, she finally took a deep breath and said, "Meme says you can have Cletus's old room until he comes back from the war. Can't believe the stupid son-of-a-bitch got himself drafted. I'll show you where it is and then that's it. I'm shed of you for the night." She snatched a flashlight from the counter and opened a skinny door on the other side of the table, revealing a rectangle of darkness.

"I told Meme to put you in with the other youngins, but she wouldn't do it. Said you'd be getting up early to tend to yer chores and she didn't want you waking them up. So you get yer own room, like some kinda little princess or something." The resentment in her voice was a reproach on me for something over which I had no control.

"Why don't the other kids have to do chores?" I drummed up my courage to ask.

She turned and gave me a scathing look. "Because they ain't the ones with a mama that thought she was better'n the rest of us. Because they ain't the ones who ran off from the family like we was some kinda low-rent trash, that's why. What you got to say about that, you stuck-up spoiled little piece of shit?"

I gulped but didn't speak, scared I would answer wrong.

"Nothing, huh? I didn't think so," she said. I followed her up the back stairs, a set of dark uneven steps that lamented our passing with mournful creaks and snappish echoes. The faint circle of light bobbed ahead of us. I was close on May-Belle's heels clear to the top. There, she ambled down a corridor and opened a door, gesturing impatiently for me to enter. She reached over my head and pulled the string that switched on a bare hanging bulb. It swung back and forth in jerky arcs, throwing weird shadows on the walls and floor.

My new room was barely big enough to be a closet; it held only a narrow sagging bed and a scarred dresser. There were men's clothes hung on pegs in one corner. I crawled up on the bed and the smell of mildew wafted from the mattress. Bedsprings creaked and rattled with my weight. I sat cross-legged with my doll in my lap.

"Didn't you bring any clothes with you?" May-Belle scowled at me from the doorway.

"No," I said. "They got left behind."

"Well, that's just fine and dandy. Wait till I tell Meme."

I could hear the stairs groan under her feet as she descended, leaving me alone in the tiny room. My heart raced as I stared around my confines. The wallpaper was very old and yellowed with rows of vertical blue flowers that might have once been pretty. Cobwebs hung in the corners. There was a window no bigger than a cigar box above the head of the bed, and the floor was wood that had long ago been painted, but was now scuffed and worn and covered with dust. The mattress was lumpy and felt like it was stuffed with corn cobs; the pillow was nearly flat, most of its feathers long gone. I needed to use the bathroom, but was afraid to venture from this room and decided to hold it as long as I could. I yearned to hide, but instead scooted to the head of the bed and stared out the window. I couldn't see much; the night was black as a witch's hat and there was no moon. Heat from the kitchen had risen, turning the small room into an oven. I tried to open the window, but the latch was stuck.

From below, I could hear the family talking on the front porch, intermittent whoops and guffaws, and the occasional slamming of the screen door. I missed my mother with an intensity that was sickening, and I gripped my doll to my chest. Lying on the bed, I looked around with wide eyes. Through my tears, the clothes in the corner looked like a man standing there and I was afraid. I had to keep reminding myself it was only clothing. Crying softly into the musty pillow, I eventually fell asleep, sticky sweat moistening my brow. I was lost and confused, not knowing what my place would be or how I would survive.

Sometime in the dead of night, I awoke to find my room dark; someone had turned off the light and was now sitting on my bed. The whimpering of the bedsprings had awakened me, but I pretended to be asleep. I was good at doing that. Fingers toyed with my hair, almost lovingly. Chills traveled up my spine in spite of the heat.

"Ah, girly. Little girly-girl." A boozy whisper caused the tiny hairs to rise on my arms. "I wish you was awake right now. Uncle Jez is lonesome tonight. Aunt May-Belle is mad at me over something; you know how women get sometimes. Bet you'd be sweet to me. By gawd, you're just a little slip of a thing, tender as a rosebud. It's a wonder yer daddy ain't been in to see you yet. But, he went off to the roadhouse, and you just here, yer first night and all. It's a real shame. He never was much of a daddy. If you was my little girl, I'd treat you right. I surely would. We'd be just like a pair of turtledoves, you and me."

This felt scary and wrong. Wrong like those two-headed calf fetuses I saw at the county fair one time. Wrong as the albino salamanders the workmen pulled from the sewage line down the street when I was six. *Wrong.* I kept pretending to sleep, hoping he would go away. But a sad hurt little part of me wanted to hold onto the drunken kindness in his voice. It was the only compassion I'd found in this horrible place.

Jez's hand drifted down from my hair to my back. He began rubbing it lightly, making little circles. His hand felt soft, like a woman's, through the thin cotton shirt I was wearing. "Yer mama was a pretty thing in the beginning. I had a little romance with her for a while; when yer daddy was off on a drinking spell. We was sparkin' real heavy, her and me. But it was ok; I mean Carl and me shared women before, so it was no big deal. I knew living with yer daddy was hard on her; and losing all them babies, too. She looked like death warmed over when she finally high-tailed it away from these parts. Yer brothers and sisters is buried up here, you know. Out back, behind the corn. Got them some nice little graves, with pretty stones. I hauled them stones in myself, from the river. 'Course they ain't engraved or nothing. But, you probably don't want to hear that old sorrowful stuff."

His hand moved lower, to my rear end. I couldn't help myself; I clenched all over, rigid as a poker. His hand froze. "You awake, girly?"

I forced myself to relax, and he chuckled softly. "Probably dreaming is all," he said in his hoarse whisper. He resumed his circular massage on my backside, interspersing his touch with light squeezes of my buttocks. "Yep, we're gonna be friends, you and me. Old Uncle Jez'll look after you. We're gonna be close as grapes on a vine, you and me. Two peas in a pod. Turtledoves. You go on and sleep, girly. I'll see you tomorrow."

With that, he rose from the bed and left the room, stubbing his toe on the iron bed leg and swearing quietly. I held my breath until I heard the creak of my door closing. I couldn't fall back to sleep for hours. A bleak dawn was staining the sky when I finally drifted off.

A rough hand jostled me awake. Trinket was standing over me, staring down at me with her weirdly skewed eyes, which I now noticed were different colors. One was hazel and the other a pale washed-out blind-looking blue. "Get up."

I felt vulnerable with her towering above me.

"I got stuff fer you," she said as she tossed a handful of miscellaneous clothes on the foot of the bed. Evidently, some of the relatives went through their kids' old clothes and came up with some hand-me-downs. I put my hands on the mattress to push myself up. They found a damp spot. Humiliated, I realized I had wet the bed.

"Oh, I think I hear someone coming up the stairs." I tried to distract Trinket so she wouldn't see what I'd done. She moved away from the bed and gazed toward the hall. No one appeared and she looked baffled. Waiting by the door, her dull features arranged themselves into a foxy expression. I knew before it happened that she planned to hit me, but I could see no way to avoid it. I tried nonetheless.

"Wait outside," I told her. She didn't move. "Please."

She shrugged her shoulders and left the room. I changed into a shabby dress and dingy underwear; and hid my wet clothes behind the dresser, reminding myself to wash them out later. I hated the ill-fitting clothes, but accepted them as I had no alternative. I wasn't about to run around naked like some of the littler kids did. The clothes had a musty smell, and were ratty and out of style. Later, I found out the family took regular advantage of church giveaways, thrift shops, and even scoured the dump for items they could haul home. They hated spending money, and even drilled into my head that stealing was perfectly acceptable, just as long as you didn't steal from family.

As soon as I walked out the door, Trinket sprang at me from where she had been hiding and slapped the top of my head. Then she skipped down the back stairs as if nothing had happened. Tears sprang to my eyes and I thought of running away. I had no idea where I was, or how far I would have to go, or even who I could run to. But, the idea of getting away from these people began growing in my mind, and it was fierce and compelling. I clung to the notion, for thinking of it brought me comfort.

The second night there, I fell into my uncomfortable bed too weary to even cry. My hands were raw from the scrubbing I had done, and my muscles and bones ached from carrying loads too heavy for my small frame. Dirt that had collected in that house for years suddenly needed to be addressed now that I was there. Meme made me sweep and scrub, scour and polish, wash and wipe until my hands felt like they were stuck with a hundred needles. The only good news was that she called it the 'yearly' cleaning. By evening, the hovel was a bit tidier, but it was still a hovel for no amount of cleaning can clear away years of filth and grime. Plus, Meme refused to throw away anything. I found in every room of the house stacks and piles of useless, spider-infested collections of assorted junk. The best I could do was dust around them.

Inside the house was one bathroom with a toilet and sink that were not functional. Close to the hog pen leaned a grayed reeking outhouse which was used for number two. Number one, I was told, could be done anywhere outside the house. The men would unzip their pants to urinate on tree or shrub, and the women hiked up their skirts and squatted where they stood. The children followed suit. The justification for this was the enormous wasp nest in the privy. No one wanted to be stung. Seems it never occurred to them to clear out the wasps, only to try and avoid them as much as possible. I could not bring myself to urinate outside, preferring to brave the wasps.

No one knew I had wet my bed the night before, and probably wouldn't have cared anyway. The second night I lay atop the moist smelly mattress, attempting to stay out of the wet spot, and fell into a deep exhausted sleep. Sometime before morning, Uncle Jez came in and woke me.

"Hey, girly," he whispered, shaking my shoulder. "Can I lay down with you? I'm lonesome."

I rubbed the sleep from my eyes. "My bed's wet, Uncle Jez."

"Ah, you had yerself a little accident, did you?" His voice was sympathetic instead of scolding and that was all it took to make me cry.

"Yes," I confessed between sobs. "Last night."

"Well, that's okay," he said as lifted me from the bed and hugged me. He smelled of hair pomade and beer breath, over a lingering odor of sweat. "We'll just turn the mattress over. Problem solved." He put me down on the floor and flipped the old mattress so the dry side was on top. "See? That's all there is to it. You hush now and lay down by Uncle Jez." He flopped down on the bed and patted the surface next to him. Reluctantly, I crawled in beside him. He pulled me close and put my head on his hard shoulder.

As he patted me and cooed to me, I began to relax a little. A nameless fear was writhing inside me like a snake, but there was nowhere to run. I wasn't even sure why I was so afraid of Jez, for he acted kindly toward me. I tried to lie very still.

It seemed the man mostly wanted someone to listen to him, and so I did. Gathering my courage, I began to ask him questions.

"What happened to my brothers and sisters?"

"Well, now, little thing like you don't need to worry on that a bit. Ah, I 'spect you are curious, though. Let me think a minute. That first boy, Grey, he was delicate, small for his age. Yer mama babied him something awful. Meme didn't like it neither. But I 'spect after losing them twin girls, she was feeling extry nervous. She kept her eye on that boy all the time, watched him like a chicken hawk, hardly let him outta her sight. Was real picky about letting people hold him and stuff. Yer mama lived here with yer daddy back then. They had the room over the porch where the youngins sleep now. Now, yer daddy has no patience with kids. He's not like me. I told you he weren't daddy material. Ain't his fault. Some people is just born with it; some ain't, and he weren't. Anyhow, one day he was fixin' to go into town and little Grey wanted to go with him. Yer daddy didn't want to take him. He was hanging onto Carl's leg, you know how kids do. And Carl was wanting to get down them stairs, and trying to shake Grey off his leg. Anyhow, it was an accident, that's all. Grey hit his head when he fell down those steps. He hit hard. Split his scalp and cracked his skull right open like as if he'd been axed. Was an awful sight. Yer mama went into hysterics. I thought she was gonna kill Carl. You see, she thought he did it a-purpose. She went after Carl with a butcher knife. We had to pull her off him. Took a while to calm her down and get her settled. She was hinky for a long time; way after the boy was proper eulogized and buried. The family had to get real strict with her to line her out, and she finally come around. But she was never quite the same after that." He stroked my chest and belly as he talked. He kept his voice low so as not to wake the rest of the family, especially May-Belle. Jez said she was feeling a mite jealous of me, and there was no point in making it worse.

"I don't want to make Aunt May-Belle mad at me," I said.

"Ah, now, don't you fret. She'll get over it. She always does after a fashion," he said in a comforting tone. "If not, Meme'll straighten her out."

"Is Meme the boss?"

He chuckled. "You could say that. Meme pretty much always gets her way. Even yer daddy does what she says."

"I'm scared of my daddy," I confided.

"Well, he's got a short fuse, that's for sure. Best you just stay outta his way, Blue."

"Tell me about Violet and Lavender," I prompted.

"Precious babies, those were. Born dead, but just as pretty as could be. Skin like rose petals, purest white. You could see their little veins if you looked close. Tiny little perfect hands and feet. And blonde hair! Like little dolls, they was. I don't know why they was born dead. Meme said it was 'cause yer mama raised her arms over her head too much while she was pregnant. Meme says that'll cause the cord to wrap around a baby's neck and choke it inside a woman's belly. But I don't know. Yer mama said that was backward talk. Said it was more likely the way yer daddy went after her all the time. She took to her bed for weeks after the funeral. Finally yer daddy had to just go in and haul her out by her hair before she would snap out of it. She carried a hard grudge against him for that. That's when I stepped in and she let me. I never did slap around on yer mama like yer daddy did. Now, don't get me wrong; a lot of women need that from time to time. But yer mama was kinda delicate. She needed a lighter touch. When yer daddy was out tomcatting around, yer mama and I got real close. Kind of like you and me are right now, but even better. We did a lot of loving, her and me. Spent a lot of nights just like this, all snuggled up. Feels good to cuddle good to cuddle up together, don't it?"

I didn't like the direction of the conversation at this point, although I wasn't quite sure why. I wanted to distract him. "So Violet and Lavender were the first; and after them Grey was born. Then I came along?"

"That's right." He took his hand off me and put it behind his head, staring at the light bulb hanging from the ceiling. "You came along and yer mama was happy again. She thought you were pert near perfect. Meme said you was ugly, but I didn't think so. You had yer mama's light brown hair and brown eyes. Didn't look like the rest of us. I think that's what got Meme so wound up and hateful. Do you remember living here before?"

"No."

"Well, you was pretty young when yer mama nagged yer daddy into leaving. He didn't want to, but she finally wore him down. They moved down to Memphis and yer daddy had to take a job there. He didn't like it one bit. The old nine-to-five just weren't for him. I'll give him this much, though. He tried. He tried to fit it with the city folk. Yer mama thought all of us Clappers was beneath her. She said we was just ignorant hillbillies. I don't know where she got her high-falutin' attitude. After all, yer daddy met her down at the roadhouse. She weren't exactly high society. But she said some mighty harsh things about the family after you was born. She said we weren't nothing but white trash. Now, that's something you never want to say about us. It makes Meme and the rest of them fightin' mad. It's the most insultin' thing you could ever say. You remember that, ya hear?"

"I'll remember," I promised. I certainly didn't want that family mad at me.

"Anyway, it was while they was living in Memphis that Baby Red was born. Do you remember him, Blue?"

"Sort of."

"Well, he died of that there crib death. But yer mama was convinced that Carl smothered him. I don't know which is the truth of it. Carl never wanted him, I know that. But I'm not sure he'd go so far as to kill a baby. When they brought his poor little

186

body up here to be buried, yer mama'd hardly even look at Carl. She was white as a sheet and kept you stuck to her side like you was glued there. They only stayed one night afore they headed back to Memphis. I suspicioned she was planning to leave my brother, but I didn't say a word to nobody. Anyway, turned out I was right. Yer mama waited till Carl was at work one day and then she packed you up and ran. We didn't know where you were till a few days ago when they found you in that hotel next to yer poor mama's dead body." He closed his eyes and shook his head. "'Bout broke my heart to hear it. I was especial fond of yer mama."

"Did my daddy ever look for us?" I remembered how afraid my mama had been that he would find us, and how we always had to be careful, going from place to place.

"He didn't really look too awful hard. There was one time he came up with some news about you living in Gainesfield and was gonna look you up, but he never did no more than pass the word around. Never did even leave the county." He chuckled. "He was always a big talker, small doer, that Carl. Still is. But don't you tell him I said that."

"I won't," I said. So many times, my mama had picked up and run when there was no need. The realization made my heart hurt. If Uncle Jez wasn't lying, then Mama and I had lived a life of fugitives when we didn't even have to. Remembering those nights when Mama brought strange men to our room or apartment and carried on while I pretended to sleep, I thought maybe it wasn't only my daddy she was running from.

"Anyway," Jez continued, "yer daddy moved back here to the farm when yer mama left. He quit that factory job he hated so much and went back to his old life. It's a good life we got here. Hell of a lot better'n most. Easier, too."

I didn't agree, but knew better than to say it out loud.

"You know, that light's bothering my eyes. What say we turn it off and get cozy?"

Again, I didn't answer. He rolled me off his shoulder, stood, and reached for the string. I was afraid of what would happen when the light went out, but Jez merely plopped back down and passed out once his head returned to the pillow, snoring softly and filling the air around me with alcohol fumes. I scooted as far as I could from him on the narrow bed, curled up around my doll, and went to sleep. The next morning as the sun tried to poke through the small window, I found myself alone.

Every part of my body hurt as I drug myself to the outhouse, trying to duck the circling wasps and avoid the wicked sticker bushes near the doorway. When I finished, I was called to the house by Meme. As she outlined my chores for the day, my sore muscles screamed in protest. It was almost as if they were weeping under my skin. She started me out in the kitchen where May-Belle and Trinket were making those hard tasteless biscuits that seemed to be the steady fare on the farm.

"Yer to learn how to do this so's I won't have to any more," May-Belle informed me. Trinket sat at the table rolling dough into little balls streaked with grey from her dirty hands. The sight made me want to vomit.

Flour, salt, baking soda and lard were the basic ingredients, with a little water thrown in for consistency. There was no measuring. I burned myself on the stove trying to open the heavy iron door. May-Belle gave me no sympathy.

"That's what happens to stupid children," she remarked. "I wish you was smarter. It's taking way too long to teach you shit. Yer gonna have to pick up on this 'cause it's yer job from now on. Yer lucky I'm a patient woman because you ain't got the brains God gave a goose. I swear!"

"I'm not stupid," I said, my feelings smarting along with my hand.

"Don't sass me, Blue. I'll whip yer ass." She stood with her hands on her hips, tapping her scuffed black shoe on the worn floor.

I shrunk under her hateful gaze. "I'm sorry."

Trinket snickered from the table and began rolling the biscuit dough into long snakes. May-Belle threw her a smoldering look. "And you!" she railed. "Stop playing with that dough and make up them biscuits before I slap you nine ways to Sunday, you blithering idiot."

Trinket huffed, her shoulders raising and lowering with the effort, but she started mashing the dough-snakes into roughly circular shapes. She had flour in her hair and rimming her lips. I could tell she'd been sucking on the dough when we weren't looking. I vowed not to eat any of the biscuits even though I was awfully hungry.

Once a large supply of biscuits was baked and stored away in plastic sacks, I was sent outside to pick corn. After the heat of the kitchen, the sweltering summer day felt almost cool. Since the men folk had gone fishing, taking a bunch of the kids with them, the yard was mostly empty. I dragged the heavy gunnysack behind me up and down the rows and wondered who had planted the corn patch. I couldn't imagine any of the lazy men doing it. Probably was left to the kids or May-Belle, I thought. No wonder she's so mean. She was their slave before I came along. But what made her stay? This was a question I could not answer. What made any of them stay? If I were older and could drive, I would jump into one of those beat-up old trucks and drive far away from this place. I would never come back.

That day, besides baking biscuits and harvesting wormy corn, I also had to pull ticks off all the hound dogs, wash clothes in the wringer washer situated on the back porch, hang them to dry, give ugly Meme a neck rub (trying to avoid touching her numerous moles), and feed the hogs. I was afraid of the pigs because they were so aggressive and butted up against the boards of the fence like they wanted nothing more than to get a taste of me. Under the hot sun, the laundry dried quickly and I had to haul it all into the house. There, it went into baskets in the pantry where everyone had to dig through the piles to find their clothes when they had a mind to put on a clean set. There was no folding or putting away in drawers and closets like my mama had done.

I'd remembered to pull out my clothes from their hiding spot behind the dresser and wash them along with the clothes they'd given me. I kept my own clothes separate from the family's things and took them to my room. Ugly as they were, they were all I had and I intended to take care of them. Trinket poked fun of me for this and managed to swat me on the head as I tried to duck past her and go up the stairs.

When the men got home with their catch, I was expected to clean them. I had no idea how to do it and cautiously admitted the fact. Growling with drunken impatience, my Uncle Willy snatched the knife out of my hands to demonstrate. "Even my four year old knows how to clean a fish," he groused. "You sure ain't the sharpest tool in the shed, are ya? Watch me so's you can learn. Here's how you do it. Cut off the head first, then split the belly and scrape out the innards. Now, you save them guts for the hogs. Dump 'em in those buckets there. Then, lastly, you cut off the tails. Ain't nothing hard about it. Anyone who can't clean a fish is either ignorant or lazy."

Squaring my shoulders, I pressed my lips together hard so they wouldn't tremble and give him another reason to criticize me. Uncle Willy was obese. All my life I had thought fat people were jolly, like St. Nick. Not Uncle Willy; he had a bad temper. I tried to follow his example and ended up making a mess of the first few fish. Eventually, I got the hang of it, although I hated the cold slimy feel of the things and the look in their dead eyes. I knew I would never get used to this particular chore.

The meal that night turned out to be one of the better ones ever served in that house. Fried fish rolled in a flour and salt mixture and then cooked in copious amounts of lard, corn on the cob with the wormy areas cut out, and gooey store-bought macaroni and cheese. I had hardly any help in the kitchen, but thought I did a decent job for a little kid, fixing that whole meal, standing on a wooden box to reach the back of the stove. May-Belle was determined I would learn to cook (so she didn't have to) and just stood by, telling me what to do and bossing me around. She hardly lifted a finger.

I wouldn't touch the biscuits, but everyone else wolfed them down. The kids drank red Kool-Aid, while the adults had beer. The Clappers had nothing against kids drinking beer, I discovered, but generally didn't approve of wasting a good beverage on a child. Children were low on the totem pole in that family, but still a step above me.

Trinket ogled me with her squinty eyes as I washed all the dishes that night. I dried them and put them away, rather than struggle to get her assistance. She sat at the table and occupied herself with her strange solitaire game, sucking on her thumb from time to time. She'd burst into intermittent laughter, which sent chills up my back.

"What's funny?" I finally asked as I passed by, my arms loaded with drinking glasses to put away in the dining room. There wasn't much to like in this place, but I did like the aluminum glasses they had in all different pretty colors.

"This," Trinket said as she knocked the entire collection from my arms. They went flying, hitting the floor with tinny sounds, and rolling under the table and into the corners of the sloping room. Tears stung my eyes as I gathered them up, glancing every so often at Trinket snickering into her hands like a child.

When I had picked up every last one and put them away, I returned to the kitchen and slammed my hand down on the rickety table with a loud smack. Trinket looked up, her small eyes registering surprise.

"Never do that again!" I yelled at her, my rage making me forget for the moment that she towered over me and could easily hurt me. I locked eyes with her and put the meanest look on my face that I could muster. As my initial anger faded, I saw my vulnerability and started to shake inside. I waited for an attack that never came.

"Fine, Stupid," Trinket finally uttered and went back to playing with her cards. I sighed and returned to the sink to wash the pots and pans. I had just finished up when the Clappers tromped in from the front porch to the living room.

And, that was my life. My days were divided between working and trying to avoid the rude hands of uncles and cousins. I grieved for my mama and dreamed of running away.

Nobody cared about me. That was soon obvious. My place in the family was servile. I cleaned the dishes, gathered wood, washed clothes, and tried to keep Trinket from hurting herself. I fed chickens, collected eggs, cooked slop for breakfast, slop for lunch and more slop for dinner. Meme's idea of stew was six cans of corn and three cans of tomatoes in a pot with some hunks of baloney. Her idea of a hearty meal was hard biscuits, oily gravy, and Spaghetti-Os. They had hogs, but we didn't eat them. They were sold or traded. Pork was only served if a sow rolled over on one of her babies or miscarried. The sight of the small pigs boiling on the stove would set me to retching. The family ate them with gusto.

They lived mainly on welfare checks, I found out. The food stamps they sold for money to buy booze. The dilapidated old house had been in their family for years and they spent no money to maintain it or fix it up.

Clapper family ties were intricate and hard to unravel. There were so many relatives in that old rambling house, it took me awhile to figure them out, and I never did get clear on all the children. I had cousins and cousins of cousins in and out, coming and going.

My Uncle Jez and Aunt May-Belle were a couple, but not legally married. She was a second cousin or some kind of relation from up by Palmyra. Meme's man, my grandfather Jim, was a pathetic shell who barely spoke and occasionally drooled on himself. According to family history, he had been a rip-roaring bull of a man until he fell into the creek and hit his head on some rocks. He hadn't been right since. Grandpa Jim collected a small pension from the railroad. He couldn't work anymore, obviously, but he had no trouble bending his elbow when there was a beer or a Mason jar of shine in his hand.

He had been very close to his four daughters before his injury, teaching them all they needed to know about life, about love, and about men folk. Meme told me this herself one day when she was in a mood of rare patience. The family joked around about the strong resemblance between Jim and the various grandchildren who called him Pappy.

"Pappy's kind of an all-purpose name," Gladys One said with a secretive smile. She was my daddy's sister and the mama of Gladys Two. Gladys's 'husband' was Ike, a dark brooding man of massive size who worked over in Silver Springs at the mill. He was only in the house occasionally, which was fine with me because I feared him. I saw him hit one of the youngsters so hard one time that the boy's ears bled for a day. It was serious enough that the family even discussed taking the boy to the hospital in Nashville, an almost unheard of proposition, but the bleeding finally stopped so they didn't have to.

Trinket was the youngest of Jim and Meme's offspring, and I reckoned she was about seventeen or eighteen years old. One of the four sisters, April June, died sometime in the past decade of a hemorrhage during a miscarriage. They'd let her lay in the downstairs bed and waste away, Meme telling them all it was normal to have bleeding after losing a baby. Meme had been wrong, and April June had died. She was buried in the same plot with my brothers and sisters. She left behind a husband no one ever sees and two children who were now being raised by Meme. Perhaps the husband returned to his people after she died, or perhaps there really wasn't one to begin with. I never found out, nor did I care to.

Of the three remaining sisters, Bentley Jane was the black sheep of the family. She had married a jazz musician she met at the roadhouse and moved to Chicago or somewhere. She never came back to visit, and the family disowned her. I envied Bentley Jane and pictured her as a pretty and vivacious woman; although, coming from the Clapper family, it would have been a genetic miracle. The family rarely took pictures, and any they'd had of Bentley were burned in the pot-bellied stove after she ran off. Leaving was the worse thing anyone could do in that family. Meme said a hundred times that families have to stick together come hell or high water no matter what any one of them says or does. She also said family secrets were to be kept inside the family. Telling family secrets to an outsider was 'treason', according to her.

As best as I could tell, there were six boys born to Meme and Jim. Besides my daddy and Uncle Jez, there was Uncle Cletus who was in Viet Nam, Uncle Junior with the crippled hand who slept in the barn, grouchy old Uncle Willy who lost his front teeth to decay and weighed at least three hundred fifty pounds, and his twin brother Uncle Nilly who ran shine for a local producer. Nilly looked nothing like Willy, being a thin nervous man with a stutter who liked to tell bawdy jokes, funnier because of his speech impediment than their content. Or so Uncle Jez would say.

Then there were the women. Nilly drug around behind a pock-faced hag named Pearl who complained constantly about everything, was quick to pinch me if I didn't respond fast enough to suit her, and had two kids from a previous relationship who were fearful and shy around the family. Pearl often made me give her foot massages, and her feet stank. She had three or four children with Nilly. Nilly and Pearl shared an upstairs room down the hall from mine and fought regularly. They didn't care who could hear their arguments and often members of the family got pulled in, taking sides, and turning the disagreements into brawls.

Most of the kids shared a room in the back, over the rear porch that had to be accessed from an outside stair. Sometimes I would see a dozen or more children traipse up those steps, and it was impossible to be sure which child belonged to which parents, or which ones might be visiting.

Besides Gladys Two, Aunt Gladys One had four other children, two boys and two girls. One of the boys was obviously sired by Ike because he looked just like him: big, dark, and surly. The other boy was blond, slight, and effeminate. How Gladys passed him off, I'll never guess. He looked like no one in the family, not even her. Her two girls were mildly impaired, had the small eyes of the clan, and whispered together all the time. They were so thin, I wondered if they had worms.

Willy and his woman, Jerri, shared a ground floor room. They had several children. It was hard to keep track of them because all of them but one actually went to summer school in town, something the other children did not do. I envied them for that. I asked Meme one time if I could go to summer school, a question which earned me a slap in the face. She said Jerri's kids only got to go to school because their mother had a waitressing job in town and could drive them. She also said their schooling was paid for by a special government program, but sending me would cost money. She wasn't about to spend money on me. Besides, I could tell Meme didn't approve of Jerri's children going to school. She said all kids should be home schooled. She said going to public school was the same as begging the welfare people to nose into your private life. I wanted so badly to read their books, but they wouldn't let me. Sometimes they stayed in town with their other grandmother, and I envied them for that too. I wished I had another grandmother.

Jerri snuck free food to Willy every time he was in town and her boss wasn't looking. Meme said that's how he got so fat. It was all Jerri's fault and she told her so many times. Jerri would just laugh and say the way to a man's heart is through his stomach.

I never quite figured out how Bonnie-Lee fit into the picture; she might have been a relative from up north, and I had no idea when she moved in with the family. She was a raw-boned woman, tall and angular, with dark gray-streaked hair, a large mouth, and teeth like a horse behind her thin pale lips. Her eyes were not quite as small as the rest of the clan, but had the same general appearance. I could tell she was blood kin. Bonnie-Lee ignored me completely. It was as if I didn't exist. Her loud raucous laugh set my nerves on edge, and I was relieved that she paid no attention to me. She regularly shook the smaller kids when they got in her way.

Over time, I noticed that Trinket would occasionally go out to the barn and sleep with Junior. I suspected one of the kids that tacitly belonged to Willy's brood was actually Trinket's. The child was profoundly retarded, unusually small, with eyes so close together they nearly touched, and a bulbous head that lolled all the time. It looked like a distorted miniature of Trinket. They called it Jewel, and I never found out if it was a boy or a girl. It was usually pushed around in an old stroller, tied in with dish towels to keep it upright, and still drank from a bottle and wore diapers even though I know it was at least five years old when I first came to the farm. One time I walked into the parlor to find that poor imbecile at Gladys's breast. Gladys One looked up at me with a sardonic grin. "You want some, Blue?" I shook my head, backing out of the room as her laugh followed me. Only babies are supposed to nurse on a woman's bosom. Everyone knew that!

Jewel died in its sleep a month or so later, and Gladys grieved harder than anyone. I think everyone else was kind of relieved. By that time, I was numb enough not to care. Everyone gathered around the hole in the ground and sang Amazing Grace before the uncles lowered the wood box and covered it with dirt. The whole thing only took about fifteen minutes and they were all back on the porch sucking down booze two minutes after that.

The endless parade of aunts, uncles, brothers, sisters, cousins, in-laws, and other kin formed the chaos that was life in the Clapper family. Sometimes I wondered how even the regulars, who knew each other well, could keep it straight. Few written records were kept, as half or more of the Clappers were barely literate. They did the absolute minimum required to qualify for government assistance, and no more. Many of the offspring had been born, and died, right there in that house. They were a huge dirty mob of heathens who had tangled their lines so many times; probably not one could be accurately traced back to his or her origins.

Shortly after my arrival, I was finishing up the supper dishes with Trinket at her usual spot playing cards when Meme called to us.

"Trinket, Blue! Get in here," she yelled. "All in the Family's on. Come on in here so's you can watch."

This TV program was a family favorite. Even a lowly slave like me was allowed to put aside the work while the show was on. I entered the room behind Trinket and found the sofa, chairs, and even the coffee table crowded with happy Clappers, all their malformed expectant eyes glued to the television. Kids were sprawled around on the floor or sitting on laps. Jewel was still alive then and the stroller was situated off to one side, but still fairly close to the screen, as if that pitiful thing could even comprehend what a television was, much less enjoy the show. I went as far as I could from any of them and sat cross-legged on the splintery floor. When the music started, they were already laughing.

"I love that piany part," Nilly said, his weaselly face lit up like a Christmas tree.

"Ah, me too, me too," Pearl bellowed from the sofa where she was crammed in between Junior and Jez.

Even my daddy's usual scowl was transformed into a look of pleasure. He guzzled something clear from a Mason jar without taking his gaze from the set. I was so tired; I leaned back against the wall behind me and dozed. Although I missed most of the show, I needn't have worried for afterwards there was a lively discussion wherein the entire program was hashed over and remarked upon by the clan.

"Did you just hear the way Archie talks about niggers?" Carl laughed, slapping Nilly on the shoulder. "That just slays me."

"Well, why not? Look at how they talk to each other," Meme said with an amused expression. "They like that kinda talk. Even call each other names all the time."

Willy laughed till his belly jiggled under his overalls. "Ain't that a fact!"

"I like that Meathead. He's such a dumb-ass," Junior said. "Cracks me up." Junior was oblivious to his own multitude of intellectual shortcomings.

"Bet Cletus wouldn't think much of him, if he was here." Gladys commented archly. The family grew quiet for a moment thinking of Cletus getting shot at over in Viet Nam.

"Ah hell, Cletus was drafted like everyone else," Pearl pointed out with her usual lack of diplomacy. "He probably hates the war too. It ain't like he's some kind of hero earning medals over there. They had to practically drag him screaming and kicking. He's a gutless wonder, scared of his own shadow. Bet he hides in the bushes more than he fights. If he'd had any gumption at all, he'd be in Canada right now instead of running after gooks in the jungle."

I turned to Meme to see if this would anger her. After all,

that was her son Pearl was insulting. But, Meme just laughed along with the rest of them. "Sad but true," she said with a grin. "He was too damn lazy to even run."

The talk returned to All in the Family. "I'd like to hop on that Gloria and ride her all the way to kingdom come," Jez said with a lascivious wink. "You see the milk jugs on that little heifer? I'm telling you, I could drill her like a new well."

"Right after me, boy," my daddy joked, hiking his pants and smoothing his hair back with his palm. "You better let the expert show you how it's done first." He and Jez laughed and snorted, winking at each other like they had something stuck in their eyes. I was ashamed of them, and for them. They weren't bright enough to be ashamed of themselves.

I rose and tried to sneak up to my room, but Pearl saw me.

"Where do you think yer going?" she said with narrowed eyes.

"To bed."

"Not yet, you ain't. Sit down here in front of me and rub my feet." She slipped off her shoes and wiggled her toes. "Come on, now. Don't make me tell you again."

With a sigh, I walked over and knelt in front of her. This was turning into a regular routine. Her feet were gamey, slick with sweat, and felt indescribably repulsive in my hands. I wept silently as I manipulated her toes and soothed her calloused heels like she told me to.

When she finally let me go, I washed my hands three times with lye soap before feeling my way up the dark staircase to my room.

There were times when I tried playing with my cousins. Some of them were mean and liked to shove me to the ground and roll me around in the dirt. Others of them were so dull-witted, they were no fun. A few of them would actually take time to play with me, but they couldn't be trusted. They were only interested in me so long as I could provide something they needed: a lookout when they were doing something forbidden, a patsy in a game of chance, or someone to fetch and carry for them. They seemed to adopt the attitude of their elders; I was nothing but workhorse, less even than an animal. I was lonely when not busy with the long list of chores assigned to me.

Meme rarely talked to children just for the sake of conversation, but she yapped all day long to the adults. Much of my information about the family was gleaned from eavesdropping on these exchanges. The rest, I obtained from Uncle Jez during his frequent visits to my room.

I had mixed feelings about these visits. On one hand, they were disturbing and hinted at a dark future threat. On the other hand, Jez was the only one in the family who had a kind word for me, and I longed for any scrap of tenderness. His presence hummed with a danger I was too young to define, but intuitive enough to detect. I felt I was walking a precipice and just barely retaining my balance. Any wrong move might send me over the edge. At times I was pathetically grateful for his attentions, at other times ashamed and deeply frightened.

At one point, I thought about talking to Meme about these visits and asking her to put a stop to it. Then, one day I saw her lay into one of my cousins for telling her that Uncle Nilly had been bothering at her. Meme had whirled the girl around by her arm and hissed into her ear, "You stop telling tales out of school, you little tattle-box. Nilly's just cherry-pickin'; ain't nothing wrong with that. Now you get on out of my way before I give you something to cry about." I knew then that going to Meme would be a mistake. I'd likely just get my ears boxed or worse.

Once when Uncle Jez was visiting me at night, I asked him if I could go into town the next time they went. He said he'd think about it, but he'd need a little motivation. I didn't know what he meant until he guided my hand down below his waist. After that, there was another massage I had to regularly perform. Uncle Jez said it was very important and not a job for just anyone. I didn't enjoy it any more than rubbing Pearl's stinky feet, but Uncle Jez was a lot more grateful for his massage than Pearl ever was. Both of them left me feeling dirty, just in different ways.

As a late summer heat wave was flexing its oppressive muscle over the land, the family decided to go into town for supplies. This time, I was allowed to go. A bunch of us piled into two rusty pick-up trucks and barreled along the dusty roads into the nearest town. I sat in back with the other kids and a few adults. Watching mile after mile of country pass by, and jostled like crazy from the rutted roads, I was relieved when we finally pulled onto a smooth highway. With the wind whipping my hair and making conversation impossible, I was almost happy. Finally, I might have a chance to escape. I determined that I would run at the first opportunity. That chance never presented itself, as things turned out.

The kids were made to wait outside the market, with Nilly keeping a watchful eye. Gladys One kept him company and she kept her hand on my shoulder like a vulture's claw, gripping me tight, as if she could read my mind. While the other kids darted around, involved in horseplay, I had to stand still. Another old truck pulled up and parked. From its doors issued a colored family.

"Amos." Nilly nodded at the man. Amos tipped his hat in reply. The woman averted her gaze, but their little girl looked around with bright curious eyes.

Remembering what Meme said about black folks, I looked right at that girl and said in a friendly voice, "Hi, nigger."

She was on me before I could blink, hitting and kicking me with a vengeance, a small spitfire of fury. Nilly looked surprised and even Aunt Pearl took a step back.

"I'll be damned," I heard Nilly exclaim.

"Carmen!" The girl's mother shouted and pulled her off me. "You stop that right now!"

Panting from exertion, Carmen stood with her mother's arms wrapped around her and glared at me. "She called me nigger! Ain't nobody gonna call me that. Ever!"

Wiping tears from my eyes, I got to my feet. I was stunned and looked from Nilly to Gladys One for help. They were hiding smiles behind their hands. The black family gathered themselves together and marched into the store. The screen

Blue

door with its metal Pepsi sign slammed behind them.

"What the hell got into you, Blue? Are you crazy?" Nilly laughed. "Why you trying to start trouble with the coloreds?"

"I wasn't!" My eyes burned with tears as I dusted off my clothes. "I was trying to be nice. Remember what Meme said? She said they like being called that."

"Oh, lord!" Gladys erupted in gales of laughter. "That's a kicker. Wait till I tell the others. You stupid girl, I would swear you are pure-D retarded. Oh, lord! That's the funniest thing I ever did hear."

"For now, I think you'd best wait in the truck. Can't trust you out in the open. Yer worse than Trinket." Nilly grabbed my arm and pushed me into the cab of the truck, chuckling the whole way. "You just sit in there till we're ready to go."

I lay down on the dusty seat and cried in great whooping sobs. When my anguish had spent itself, I wiped my runny nose on my shirt tail and sat back up. Before long, the black family exited the store with their purchases. Carmen looked around until she found me sitting in the truck. She paused and gave me a long look. Her mother bent down and said, "Never you mind, girl. Them people don't know no better. They ain't worth your time."

Her words made me cringe with shame. I still wasn't sure what I'd done wrong. Carmen pulled her eyes from me and followed her parents to their truck. As they drove off, their wheels kicking up small clouds of dust on the dirt road out of town, I was pierced by longing. Longing to be away from these people who were my family, and into a clean world where things were well-ordered and clear-cut. I figured right then I could never again trust anything I heard from the Clappers without verifying it myself first. It was a hard but valuable lesson.

Of course, the embarrassing tale of my misadventure was fodder for much family amusement once we got back home. My trip into town had been ruined and now I was the target of even more jokes and taunts. I hunched my shoulders against the onslaught and crept away to do my chores.

The idea of going to summer school stayed in my head. Nothing I said would convince Meme I should go and if I badgered her too much, she would simply slap me around and find more work for me to do. I soon gave up the notion, knowing if I persisted, I would risk a severe beating. There was an abundance of old magazines around the place, however, and I practiced my reading on articles like "Ten Ways to Add Spark to Your Romance", "Secrets to a Clean Bathroom", and "True Stories of Animal Heroism". These publications I spirited to my room where I could read without being taunted by the family, but there was precious little time for study.

I soon learned to fly through my chores and make myself scarce. There was a new worry in my life. Junior had started lurking around behind me, dogging my steps, with an odd gleam in his eye. It became imperative that I find some good hiding places.

I had been in the clutches of these trashy people for several months when I found the pretty creek about half a mile from the farm. It was a day of unnatural beauty in my ugly world, the trees aflame with the colors of changing leaves and a thin haze of wood smoke wafting in the breeze like ghostly fog. Nearby farms were curing hams and clearing fields in preparation for winter; the air was filled with tantalizing aromas.

Sneaking away from the house of horrors, I wove my way through the trees, venturing further than I ever had, when I came upon the small stream. I was skipping over the flat rocks protruding from its bed when I heard a rustling sound in the surrounding foliage. I was afraid Junior had followed me. Scared, I searched the banks with my eyes. To my surprise, Carmen stood just inside the trees, watching me. Relieved, my shoulders sagged. She might want to beat me up again, but I was confident that I could outrun her if she tried, and being whipped by a little girl seemed infinitely better than what I feared Junior had in store for me.

"Hey, Clapper girl!" she called, stepping into the open. "What you doing at my creek?"

"I didn't know it was yours," I answered.

"Well, it is. It's on our property." She came down the banks, nimble as a squirrel.

"I guess I'll leave then." I started to leap over the rocks, back to my side of the creek.

"Wait," she said. "You don't have to go."

I turned to face her, bracing for her reply. "Are you still mad at me?"

"Nah," she said, her braids bobbing around her head. "I done forgave you because the Bible says I'm s'posed to."

Relief washed over me. "Well, that's good," I said. "Because I didn't mean to make you mad. Somebody lied to me. Somebody told me it was the right thing to say."

"Who?" Her brown eyes were curious. "Who told you to say it?"

"My grandma. She didn't exactly tell me to say it, but she said colored people like to be called…that word. I hate her." It was the first time I had been able to openly express my feelings like that. It felt good, so I repeated it. "I hate her guts."

"Well, we don't really like being called colored either," she said with eyebrows raised and lips pursed.

"I figure I don't know the right thing to say. I'm best off keeping my mouth shut." I rubbed my hands together nervously and then wiped my palms on my pants.

"Ah, just never you mind all that. You want to play?" she asked with a smile.

"I sure do!" I returned her smile. My face felt like it might break and I realized I hadn't smiled in quite a while. "My name's Blue," I told her.

"Like the color?" she cocked an eyebrow. "I like it."

We traipsed up and down the creek that day, picking up feathers and stones and other interesting things, and talking a mile a minute. We agreed that we should meet in the same spot the next day and bring our dolls with us so they could meet. When the sun began to set, she told me she had to go home. I hated to see her go; it was the most fun I'd had for a long time.

"Me too," I said. "I'm already looking at a beating for being late. I was supposed to cook supper."

"You were supposed to cook supper? All by yourself? And what do you mean, a beating? You mean a spanking?" Her eyes were wide.

"I wish it was just a spanking. No, I'll likely get the strap this time. Meme might even punch me. I don't know. But don't worry; I'll be back tomorrow if I'm able."

"Okay," she said, giving me a dubious look. "I'll see you tomorrow, Blue."

The beating I got when I returned to the farm was worth it to me because now I had a friend. It was a small price to pay, but it hurt something awful.

I didn't want anyone to know about Carmen, so I told Meme I had been wandering in the woods and got sidetracked. Meme told me she didn't give a living shit what I did as long as I was back home in time to do the cooking, and I'd better not disappear like that again unless I wanted my feet hobbled. Between the blows, I tried to shut off my body so I wouldn't feel the pain. It was hard to do and I cried for hours that night in bed lying next to Uncle Jez. While his sneaky hands roamed my body, he muttered low sounds intended to quiet me.

I thought about my mama and all the lectures she gave me over the years. She didn't live the same way she talked, but her lessons stuck with me nonetheless. She made me believe in a Mayberry world, even though we didn't live in one. She made me believe that someday we *would* live like that. I felt robbed of that possibility now with her gone.

She had preached to me about being clean, and honest, and kind. We read books together and went for walks. I could ignore what went on in the dark with her gentlemen callers, because she would erase it the next day by painting pictures with bright words of hope. She described our future so well, I could see in my mind the little house we would have, safe and snug on some pretty street. Mama said the hotel rooms and apartments were temporary, until she could make things better. It was because of her relentless fantasy stories that the Clappers could not corrupt me too much. I still remembered what life was supposed to be like, at least according to my mother.

She told me many times that she had to keep me from my daddy's family because they were bad people, horrible people, and she was right.

I thought about the television shows that I loved and the TV families who treated each other with kindness and respect. My Three Sons, Leave It to Beaver, Lost in Space, Lassie, and Dick Van Dyke all featured the kinds of families I wanted to be a part of. I tried to express this to Uncle Jez that night between sobs.

"That ain't real life, Blue. That's all made up stuff. People ain't really like that." He nuzzled the top of my head, his beery breath blowing over my face. "It ain't bad here on the farm, eh? You just got a wholloping, that's all. Happens to everybody. You'll live."

Jez said I reminded him so strongly of my mama that he didn't know what to make of it, couldn't get it out of his head. "Cherry-pickin's nice, but it's more for the little bitty kids. I think yer about ready for me to teach you something really special, something that sweethearts do to show their affection for each other," he murmured next to my ear. "Would you like that, Blue? Yer so grown up for yer age, you could be my sweetheart. Whatcha think 'bout that, girly?" I just shook my head and wept.

Jez sighed his disappointment, conveying his long-suffering patience with me. He shifted tactics. "Well, then, I got something else that'll make you feel better. I been a-keeping a special secret," he whispered. "And yer the only one I'm gonna tell. Just calculatin' on the time and all, I think you might be my youngin'. Yer mama and I was real sweet on each other some months afore you was born. I've got a notion that you might be my little girl. You'd like that, wouldn't you? Being my little girl 'stead a Carl's? Wouldn't that be something if I was yer daddy, Blue?"

He kept trying to pull me closer, but I kept pulling back. Eventually he gave up and contented himself with patting my head and smoothing my hair back from my face. "We'll save all that other stuff for another night, I guess," he said. "When yer feeling more yerself."

The problem for Jez was that he had started to like me. When you like someone, you want them to like you back. It made him softer on me than he might otherwise have been. I knew he wasn't soft on the other kids. But for some reason it was different with me. I could tell he wanted me to go along with him, with a willing heart. He would wait, but not for long.

I finally cried myself to sleep, ignoring Uncle Jez the best I could. Sometime during the night, he left the room.

Carmen and I became good friends and played together as often as possible. We did all the things little girls do and ultimately shared all our secrets. She told me about the money trouble her family had, how they still couldn't use public bathrooms in some places, and how her cousin teased her for having dimples. I told her about my chores, how my mama had died in that hotel room, and about the cherry-pickin' between my uncles and the kids in the family.

It wasn't long after that that the social worker drove up to the farm with a couple of sheriff's deputies in tow to talk to the Clappers. I guess Carmen didn't keep my secrets after all. She told her mama and daddy, and they called the welfare people.

My first foster home after that was a good one; my second not so great. And so it went until I was old enough to be on my own. For a time, I was able to go to the same school as Carmen, and we were thick as thieves until the system moved me too far away. Even after that, we wrote letters back and forth for years.

I didn't care one whit what happened to the Clappers. Still, I couldn't avoid the gossip completely, and I heard that some of them went to prison and that the kids were taken away. Meme had a heart attack when the family was dismantled. It was a bad one and she had to be put in the county nursing home over near Sandy Hollow. So did Pappy Jim.

I took my mama's last name and the welfare people said that was just fine. They said I didn't have to call myself a Clapper if I didn't want to. The social worker was very understanding about the whole thing, said she didn't blame me a bit. Finally, someone believed me when I said I wasn't part of that family.

Once I was out of there, I decided I'd never again let someone put their hands on me without my consent. I never wanted to feel that vulnerable again. And I would never be any-body's slave again. As I grew older, I naturally developed a size and strength I didn't have when I was a defenseless child; I learned how to take care of myself.

I vowed someday to have the tidy little house on the pretty street, inside of which things would be normal and I'd never have to be afraid again. It might not be real life for some people, but it's damn sure going to be real life for me.

Notes of Interest

Cover photo for *Blue* by Sascha Burkard

The following is a list of short stories included in this collection along with the sites where they appeared prior to this publication.

HubPages (http://hubpages.com/)

> Life of a Beat Cop
> Ruby & Pete and Rex the Cheat

Associated Content (http://www.associatedcontent.com/)

> The Erotic Adventure of Dick Speed, September 2010
> The Rustling Dark Shadows of Autumn, October 2010

Necrology Shorts (http://www.necrologyshorts.com/)

> Death Hates His Job, March 2011

Coming soon:

Betrayed by Wodke Hawkinson. A novel of abduction, torment, escape and redemption in the wilderness of Colorado.

Tangerine by Wodke Hawkinson. A tale of intrigue set in a future time when aliens are a natural part of everyday life and travel to distant planets is commonplace.

Alone, Selected Short Stories, Volume Three by Wodke Hawkinson

Available now:

Catch Her in the Rye, Selected Short Stories Volume One by Wodke Hawkinson.

Half Bitten by PJ Hawkinson. A tale of vampire revenge.

James Willis Makes a Million by K Wodke. A book for young readers about a boy who starts his first successful business at only eight years old.

Contacts:

Website: http://wodke-hawkinson.com
Blog: http://wodke-hawkinson.com/blog1/
Like us on Facebook: http://www.facebook.com/wodke.hawkinson

Author Biography

Wodke Hawkinson enjoys a split personality which gives him the advantage of two unique perspectives when writing. It also grants him the ability to operate two completely independent households. Sometimes he disagrees with himself which can skew a storyline, taking it into unforeseen territory.

In all seriousness, Wodke Hawkinson is the name under which writing duo PJ Hawkinson and Karen Wodke produce their collaborated works. The authors have been friends since high school, but only recently formed a writing team. Before combining forces, each completed a solo project in addition to publishing various short stories and/or articles. Together, the two published *Catch Her in the Rye, Selected Short Stories Volume One*. Separately, PJ published *Half Bitten*, a novel of vampire revenge and teen angst. Karen completed her book for young readers, *James Willis Makes a Million*.

Both PJ and Karen attended school in Kansas. PJ graduated from Hutchinson Community College, and Karen attended HCC and Kansas Wesleyan University. Both reside in different Midwestern towns, and do much of their collaboration via telephone and the internet. However, they have been known to discuss ideas while casting their lines at a quiet lake, as they both enjoy fishing.

We hope you enjoyed the stories in this collection and will take the time to peruse our other works as well.

Wodke Hawkinson

Enjoy this preview of *Betrayed*,
the exciting soon-to-be-released novel by Wodke Hawkinson.

Chapter 1

Clark and Brook entered their six-car garage together. Brook reached for the keys to the Cayenne Turbo S. With its 520 horsepower, it was capable of handling even the most extreme conditions and Clark always insisted Brook drive it in the winter. Now, however, Clark placed his hand over hers to stop her from taking the keys.

"Why don't you drive the Ferrari? This might be the last day of the year you'll be able to take it out." He smiled and kissed her cheek as he grabbed the keys to his Spyker D8. After tossing his briefcase through the backwards opening rear door, he slipped into the driver's seat. He pressed the garage door opener, blew Brook a kiss, and exited into the early winter morning.

Brook took the keys to the Spider, slid into the luxurious interior, and backed out of the garage. Moving into the street, she glided past million dollar mansions that sat on two to three acres of well-manicured land and exited the gated community, nodding to Jerry in the guardhouse. Jerry waved and smiled. He recorded the time she left and what vehicle she was driving. Security at Pinion Plateau was state-of-the-art. No one entered or left without their presence being noted.

Brook made her way through town. Clark was right, the day was beautiful. They'd had a couple of small snowfalls, but now the roads were clear and the Spider moved in and out of traffic like a red blip on a radar screen. It wouldn't be long before the first big snow hit and then driving would become a chore; if the town didn't shut down completely. Forecasts were calling for a real whopper. Although the brisk air held the threat of impending snow, bright morning sunlight slanted through the windshield as Brook went about her errands.

Glancing at her city map, she signaled for a right turn

and zipped down an unfamiliar byway. The Ferrari was as responsive as a lover under her hands.

Soon, Brook had left the city-major behind. She didn't like the looks of the area she was now entering. She tapped her manicured nails nervously on the steering wheel of the Spider as she sat at a stoplight. Several groups of young men noted her discomfort and watched with amused looks on their faces. She pulled away quickly as the light turned green.

This would be the last stop on her list. After this, she decided, she would grab some lunch at Maurice's. Then, she could go home, tend to daily household chores, and relax in the hot tub before Clark arrived home from work. Maybe she would have Rachel whip up something special for dinner. She could use some intimacy. Clark had been working long hours lately and they'd had little time together. As she drove, she reflected on the reason for this particular errand.

That morning at breakfast, completely out of character, Clark had asked her to do him a favor. He wanted her to go to a bookstore on the south side of town. He said he had done some research and this was the only shop he could locate that carried a copy of a rare book his boss had mentioned. Clark wanted to surprise Harold with the book on his upcoming birthday. He had stressed several times that this was the only store in the state with a copy and he didn't want to miss the opportunity to make the purchase. The book was being held under his name. She had watched him as he finished eating, took a final sip of coffee, and then began stuffing papers into his briefcase. He had seemed nervous, fidgety, but she couldn't imagine why. Their usual morning conversation had been stilted and they had parted in the garage shortly after.

Brook assumed Clark hadn't sent his assistant on this errand for fear Harold would hear about the book and the surprise would be ruined. She felt anxious as she found herself amid abandoned stores intermingled with porn, tattoo, and head shops. Splashes of graffiti scarred the forsaken buildings. In a weed-choked lot, two groups of rough-looking youths sat atop parked cars and hollered lazy insults back and forth. Further ahead, posturing gang bangers strutted their colors, advertising their menace. A ragged homeless woman shuffled through the garbage-strewn streets. Brook was certain a shadier slice of humanity couldn't be found.

To top it off, her shiny red car was drawing unwanted stares from watchers with desire written on their faces. With each passing block, her surroundings became more sinister. Low-riders were cruising up and down the street, and men with low-hanging pants that exposed their underwear were standing in small groups shouting banter and invective between them. They all stared at her car, some blatantly, others from under downcast eyes.

Brook peeked again at her map and checked it against the paper on which Clark had scribbled the name and address of the bookstore; Bill's Bookstore. She scanned the names on the buildings and found Bill's Bawdy Book Barn stuck between Fanny's Massage Parlor and The Dragon's Den tattoo shop. She compared the address with that on the note paper, muttering in disbelief. *This is the place? Oh, lord!* On her right was a narrow parking lot, the cracked asphalt strewn with wind-blown debris. She pulled in and guided the car into an empty space.

She hesitated before stepping from the vehicle. Why would Clark send her here? He couldn't possibly have realized how bad this part of town was, or he surely would have taken care of this himself. Although Brook wasn't easily intimidated, she also wasn't usually exposed to this sort of living or the vibes of danger that radiated from the men on the street.

Brook finally gathered her courage and stepped from the car. She felt exposed and vulnerable. Holding her Bottega Veneta handbag close to her midriff, she walked briskly from the lot to the sidewalk. Turning the corner, she took perhaps half a dozen steps before she was accosted by a young man.

His shaggy brown hair hung in greasy strands around his face and his clothes were torn and dirty. "Well, well, well. Whadda we got here?" He moved to block her way and Brook stopped, uncertain how to proceed. "Come to Bobby, baby," the man said, rubbing his crotch suggestively. "Let me show you what a real man can do for you."

Brook turned and headed back for her car, her heels tapping a quick staccato on the pavement. Behind her, Bobby laughed derisively but made no move to follow. She pressed the keyless entry as she approached the car. She was intent on getting inside, locking the door, and getting away from this place. Anger flared within her, distracting her for a second or two. *What* had Clark been thinking? She didn't belong here. He could send someone else or call and have the book delivered to the house, because *she* wouldn't be picking it up for him.

As Brook slid into the car, she sensed a movement behind her and turned her head in time to see a fist coming towards her face. She managed a small scream that was cut off as the blow caught her on the side of the head. Brook fell, dazed, backwards into the car. Tears sprang instantly to her eyes.

She heard a man's gruff voice mumble, "Shit! People!"

He reached in and shoved her roughly across the console, gouging her back on the gearshift before unceremoniously pushing her legs across to clear the driver's seat. "You say one fuckin' word and I'll kill you," he snarled. "Get down on the floor. Now, bitch!"

Brook dropped to the floorboard, shaking in fear and confusion, tears rolling unchecked down her cheeks. Bewildered, she watched the man slide a key into the ignition; not her key, she still had wits enough to realize she held that in her hand. She opened her mouth and took a deep breath, prepared to scream bloody murder. Before she could even squeak, a gun was pressed to her temple. "Don't do it, lady." Brook clamped her mouth shut; cutting off the scream before it even became one. "Put your head down and cover it with your hands."

Brook complied, heart trip-hammering against her chest. *What's happening? What does he want? Where is he taking me? Oh god, I've got to get away!* These thoughts and more raced through her head as the car moved into the street and away, the sound of the tires on the road keeping pace with her rapidly beating heart.

"Don't hurt me, don't hurt me, don't hurt me," Brook pleaded through her tears as she huddled on the floor. She could barely hear her own voice through the ringing in her ears. They had only gone a short distance when she felt the car bump and then rise up a ramp into darkness. She peeked up through her hair and tried to see where they were. The driver got out and her hopes rose. *Maybe he was leaving. Maybe he was going away.* She was reaching furtively for the door handle, heart slamming against her chest, when the door was jerked open and a hand grabbed her by the hair and pulled.

"Out, now," her assailant's voice demanded.

Brook cried out as pain ripped along her scalp. She fell from the car to a dirty surface, bruising her knee through her custom designed slacks. She stood, turning toward the sound of voices, rubbing at her scalp and checking her hand for signs of blood; there were none. She realized she was in the trailer of a dark and musty semi-truck. The only light came from the open loading door, its feeble glow barely enough to illuminate the three men who stood staring at her. Even in her terror Brook tried to record their faces into her memory. She wanted to be able to give accurate descriptions to the police when she got out of this mess. She stared openly.

Arguing with the man who had attacked her was a tall, skinny man whose straight, medium-brown hair fell over one eye and most of the other. He had a mustache and small beard. Brook noted his bad teeth when he bared them in a snarl at the first man. "Damn it all to hell, Benny. What the hell is *this*?" He gestured towards Brook who regarded them with a look of fear in her eyes.

Ok, Benny! Benny! He's the one that attacked me. Watch him. Remember him!

Benny glared at her from deep-set, dark eyes. He was of medium height and build. His face was long, tapering to a pointed chin with a scraggly thin beard. Sparse whiskers grew over his lip and down the sides of his face. His hair was over-the-collar length, neatly combed and swept across to one side, barely missing an eye. His clothing was more like that of a business man and totally inconsistent with his actions, she thought as she noted his khakis, button-up shirt, white sports jacket, and loafers and filed them away for future reference.

"She came back to the car too soon. Fuck! She wasn't supposed to be there. And then there were too many people around. I couldn't just dump her out in the parking lot without being seen," Benny explained. He gave Brook the once-over.

"Besides, she's kinda cute."

"Kind of cute? Are you for real? Kind of cute, jeez!" Pete shook his head.

The third guy was a trucker through and through. Jeans, button up shirt open over a wife-beater t-shirt, and tennis shoes. His belly hung over a large belt buckle shaped like Texas. Graying on top, he wore a crew cut and was clean-shaven. He spat to one side as he said, "I don't give a flying fuck about none of this. Ya all need to get the hell out of my truck. I need to move this merchandise and don't want no part of whatever trouble this little lady is gonna bring." He pointed to Brook when he made this statement. Her heart squeezed painfully in her chest as all three looked her way.

Benny said, "Mind your own fucking business, asshole." Oblivious to the flash of anger on the trucker's face, he turned to the tall guy. "We'll just have to take her with us, Pete. Come on, let's move."

Brook filed away this new name.

"Man, Benny! Jase is gonna be pissed," Pete proclaimed.

"Fuck Jase," Benny spat angrily, but Brook detected a hint of concern behind his bravado.

As the two argued, Brook saw a chance to get away. She started backing towards the open loading door. Slow and easy, shaking badly, she put one foot at a time behind her and moved backwards, keeping an eye on the men the entire time. She reached the door, turned and ran awkwardly down the ramp, her heels slowing her. Behind her, she heard the trucker laugh and say, "Your little woman is leavin'."

"Shit!" Pete yelled.

Brooklyn ran. She fled for her life down a deserted alley. She heard a thump as someone hit the ground behind her.

She needed to lose the heels but wasn't going to stop and take them off. Keeping her eyes straight ahead and gasping for breath, she screamed, "Help! HELP!" She could see no one and no one responded to her yells.

Brook didn't make it far before she was tackled from behind, knocked off her feet. Her face hit the pavement and bounced back off, abrading her cheek and scattering a pile of rubbish. The sleeves of her beautiful jacket were stained with rotted garbage, the odor stinging her nostrils. She cried out in pain and fear as the weight of her assailant held her down.

"You stupid bitch," Benny, lying across her, growled. "Why do you want to be this way?"

Brook heard the screech of tires, and hoped against hope that it was someone coming to rescue her. She tried to raise her head to call for help again, but was saved the trouble when Benny crawled off her and yanked her to her feet. An SUV skidded to a stop beside them, its deep green paint sparkling in the sunlight, and the windows so dark Brook couldn't see the driver. Benny opened the rear door and flung her inside before he crawled in behind her. He shoved her head down into the seat.

"Go," he growled to the driver.

Enjoy this preview of *Half-Bitten* by PJ Hawkinson
Available now.

Prelude

"I'm bored," a young woman, by appearance maybe eighteen years old, said for the hundredth time. "Why can't we move, we've been here more than long enough.

A boy who appeared to be the same age as the girl agreed with vigor, "Come on Damien, it's time to go somewhere new. These hills have lost their appeal," he referred to the hills near the surrounding city of Edinburgh, in Ireland, where they lived in luxury in a smallish castle.

Damien looked at the two complainers, and then turned to the third member of his family, "What about you? Do you want to leave also?"

A boy, around the same age as the other two, or at least by appearances, glanced up from his studies of Divinci's art with mild confusion. "Leave," he said, "and go where?"

"Spin the globe Damien," the girl suggested. "It's my turn to close my eyes and stop it from spinning. This will be fun; I know I'll stop it at a good place."

"Sure," the first boy said with sarcasm, "and if your finger lands in the middle of an ocean are we suppose to go there?"

"Ha, ha," she laughed falsely. "Come on Damien, what do you say?"

Damien sighed and rose from his position at an exquisite grand piano. He had been playing a haunting tune when his oldest two *children* had rudely interrupted him. Now, he moved to a beautiful globe centered on an ornate mahogany stand. Reaching out a long finger, he gave the globe a nonchalant spin. The young girl closed her eyes, stuck out a finger, and stopped the globe from spinning.

"Where are we going?" asked the first boy.

She squinted at the globe, and then frowned, "Spin it again, Damien," she demanded.

"Nope, that's not the way it is done," said the first boy. "Where are we going?" He moved forward and looked, "Oh lord," he groaned. "She's right, spin it again."

The second boy came to look and said with a laugh, "You know the rules. As long as Damien spins the globe, where it stops is where we go. Peering at the globe, he said, "And it looks like we are off to the center of the United States of America. Better start packing."

Damien frowned and then sighed hugely, "I'll contact movers, and find us a place to live." Turning, he was gone.

The center of the United States of America was the home of a young girl who was exactly the age she appeared. This girl was living her live in a decent way, going about in the ways of fifteen year old girls, but for the last year she has been teetering upon turning a corner of life; the wrong corner.

As she moves towards this corner, another family moves towards her; a family that could mean her salvation; or her death. Let's meet her and find out...............

CHAPTER 1

My name is Gertrude Penelope Purdy. I know, terrible hunh; I'm named after both my Grandmothers so I honestly can't complain, at least not aloud.

I'm not much to look at; I'm 5'6" tall, 102 lbs, built on the slight to medium side. I've got pretty nice tits and my ass isn't big, but, I wish my waist was smaller. My eyes are liquid green. I have heart-shaped lips and a slight crook to my nose.

My hair is plain old brown, wavy, and tends towards curly when the weather is damp; I usually iron it when it gets that

that way. My voice is medium. I'm just your average plain-Jane, your ordinary, everyday girl. That is, right up to the time I am bitten by a vampire. However, that is yet to come.

As to my personality, well, I think it is lacking; I never seem to be able to be 'cool' like the other kids no matter how hard I try. Consequentially, I tend to over try on everything to make others like me. I certainly don't care about girls much, but boy do I want the boys to like me.

When I was growing up, I always tried to act sexy around the friends of my brother Davy. Davy is six years older than I am and I'm sure I embarrassed him when he had friends over to our house. Whenever they came over, I would hang around, swing my hips, and poke out my non-existent tits. Not that any of them ever laughed at me; they just ignored me, which definitely did not help my low self-esteem problem.

I'm 15 now, and me and a lot of kids my age go to the races every weekend. Most kids are dropped off in groups by one of their folks about 7 pm, and then picked up by another about 11 pm when the races are over. Need I say that I don't have a close friend to ride with to the races? I always ride with my next-door neighbors; I jump out as soon as we get to the track yelling that I will see them after the races. I don't want the other kids to know that I have to catch a ride with adults instead of friends. Oh, and do I even need to mention none of us have ever watched a race?

All of us kids usually hang out near the concession stand with us girls flirting with the boys that hang around. I always have to resort to measures I am not at all proud of in order to be noticed above the rest of the girls. While they all flirt in a no-contact manner, I have to resort to full contact.

Take for instance the time Peter Remsky, a cute 19 year old, was the target of the flirting for a couple of months. Peter was eyeballing all the other girls and no matter how hard I tried, he never seemed to see me. I started dropping hints that I could offer more then the other girls: I would coyly suggest that I like to French kiss or suggest that it was kind of cold and maybe we could get warm by getting closer. Finally, my hints got his attention and we started to do a lot of hugging, and even managed some French kissing (it was new to me but I caught right on). However, the whole time he had his body smashed against mine, he was still looking at the other girls, and all the while, the other girls were calling me a slut under their breaths or, sometimes right out-loud. Hurt!

Made in the USA
Monee, IL
22 May 2023

34317255R00134